CALL ME CARMELA

Call Me Carmela

A Dot Meyerhoff Mystery

Ellen Kirschman

OPEN ROAD

INTEGRATED MEDIA
NEW YORK

ISBN: 978-1-5040-9575-4

Published in 2024 by Open Road Integrated Media, Inc.
180 Maiden Lane
New York, NY 10038
www.openroadmedia.com

CALL ME CARMELA

1

Fran and Eddie's café is a shrine to the past. Formica counters, stools tipsy with age, and scarred tabletops. Nothing's changed here but the person frying eggs and flipping pancakes with a Sheetrock trowel. It used to be Fran, now it's retired cop Eddie Rimbauer, his face red from the heat. I'm dropping by, as I often do, to get coffee and a bagel to go before heading to my office. The screen door to the restaurant bangs open several times in a row. It's not quite lunchtime, but cops eat when they can, not when they should. At Fran's they can eat in peace, without being accosted by irate citizens complaining about traffic tickets they most certainly didn't deserve.

Eddie waves me over. "Just the woman I want to see." He leans across the counter, holding his trowel in the air. "Something's going on with Fran. I caught her this morning, hiding out in the back booth, crying. She thinks I didn't notice, but you can't fool an old cop. When I asked her what's wrong, she just clammed up."

Fran's had a lot to cry about in her life, but mostly she's sturdy and cheerful. Always good for a joke. The café has been her bully pulpit for decades, long before her husband, BG, was killed in the line of duty chasing a twenty-year-old armed felon who had robbed a convenience store. It was only the second line of duty death at the Kenilworth Police Department in fifty years. A photo of him in uniform and the glass-encased American flag they handed to Fran at his funeral sit high on a shelf over the long front counter. Never one to—as she says—"play the widow card," she's always ready to help anyone, especially her cop customers.

"Look who's here." Fran's voice reaches me from her booth in the back where she's rolling flatware in cloth napkins.

"I thought you were retired." I walk toward the back. From a few feet away, I can see that her face is blotchy and her eyes puffy.

"Stay home and let Eddie run this place unsupervised? I been watching that boy since he was a child. I'm not letting him out of my sight. At least I'm sitting down for a change." Fran's legs, swollen and riddled with varicose veins, were just about to give out when Eddie put in his papers at KPD and took over.

Fran tells me to grab a cup of coffee and sit. And while I'm at it, pour her one too. As soon as I do, Eddie joins us. "Too early in the morning for the doc to look at your ugly mug," Fran says. "She needs more coffee first."

This isn't bickering. It's love, pure and simple. It's how they are, the two of them, a widow with bad legs and a recovered drunk, twice divorced, still mourning the only thing he had left in life, his job as a cop. I'd worried Eddie wouldn't survive retirement, that he'd kill himself or start drinking again, but here he is, king of the café. Cops flock from all over to hear his war stories.

"Don't you have anything else to do, Eddie? Prep work? Taste today's soup? Wiggle the Jell-O?"

Since he's taken over, Eddie has expanded Fran's menu. After what we'd all been through last year, Frank and I invited Eddie and Fran to our wedding in Iowa. Eddie went crazy for the local food. Despite Fran's opposition, he put Iowa potato salad and three kinds of Jell-O on the café menu.

"How is my man Frank? Tell him I said hello. I'm going to be calling him one of these days to talk about remodeling this joint."

"Will that be before or after you call the bank for a loan?" Fran says. "I'm not fronting the money. This place is fine as it is."

"This place is older than you. It needs a total do-over. If there's any money left, you can get a facelift." He turns to me. "What's up at the PD? Cops still turning the other way when they see you coming?" Eddie swipes at the table with the corner of his apron. "I know a couple of guys who are in the middle of nasty divorces. They'd rather talk to me than a psychologist. I don't charge for my time plus I'm an expert on nasty divorces."

"Are you finished?" Fran looks disgusted. "Get back in the kitchen and make yourself useful."

"See what I got to put up with? Twenty-plus years on the job chasing crooks and directing traffic in the rain is nothing compared to working for Ms. Slave Driver over here who forgets she's not the one in charge anymore, I am." He snaps his towel against the tabletop and storms off in a mock rage.

Fran shakes her head. "He's never going to grow up. Never. Still doesn't have a life. All he did was trade his addiction to police work for an addiction to this place."

"Better than his addiction to alcohol," I say. "What's going on, Fran? Eddie said you were upset but you wouldn't say why."

"None of his business."

"Your eyes are red and your face is spotty."

"I'm old. Those are age spots."

"Those are not age spots. Talk to me, Fran."

I stretch my hands across the table. She reaches back. Hers are sandpaper-rough, the backs covered with knobby veins. I've developed an abiding affection for Fran's tough-on-the-outside, soft-on-the-inside personality. The fortitude it took for her to keep going after BG was killed. How she honors his legacy and love for police work by mothering the cops who came after him. I have warm feelings for Eddie, too, as erratic as he can be in his still wobbly sobriety.

"It's my eighteen-year-old goddaughter, Ava Marie. She's in trouble. Things haven't been great for her at home, but, until a few days ago, I didn't know how bad. Her parents think she's gone off the rails. They had a big fight and she took off. Nobody's seen or heard from her for two days. They think she might be headed my way." Fran pulls her hands back. "This is killing me."

"Has anyone called the police?"

"They live in Moss Point on the coast. It's a little one-horse town with a one-horse sheriff. He thinks she's a runaway. Told her parents to give her a few days to get over being mad and she'll come home."

"There is no waiting period in California for reporting a missing person. He has to take the report."

"He knows that. Ava's father told him. Dan used to be a KPD cop. BG was his field training officer. The only way anybody in that two-bit agency is going to find her is if she runs in front of a patrol car. I keep thinking about that coastline, that skinny road over the mountains. What if she drives off the road? Or over a cliff? Or into the ocean?"

"Has she ever tried to kill herself?" One of my psychology journals just issued a report that teenage girls are experiencing record high levels of violence, sadness, and suicide. I keep this unhappy bit of information to myself. Statistics are about groups. Fran's goddaughter is not a number.

"Not that I know of. Except now I don't know what I don't know. She used to tell me everything until about a year ago."

"What happened a year ago?"

"She was adopted. I think she started asking about her birth parents."

"How can I help?"

"When they find her, could you talk to her?"

"Doesn't she have a therapist?"

"Her parents tried to get her to go to counseling. She refused."

"So why would she agree to see me?"

"I'll tell her you are good people. She'll listen, she trusts me. At least she used to."

"I don't have any experience with teenagers."

"Not to worry. If you can help cops who don't trust civilians and hate asking for help, you can help anybody."

2

I take my bagel and coffee and drive to my private office on Catalan Court. One of the many things I love about Fran is that she never sees my flaws, only my assets. What she doesn't know or doesn't want to acknowledge is that, after four years on the job at KPD, there are still officers who avoid me like the plague, believing I have a video cam in this office and in my office at headquarters, both of which go straight to the chief. As for my ability to help, Fran seems to have forgotten Ben Gomez, the young rookie who killed himself. I have mourned for him in silence almost every day since. Tortured myself with questions about what I missed, what more I could have done to prevent his death. Fran will have to find a different therapist for her goddaughter. I am not ready to work with another potentially suicidal young client.

I pull into the parking area behind the building where my private office is located, noticing for the first time what a beautiful summer day it is, sunny and hot. I wave at the gardener who is pulling weeds and deadheading bushes along the walkway. Gary Morse is sorting mail in the lobby. Concentrating so hard he doesn't hear me come through the door. He's dressed, as usual, in a beat-up corduroy jacket with leather patches on the elbows. Gary, his wife, Janice, and I have a long history. I've known them both since grad school. They were the ones who warned me off Mark, my ex. After our divorce, when I was convinced the romantic part of my life was dead and gone, they introduced me to Frank, who was remodeling their house. When Frank proposed and I had a serious case of cold feet, they kept nagging at me until I agreed to marry him. It was the right decision and I'm forever grateful they knew it before I did.

"Coming to the staff meeting today?" Gary's mellow voice is as soothing as the sticky sweet aroma of pipe tobacco that clings to his clothes.

Once a month, all the therapists in our building get together for coffee and companionship. I don't have much in common with the other therapists. They all have conventional practices, treating the usual grab bag of presenting problems. My clients carry weapons and live in a kill-or-be-killed world.

Gary hands me my mail. I walk up the stairs to my second-floor office and dump the pile on my desk, toss the circulars and the ads, and stack the professional journals on top of the eight-inch pile of unread past issues I'll probably never get to. I'm about to check my schedule for the day when Fran texts me.

She's here, at the café. Showed up out of nowhere. She's been sleeping in her car for two days. On my way to U.

Fran looks worse than she did an hour ago. Standing in my waiting room, her hands clamped over Ava's shoulders, holding her steady. I tell her I have forty minutes until I have a preemployment interview. Forty minutes I need to review the applicant's test results and background packet. She tells me she won't take that long, she just wanted to introduce me to Ava.

"Is this a doctor's office?" Ava looks around. "I thought you said we were going to see your friend and then out to lunch."

"Dot is my friend. She's also a doctor, a psychologist."

Ava wheels toward the door. She's a tiny girl with an unruly mound of dark curly hair and deep brown eyes. Her skin is the color of weak tea. Bony knees stick out of the holes in her jeans.

"I don't need a psychologist."

"That, my dear Ava, is a matter of opinion."

"I'm eighteen. I'm an adult. I don't have to do anything I don't want to do."

"What you are is mixed-up, confused, and highly emotional. It comes with being eighteen." Fran turns to me. "This is as much as I know. Ava and her parents had a big fight. Ava threw a tantrum and left home."

"I did not throw a tantrum. I got angry. There's a difference. My father doesn't need to know where I am every minute of every day, which is what he wants."

"If you're going to stay with me tonight, I am going to call them and tell them where you are, so they won't worry. This is not negotiable. Unless you'd rather sleep in your car."

"Whatever," Ava says.

Fran takes her phone and walks into the waiting room, closing the door to my office behind her.

"Might as well have a seat while you're waiting," I say.

"No thanks." Ava walks over to a set of colorful framed textiles that hang over a bookcase. Hand-embroidered little boy's pants and huipils from Guatemala. "These are pretty. Are they from Mexico?"

"Guatemala."

"Have you been there?"

"Once, when I was in college. It's very beautiful."

She circles around the room, touching things with her delicate hands. She moves with precise steps like a dancer.

"What's this?"

She stops in front of a blue-and-gold ceramic bowl that sits on a low coffee table in front of the couch.

"A client made that for me using a Japanese technique called kintsugi, mending broken pottery with lacquer that's mixed with powdered gold."

"Why?"

"Why what?"

"Why did she make it for you?"

"It was a thank-you gift for helping her. She wanted me to keep it here to show my other clients that the woman who made it is no longer broken. That if she could put herself back together, so can they."

Ava runs her finger along the rim of the bowl. "It's hella beautiful."

Fran's muffled voice, but not her words, comes through my office door. Ava keeps walking.

"Fran's my godmother. I call her my aunt. It's easier. I guess she told you that I was adopted." Ava looks for my reaction. I do my neutral screen face thing.

She continues to circle the room. Stops in front of another bookcase. "Have you read all these books?"

"No."

"I love to read."

"What kind of books do you like?"

She shrugs. "Fiction mostly." She tracks her hand over the top of the bookcase, picks up a small pine needle basket, turns it over, glances at the bottom, and puts it back. "Cool. Who made it?"

"Not sure. I think it's Ohlone."

"So what kind of shrink are you?"

"I'm a police psychologist." Her dark eyebrows lift slightly.

"You see cops after they shoot people?"

"Sometimes. Mostly they don't shoot people."

"My father was a cop, here in Kenilworth. He quit and moved to Moss Point when I was a baby." She's still pacing. "Do you see many cops' kids?"

"A few."

"My father acts like he's still a cop. Watches my every move. Wants to know where I am all the time. Is that normal?"

"Cops see a lot of bad stuff that happens to children. It makes them afraid."

"But is it normal? He only sees the bad stuff, never the good. Acts like there's a bad guy around every corner. Talks to me like I'm a crook."

The door opens, Fran comes back into the office.

"That wasn't easy, but your parents said you can stay for the night. Your father's hopping mad and your mother is on the verge of hysterics she's been so worried about you."

"He's always mad and she's always a nervous wreck. I want to stay with you for the whole summer." Fran looks surprised.

"One day at a time, please. That's a big ask. First things first, you need a shower, a shampoo, and a good meal. You're skinny as a scarecrow."

"He hit me, I bet he didn't tell you that." Fran and I freeze. "He was mad. So was I. Didn't give him the right to slap me."

"How often has this happened?" I ask, switching into therapist mode as a mandated reporter of child abuse.

"Just once." Her voice is so soft I can barely hear her.

"Again, please."

"Once. But he says shit all the time."

"What do you mean?"

"I'm eighteen, I want to look for my birth parents. Just like millions of other adopted kids. Dan and Sharon go mental every time I bring it up. That was what the fight was about. Dan said he hoped my birth mother would turn out to be a slut who gives blow jobs to vagrants for money. My mother told me he didn't mean it. It was just cop humor. She always says that after he's had a few beers and says something gross. My dorky friend Cody thought it was funny, told me to lighten up." She turns to Fran. "And you probably think I'm too sensitive."

"What I think is not for print and it has to do with Dan, not you."

Ava turns to me. "You're a doctor, what do you think?"

It's not so much a question as a test. Am I going to judge her or understand how painful this was?

"I think that was an awful thing for him to say. It was cruel."

Something softens around her eyes, then just as quickly tightens again. "No biggie. He can say whatever he wants, I don't care. I already know who my birth mother is and that she lives in San Francisco with my grandmother." She walks to the window, gazes out as she's talking, her face dappled with shadows from the maple tree outside. She's so petite that if I didn't know she was eighteen, I'd think she was much younger. Fran looks at me and shrugs her shoulders.

"You've already met your birth mother?" I ask.

She hesitates a second. "I talked to her on the phone. Once."

I start to ask why only once when she turns away. "I'm hungry, Aunt Fran. Let's get lunch."

Fran gets up, shaking her head at the rapid change in Ava's mood and muttering something about needing a drink, not a sandwich. "Thanks for your time, Dot. I owe you."

"Bye, Ava," I say. "Nice to meet you."

"Same here." She gives me a little wave and walks out.

I close the door. If I work fast, I can read my applicant's records. I open his file, but I can't concentrate. Ava is not who I was expecting. She's bright and curious. And way more forthcoming than I imagine most teenagers are. Her home life sounds difficult. An angry, controlling father who drinks too much and an emotionally volatile mother. I don't know anything about her history, but she strikes me as angry and rebellious—probably normal for her age—not depressed or suicidal. Then again, I knew a lot about Ben Gomez. I didn't think he was suicidal either, not until he shot himself in the head.

3

Frank wakes me the next morning at 6:30. He's been up for over an hour. Contractors start their days early. He's holding our landline and a mug of coffee for me. We're still using a landline because my mother, Rivka, is adamant that she hears better talking landline to landline. It's her way of getting back at me for insisting she carry a cell phone with her when she goes out. She says it feels like an umbilical cord with a tracking device. From her perspective, parents are entitled to know where their children are, not the other way around.

"Sorry to bother you at this ungodly hour," Fran says. "I'm at my wit's end. Dan is on his way to my house. He's threatening to drag Ava home. She's threatening to run away before he gets here. I could call the cops, but I don't want to do that. They have more important things to do. I could call Eddie, but he'll only make things worse. I owe you big-time, but could you come over? Help me settle things down."

I sit up, still groggy, and check my calendar. I have reports to write, but no meetings until early afternoon. Fran always shows up when she's needed and asks for very little for herself. I'd feel like a bad friend if I turned her down. This is a small ask. She only needs a little support. I can spare an hour.

I tell her to keep Ava calm. "I need to shower first, then I'll be over."

The door to Fran's house is open and there's an unfamiliar pickup truck in the driveway. I slam my car door hard enough to be heard inside. Fran appears in an instant.

"Thank you, thank you for coming." She pulls me inside.

Dan Sower is sitting on the couch, glaring at Ava, who is bunched up on a dining room chair, her knees pulled into her chest, her face hidden. A duffel bag with her name written across it is lying haphazardly next to the front door, as though someone has thrown it across the room.

Fran introduces me to Dan. Ava wants to know why I'm here.

"I called her," Fran says. "Because I'm stuck in a room with two lunatics who don't seem to be able to talk without shouting. I thought maybe a psychologist would know what to do with the two of you."

"I don't want to talk to her. Tell her to leave."

"This is my house, Ava. I can ask anybody over that I want."

Ava uncurls. "Then I'm leaving."

Dan sits up. "No, you're not. Unless you want to come home with me."

Ava sits down again. Pulls herself into another knot. I ask Fran for a cup of coffee. No way I'm getting through this without more caffeine. As soon as Fran pours me a cup, I ask Dan if he'll step outside with me. I learned this from the cops. Separate the warring parties.

"Don't lie to her; tell her you slapped me." Ava's voice is pitched high. "He's been lying to me my whole life. So has my mother."

I open the door. Dan stands slowly and follows me outside. He's in good shape for someone I judge to be about my age, early fifties. Trim except for his beer belly. Clean-shaven, his hair starting to gray at the sides.

"I know what this looks like," he says. "I used to be a cop. But believe me, there's nothing going on. If there's any abuse, it's her"—he cocks his head toward the house—"abusing us."

I smell beer on his breath. It's eight in the morning. I hold my coffee cup close to my nose to dampen the odor.

"She's been lying, going behind our backs, looking for her birth parents for over a year after promising us she wouldn't, not until she was eighteen. I don't care how old she is, she doesn't have the right to lie to us." A slight tic pulses under the ribbon of tendon that runs from his shoulder up the side of his neck. "As long as she's under my roof, I want to know where she goes and who she goes with."

I've heard this before. Cops see more cruelty in their first years on the job than I'll see in my lifetime. Harm to children is the worst. Girls and boys, Ava's age and younger, being abused and exploited sometimes by the very people who are supposed to protect them, parents, teachers, and priests.

"Something's wrong with her. I don't think it's drugs. I'd know if she was on was anything heavier than a little pot." Dan's pacing, tamping a path back and forth across Fran's front lawn. "Did she tell you what she did on the Fourth of July? We had a big party, always do. The wife works her ass off for it. It's her thing. Ava's friends were there too. All of a sudden, in front of everybody, Ava starts yelling at Sharon and me, saying she wasn't adopted, she was stolen. That we bought her off a baby trafficker. Sharon got so hysterical she fainted. That's when I slapped Ava. Just the once. Sharon gets carried off to the hospital in an ambulance. We got cop cars everywhere. Do you think Ava was concerned about her mother? All she wanted was for the sheriff to arrest me for slapping her. It was a freaking circus."

"Did he?"

"Did he what?"

Dan's eyes are red. From lack of sleep, from booze, from crying, hard to tell. "Arrest you?"

"Of course not. I used to be a cop."

Ava's nowhere to be seen when we go back in the house. Fran says she's asleep in the guest room. Her duffel bag is gone.

"What's she been telling you, Fran?" Dan asks.

"She told me you hit her."

"Once in her entire lifetime. I thought Sharon had a stroke. I was just trying to get Ava to shut up so I could help Sharon."

"You shouldn't have," Fran says.

"I know. If I could take it back, I would. Sharon's pissed at me. Ava's pissed at me. And I'm so freaking mad at myself I could eat my gun." He realizes what he's just said. "Code 4, Doctor, everything's under control. I'm not serious. I don't have a plan. I'm not giving away my shit. I got a wife on the verge of a nervous breakdown and a daughter who's headed for the loony bin. I don't have time to kill myself. Freaking Jekyll and Hyde personality is what she is. Good kid, great grades, loves camping, fishing, lots of friends. Turns eighteen and suddenly we're monsters for giving her a home, a loving home. Sharon has turned herself inside out for Ava. Inside out."

With that, he runs out of gas. "Sorry, I need forty winks. Can't keep my eyes open. Been up all night." He stretches out on the couch and closes his eyes. In less than a minute he starts snoring.

Fran walks me to the door. Tells me she'll be okay. Dan will drive home after he wakes up. She's pretty sure he and Sharon are on board with Ava spending the summer; because of the way things are between them, it's better if they take a break. She thanks me again for my help and apologizes for her family mishegoss. She uses the Yiddish word for craziness because she knows I'm Jewish and she likes that Yiddish sounds so like the thing it describes.

"Dan told me Ava thinks she was stolen, bought from a baby trafficker. Could it be true?"

"Of course not, her parents loved her from the minute they got her."

"That's a different question. What she's alleging is serious. Too serious to ignore. I think you need to ask her about it."

Fran leans against the doorjamb as if it's all that's holding her up. "Whatever you say, Dot. You're the doctor."

Neither Frank nor I have kids. My first husband, Mark, said he didn't want children. Then he left me for the wasp-waisted Melinda and had a child with her. Sometimes, not having children is a deep ache. Other times, like now, watching Ava turn spiteful and angry, I feel like I've dodged a speeding bullet.

Dan is an imperfect parent with a willful child. I can relate. I was a willful child. Headstrong with a value system of my own. My mother tried to cure me with organic food and chamomile tea. My father tried to correct me with endless rants about oppression. When I chose psychology over labor organizing, he told me psychologists were minions of the state preaching adaption to a corrupt system that called for revolution. When I started working with the police, he accused me of consorting with the enemy.

All Ava wants is to find her birth parents. This seems normal to me, particularly as she gets closer to the age where she might have children of her own. So why do Dan and Sharon feel so threatened? I can understand feeling a little wary, but not to this degree. What are they afraid of? Why are they treating Ava's birth parents like the enemy?

My cell phone buzzes with a reminder. Ten minutes to my next appointment. My head is swirling with questions. Ava believes she was stolen or trafficked. Is she making things up so she has an excuse to leave home? Could she be delusional, showing signs of incipient mental illness? She seems to want help, but is she so bent on establishing her independence she won't ask for it? Ben Gomez was too proud to ask for help and too proud to accept it when it was offered. The consequences were disastrous. Despite the similarities, I tell myself Ava's not Ben and Ben wasn't Ava.

Ava's parents think she needs counseling. So does Fran. I think back to my own willful adolescent self. I didn't want a therapist. What I wanted more than anything was to be seen and believed. To have somebody on my side who understood that despite my parents' eccentricities, I was trying as hard as I could to grow up and be normal. There's a knock on my door. My client is here. I warn myself not to over-identify with Ava because she reminds me of myself. Still, the more I think about it, the more I am convinced that what Ava needs most, more than therapy, is an advocate.

4

Things must have gone well after I left Fran's yesterday because the phone doesn't ring all night and I have no texts in the morning. Frank is happy about this. My dedication to work has been a particularly sticky point in our relationship. Frank owns a remodeling business. He's in charge of his own schedule. If I don't fulfill my contractual duties as a consultant—meaning I'm on emergency call 24/7—Chief Pence can give me thirty days' notice and terminate my contract. Frank doesn't have emergencies. Not unless you count the occasional panicky call from one of his clients who knows how to run a venture capital firm but doesn't know how to change a light bulb. When something goes wrong with my job, people can die.

First thing on my schedule is meeting Pepper Hunt for our monthly appointment. We're meeting at Fran's. Pepper hates coming to my office. It triggers her, makes her feel like she's still a client. She's almost fully recovered from last year's trauma when she was kidnapped and beaten by a gang of thugs; but it's been a struggle. Pepper has finally recognized, though, that she's not invincible and that less than perfect is sometimes the best even supercops can do.

By the time I arrive, Pepper's in a back booth scarfing down a huge plate of ham and eggs. She's in street clothes. At six feet tall, she can consume all the calories she wants without any penalty. My postmenopausal metabolism means I only need to glance at a plate of food to gain weight.

"What do you want to eat?" Ava's small hand shoves a menu in front of me. She's holding an order pad and wearing a cobbler's apron embroidered with the words *Fran's Café*. She does not look happy. Fran steps behind Ava, leans next to her ear, like a ventriloquist.

"May I have your order, please?"

Ava sighs. "May I have your order, please?"

I tell her I want two eggs scrambled hard, a piece of dry rye toast, and coffee.

Ava turns toward the kitchen. Fran stops her, turns her around.

"And?"

"Thank you, Dr. Meyerhoff, I'll be right back with your eggs."

"I hope she catches on quick," Fran says, "or she's going to end up in the dish room. If she's going to stay with me for the summer, she needs a job and I need a new server." She checks on Ava's progress with the coffee then turns back to our table. "Morning, Pepper. How were your eggs?" Pepper gives her a thumbs-up and starts to scroll on her phone.

"Did you ask her?" I say to Fran.

"Ask her what?"

"About being stolen." Pepper looks up.

"Don't you think she's just being dramatic?"

"What if she's not? Dan said she's been a good kid. Never caused any trouble until recently."

"That's because they've never said no to her. Not until she started looking for her so-called real parents. Can you imagine how that hurt? Dan and Sharon bathed her, fed her, stayed up nights worrying about her. They're her real parents."

"I get that they're hurt. Totally understandable. And I get that her story sounds unbelievable. It's possible she's misinterpreting something she heard or read. All the more reason to ask her about it."

"Somebody, something got stolen?" Pepper looks concerned.

Fran sits down. "It's my goddaughter. She was adopted. She's been trying to find her birth parents and lying to her adoptive parents about it because they didn't want her to look. She recently found her birth mother. Now she believes she was stolen, not adopted. There was a big family fight over this. That's why she's living with me."

Pepper frowns. "This birth mother sounds a little off."

"Who knows if she's actually Ava's birth mother? Couldn't we look it up? There must be a record." Fran starts to gather Pepper's empty plates.

"Not that easy," Pepper says. "California is a closed adoption state. Birth records are sealed and can only be opened if the birth parents agree." She looks at her watch. "I got to go."

"Me too," Fran says as she clears the dishes. "I'll check on your eggs, Dot."

"This wasn't much of a meeting, Pepper; how are you doing?" I say.

"Chomping at the bit. I need off this school resource gig. I want back on the street."

I'm the one who suggested Pepper take the school resource officer position after her stress leave was over, thinking she needed more time off. Traumatic wounds are invisible to all but the wounded. Pepper's emotional injuries have taken longer to heal than her bruises and broken ribs. Being a school resource officer was a good way to pace her return to police work.

"I'm bored out of my gourd. Phone in a bomb threat, would you?" She sees the look on my face. "Sorry, cop humor."

Ava returns with a check for Pepper, coffee, and my perfectly done eggs and toast, a smile plastered across her face. Fran is watching her from behind the counter. Pepper lays her money on the table.

"Got time for a break, Ava?" I say.

She looks at her watch. There are very few people in the café.

"Sure, Aunt Fran said I could take a break when things slowed down." She puts the coffeepot on the table. Pepper excuses herself and leaves. Ava slides into Pepper's empty seat.

"Did my dad tell you he hit me?"

"He did. That must have hurt. Emotionally, not just physically." Ava drops her eyes. "Has he ever hit you before?" She shakes her head. "Are you afraid of him?" She shakes her head again. "He told me you and your mother had been fighting, that your mother fainted and he was trying to get you to stop yelling. Is that how you remember it?"

A faint blush rises in her cheeks and along the sides of her neck.

"That doesn't give him the right to hit me."

"No, it doesn't. I agree. Your father said you and your mother were fighting because you had accused her of buying you from a baby trafficker. That's pretty serious. How did you come to believe that?"

Ava looks around for Fran, who is sitting at the counter, talking to a customer.

"It was something my birth mom said on the phone. She said I was taken without her permission; I added the baby trafficker part. Who else would take a baby without permission?"

"Taken without her permission? That's a pretty heavy thing to say. Did she explain further?" Ava shakes her head.

"Sounds traumatic. Traumatic memories can be confusing or a little blurry. Any possibility that your birth mother may not remember exactly what happened? Could you ask her to tell you more?"

Ava's back stiffens and her eyes narrow. I'm questioning the veracity of the idealized mother who lives in her head. The mother she's been searching for. The mother who is surely better than the imperfect one who adopted her.

"No. She doesn't want to talk to me again or meet me."

"Ouch," I say. "That must hurt as bad as getting slapped."

"Worse," she says. "Way worse." She looks away.

"Did she say why?"

"What do you think? She doesn't care about me. If she cared about me, she would want to meet me now, wouldn't she?"

"I don't know."

"You're a psychologist. You know how people behave."

"I don't know your birth mother. I don't want to speculate."

Ava's eyes widen. "Would you call her for me? Ask her to meet me. She'll listen to you. I know she will." Something in her face changes. "If she says no, you could tell her I'm going to kill myself if she won't."

I put my fork down next to my eggs. If it's this easy for Ava to lie to get what she wants, maybe those things she said about being stolen and trafficked are also lies.

"Are you serious?"

She looks at me like I'm too dumb to be a counselor.

"Nooo." She drags out the o's.

"I'm not going to lie for you or threaten your birth mother with your suicide. That's a terrible thing to do. A terrible thing to ask me to do."

Ava grimaces. "Sorry. You're right. That was stupid. And mean. Just call her. Ask her to meet me. Please." She puts her hands together in a prayer position. "You're the only person who believes me enough to even ask me about being stolen. Everyone else thinks I'm making it up. They don't want to listen. You do."

"I said you could have a break, not a day off." Fran is walking toward our booth, wiping her hands on her apron. "Look at all these tables that need clearing. They are not going to clear themselves."

Ava gets up without a word. Fran sits down.

"So what's she saying?"

"Not a lot. Nothing different."

"Still think she's telling the truth about being stolen?"

"I don't know. We didn't have long. I'd like to talk to her again."

"Be my guest, Dot. Anytime. Anyplace. I'm not her mother."

"You're what she's got for now. I have some time tomorrow at ten. Will that work?"

"Not a problem. At the moment, she's more trouble as a server than she's worth."

I check with Ava. She's more than happy to meet me. Unlike Pepper, she prefers my office to the café, because it's private and she will have my undivided attention. Undivided attention may be what she's been searching for all along. Despite what Dan and Fran say about how much Sharon is devoted to Ava, if there wasn't something off about their relationship, would Ava be working this hard to find another mother?

5

It's early morning the next day and the sun is blinding; the inside of my car is suffocating with heat. It's unseasonably hot. I turn on the AC, readjust the vents until I feel cool air on my over-heated face. I savor the relief, then ruin the moment with my father's voice bellowing his disdain for American consumerism, for polluting the planet with our cars, for lives so privileged we feel entitled to control the ambient temperature. I shake off his voice, his never-ending guilt-provoking bred-in-the-bone Jewish concern for the unfortunate. I'm going to my private office to meet Ava. But first I have some research to do.

There's no one in the lobby of my office building. I zip up the stairs to my office. Drop my briefcase on the desk and boot up my computer. Pepper said California is a closed adoption state. How can that be? California is the bellwether of all things progressive. Legalized marijuana. Women's right to choose. Jerry Brown. Gavin Newsom. Nancy Pelosi. Closed adoptions are from an age of secrecy and shame.

I google *Adopting a child in California*. California *is* a closed state. If your birth records are sealed, the only way to connect with your birth parents is through something called a mutual consent registry. It requires both parent and child to sign up.

Same for the genealogical sites I look at. Bottom line, it's almost impossible to find someone who isn't also looking for you.

A link suggesting other sites for children searching for their birth parents pops up. I click on it. The screen fills and I fall into a universe I've never known, a universe of joy and sorrow. Children searching for parents, parents searching for children. For every one of them, there are adoption agencies, adoption angels, and adoption detectives willing to help. Some advertise their services are free. Others are "reasonable." I wonder how many of them are legit and how you can tell who is and who isn't.

I keep reading. There are literally hundreds of testimonials about the miracle of finding the mother who's been looking for you as hard as you've been looking for her. The excitement of seeing your face in hers. The thrill of finding siblings who love the same bands and the same movies you do. Tributes to the satisfaction of forgiving and healing. It's like I'm wading through my high school yearbook—nothing but happy stories and impossible-to-keep promises to be in each other's lives forever.

After forty minutes of reading these happy testimonials, I find something that feels real and balanced. It's a checklist of things searchers need to think about before starting to investigate. The title is "Forewarned Is Forearmed." The writer had been adopted herself and doesn't want to discourage anyone from starting a search, it's just that, *Searchers shouldn't count on whatever happens during the search—or the reunion, if there is one—to change their lives. They'll be the same people they were before they began.* I find this statement puzzling. How could Ava not be changed by connecting to her birth mother or father? She has so many questions. If she could get the answers, wouldn't she feel better? At least she could stop looking and turn her attention to the rest of her life.

The checklist writer goes on with her warnings to the searcher. *Prepare yourself for the unexpected. Your birth parents may be dead. They may not want to be found. Your adoptive parents may give you a lot of grief for looking, especially if they are insecure. Last, but not least, you should be prepared to learn painful, long-hidden secrets from your past.*

I turn my computer off. Force myself to stop reading. I've just walked into Ava's world. A big world, full of despair, disappointment, and deceit. And she's been in it all alone. Now she's reaching out to me for help in that confusing way teenagers do. *Come here, go away. Help me, I can do it myself.* Once again, she reminds me of my teenage self. How desperately I needed an ally. How hard I tried to hide it. And how sad and angry I was that the adults around me were so easily fooled.

"My birth mother's name is Iliana Ester Ortega. She works for a medical transcription service." Ava has settled on my couch like she's been here dozens of times. Shoes off, her legs folded, hugging a decorative pillow against her chest. Her curly hair is pulled into an off-center ponytail. She complains about the heat. How it never gets this hot on the coast because of the fog. "I'm half Mexican. I know that much at least. The Mexican kids at school think I'm Iranian. They call me 'raghead.' The white kids call me 'taco girl.' Sharon thinks I'm only brown because I'm outside so much and I don't wear enough sunscreen."

"She really said that?"

Ava rolls her eyes. "I don't look like either of my parents. You met Dan. Do I look like him?" She doesn't wait for an answer. "I don't think like them. I don't want to do what they want me to do."

"You're eighteen, Ava. That's normal for being eighteen."

"They didn't pick me out of a cabbage patch. I didn't float down the river like the baby Moses. I want to know where I came from, why my birth parents gave me away. Doesn't every adopted kid want the same? Maybe I have brothers or sisters or cousins? What if I've inherited some nasty genes and shouldn't have children?"

"You have a lot of questions. More questions than answers for sure. All of them important."

"The only way I'm going to get them is from my birth mother who doesn't want to see me."

"Why do you think she doesn't want to see you?"

"For the same reason she gave me away. She hates me."

"You don't know that, Ava. There could be many reasons your birth mother is reluctant to meet you. She might have another family, a husband and children who don't know about you. Hearing from you out of the blue must have been a shock. You need to give her a little time."

Ava's eyes are hard as pebbles. Am I on her side or not? If I were on her side, wouldn't I be picking up the phone, calling her mother? Why am I dragging this out? Making her wait? Asking so many questions?

"How long have you known you were adopted?"

"Always, ever since I was a baby. Sharon must have read a thousand books to me about forever families and bears who adopt piglets. She tried really hard to make me feel good about being adopted. Nobody understands this. I've always felt loved. That doesn't change the fact that I feel different and look different. Finding my birth parents is not about what Dan and Sharon did wrong; it's about me. Who I look like. Where I came from. Why I wasn't wanted."

She hunkers down, crushes my pillow in her arms.

"How did you find your birth mother? That must have been difficult."

"It was hella weird, for sure. On my eighteenth birthday,

Sharon told me the social worker who did my adoption was named Barbara Jensen from New Leaf Adoptions. She didn't want me to tell Dan she'd told me, but she wouldn't say why. Weird, huh?" She looks for my reaction. "She was lying. Trying to get me to stop looking. Nobody at New Leaf had ever heard of a social worker named Barbara Jensen."

"What about your adoption papers?"

"There were none."

"Do you have a Social Security card? A birth certificate?"

"Both. Dan and Sharon's names are on my birth certificate."

"I understand that's the normal procedure after an adoption."

There's a flush on Ava's cheeks, a coppery glow. It's as if my questions are fanning a hidden fire. She's been eager to tell her story, but until now, no one but me has wanted to hear it.

"I kept looking. Calling people. Asking questions. Turns out the year I was born, a social worker named Barbara Johnson, not Jensen, lost her license for DUI arrests and doing illegal adoptions. I tracked her down. She lives in a rehab place. Works as a counselor. She's the one who told me my birth mother's name."

"Barbara Johnson remembered your mother's name after eighteen years?"

"She had a list, must have been four or five names with dates of birth. I think she was planning to blackmail us or our parents. She was skanky."

"You went to see her by yourself?"

"She was old. What was she going to do to me?"

A menu of possibilities spools through my mind. Ava at eighteen, on her own, walking into a world of back alleys, stolen babies, and extortion.

"I couldn't take Dan or Sharon with me. I couldn't even talk to them about it. Every time I did, they'd go ballistic, start fighting with me and each other."

"If Sharon didn't want you to find your birth parents, why did she give you the name of the agency who handled your adoption?"

Ava shrugs. "How do I know?"

"I'm not accusing you of anything, Ava. I'm just a little bewildered."

"She was trying to confuse me. She gave me the wrong name on purpose."

"Why would she do that?"

"Because she doesn't want me to know she and Dan stole me. Jeez. How many times do I have to say this?"

Ava has had enough of my probing. I've pushed her, maybe too far. She unfurls her legs, sets the pillow aside. "I should go. I told Fran I'd be back in time to set up for lunch."

She stands. I've let her down, damaged her fragile trust. If she walks out my door, she's never coming back. She pinned her hopes on me and I dropped the ball. Validated her belief that adults can't be trusted. No matter how dangerous or difficult it will be, she's better off going after her mother on her own. I need to fix this fast.

"Thanks, Ava."

"For what?"

"For taking me into your confidence. Give me a little time. I am going to think seriously about calling your birth mother."

"Whatever," she says and walks out.

6

It's the weekend, finally. Frank is making his famous braised chicken and onion stew with mashed potatoes. I'm making salad. Not that I'm incapable of cooking, it's just that he's so much better. And quicker. When I cook, the kitchen is a disaster. Cleanup takes twenty minutes. Frank cleans as he goes. It's a habit he's developed remodeling houses. His clients have children and dogs and lives to manage, they don't want to live in a construction site 24/7.

I've invited Fran and Ava to dinner. Fran needs a break from staring at Ava's sullen face. I'm eager to touch base with Ava again; that is, if she's still talking to me. It's a balmy night. We can eat on the back patio next to the garden. If we run out of things to say, we can at least listen to the songbirds and the melodious sound of the water fountain Frank built.

Fran is standing on the front step holding a lemon meringue pie. I haven't seen her for a few days. She looks exhausted. Ava looks better than I anticipated, dressed in a crop top and jeans, her hair in a scrunchie. Frank comes out of the kitchen with two glasses of red wine, one for Fran, one for me. He introduces himself to Ava. Asks if she wants a glass of wine.

"I don't like wine."

"Come with me," Frank says to Ava. "Let's see what else I can come up with." He shows her into the kitchen.

"How's it going?" I ask.

"She's in a good mood for the moment. Her friend Cody is coming over tomorrow."

"And at the café?"

"She's catching on. All the young coppers think she's a great addition. She won't admit it, but I think she likes the attention."

"What about the two of you?"

"So-so. She comes back from the café, doesn't want to eat, and goes to her room. Texting with friends, FaceTime, whatever they call it. I told her to tell her friends to come over. They all have summer jobs, so I guess they can't, except for Cody, who works with his father and makes his own hours."

Frank and Ava come out of the kitchen. Ava's carrying a glass of something bubbly garnished with an orange slice and two Luxardo cherries that cost twenty dollars a bottle. Cherries that are meant for our rare, celebratory Manhattans. Frank pulls Ava's chair out from the table and motions her to sit.

"Mademoiselle, s'il vous plaît."

She smiles despite herself.

The air is warm and silky. Frank's stew and home-baked bread are delicious. Hummingbirds dart around our heads and through the butterfly bushes. Quail rustle in the undergrowth, their soft voices calling to each other. Frank is enthralling Ava with his Iowa gift for gab. He seems to never run out of things to talk about. She finishes her dinner and her second secret sauce nonalcoholic cocktail just as Frank slips her a question, smooth as a knife cutting butter.

"I understand you were adopted and you recently found your birth mother. What's she like?"

Fran and I gulp. We've been walking around Ava on eggshells and here's Frank asking her a very personal question.

Ava answers without hesitation. "Beats me. I only talked to her on the phone. She doesn't want to meet me."

"Well, then," Frank says in the space of a heartbeat, "she doesn't know what she's missing, does she?" He stands. "Ready for dessert? How about some coffee and Fran's amazing, other-worldly lemon meringue pie?"

He heads to the kitchen. We sink into silence. Our next-door neighbors are in the backyard playing with their children. Their squeaks and squeals are punctuated by a barking dog who wants in on the game. Ava fills the awkward silence talking about how hard it is to see the stars from here. Over the hill, in Moss Point, unless it's foggy, you can see millions of stars every night. I take this not so much as a complaint but an expression of how much she misses her home, her friends, and her little coastal community. And how much she's willing to give up to find her birth parents.

Frank comes back to the table with pie and coffee. We tell Fran how good it is. She brushes off our compliments, although she's obviously pleased. Lemon meringue was BG's favorite. She hasn't made one in ages.

"So, Fran," Frank says, "how did you get to be Ava's godmother?"

"Ava's father, Dan, was a Kenilworth cop. BG was his field training officer. They were very close."

"Aunt Fran knew them before they got me and when they got me."

Something about this statement causes Fran to stiffen.

"Don't ask me about your adoption again, please. I don't know anything about where you came from. All I know is that once Dan and Sharon decided to adopt, there you were. Quick as a wink."

"Too quick? Weirdly quick?"

"No. I didn't think it was weird. I was happy for them. Truthfully, I didn't think about it or you very much. BG had just been killed. I had a lot on my mind. I was running a restaurant by myself. Every spare minute I wasn't working, I was crying over BG or trying to sleep."

Ava reaches over the table and touches Fran on the arm. "I'm sorry, Aunt Fran. I wish I had known BG. He sounds like a great guy. My dad loved him. Talks about him a lot." She takes her hand away. "I know it was a terrible time. I'm not blaming you for anything."

"Are you sure? I feel like you are."

"See what happens?" Ava balls her hands into fists. "Every time I talk about being adopted, somebody gets mad."

She spears a forkful of pie, lifts it to her mouth, puts it down, and shoves the uneaten portion away. "Can we go home soon? My friend Cody is coming over tomorrow. I want to get up early. We're going hiking."

"I think you mean your boyfriend Cody," Fran says.

"He's not my boyfriend. He's more like my baby brother, even though he's older."

"Then why does he follow you around like a lovesick puppy?"

"Because he doesn't have any other friends. I'm his bestie. I keep telling him he needs to make more friends."

Ava changes her mind about the pie and starts to eat. The neighbor's ball comes flying over the fence. Ava is out of her chair in a flash. She sprints into the garden, finds the ball, and pitches it back over the fence.

"Nice throw," Frank says. They do a high five.

"Aunt Fran." Ava puts her hands on her hips in a mock display of displeasure, then taps the face of her watch. Fran gets out of her chair with some difficulty. We walk to the front door. Ava turns to face us. "Thanks much for inviting us. Nice to meet you, Frank. Thanks for the mocktail and the food. Everything was de-lish." She gives Frank a big smile.

"Our pleasure, come back again." He opens the door.

It's only then that Ava looks at me directly. She hasn't said a word all night about my calling her mother.

"Still thinking," I say.

"Still waiting," she says.

"She's a quick one, isn't she?" Frank asks. I'm washing, he's drying. "What's with her adopted family? Why are they so against her finding her birth parents?"

"I don't know."

We go back to the patio with after-dinner cordials and sit in silence, listening to the crickets serenading one another. It's still warm. The air smells deliciously damp. It's getting dark, and the line of trees behind our house is barely visible against the deep purple sky.

"Nice dinner, Frank. Everything was de-lish, to quote someone we know. You were great with Ava. Had her literally eating out of your palm."

"I do that to all the women. That's how I got you." He rubs his foot on my leg. "She's a smart kid. I liked her. A little prickly but that comes with the territory. Put a little fat on her she'd be very pretty. How come her birth mother doesn't want to meet her?"

"I wish I knew. I started checking online websites for reuniting families and finding lost relatives. It's a huge industry. The potential for deception and abuse is enormous. Poor kid's wading through all this by herself. At eighteen."

"Eighteen is the age of maturity."

"The human brain doesn't fully develop until you're in your mid-twenties."

"Or, in my case, even later than that."

"I'm not joking around, Frank. There's something off here. Something doesn't fit. She doesn't have any adoption papers. At least, that's what she's been told."

"Ask one of your police buddies to look into it."

"Ava's adopted father, Dan, was a cop. He doesn't seem concerned."

"Of course not, he's her father. Anyhow, good for him. You tell me all the time the biggest mistake cops make is to be a cop at home."

I do say that. After a few years on the job, they start suspecting everyone of being a predator, judging one hundred percent of the world by the ten percent they see at work. They do stupid things, illegal things, things they could lose their jobs for doing, like running their babysitter's license plates through computer records, looking for criminal activity. I tell them to stop, but no one listens. I'm a civilian, which makes me inherently naive. Civilians live in a world of possibility where bad things *could* happen. Cops live in a world of probability where bad things *will* happen.

"Ava asked me to call her birth mother. She thinks because I'm a psychologist, I can persuade her mother to meet her in person. She wanted me to say I think she's suicidal."

"Is she?"

"I don't think so. But I haven't done a formal assessment. I'd send her to see Gary if I thought she was; he sees adolescents."

"So what are you going to do? Are you going to contact the birth mother?"

"I don't know. What do you think?"

"You're asking me?"

"You're my husband. I value your opinion."

"This is above my pay grade, Dot. Ask me about fixing a

double-hung window or putting in a skylight, I'm your man. But teenagers? Girls?" He leans over, puts his hands on my knees, then skewers me gently with the truth. "You don't really want to know what I think. You're going to do what you want to do, no matter what I say. She seems to need your help and you love being needed. From where I sit, it's a marriage made in heaven. Take it for what it's worth, count to ten, look both ways, eat your veggies, and don't make any decisions until you've had a good night's sleep."

Getting a good night's sleep was a great idea, if only I could sleep. I turn over and look at the clock for the third time. Frank is out like a light. I can hear his slow, even breaths. I stare at the ceiling, still that same ghastly sprayed-on cottage cheese stuff Frank has been promising to replace. I turn over for the fiftieth time, trying to find a comfortable position. Frank pulls on the covers and mumbles something. I get out of bed, put on my robe, and go downstairs to the kitchen. The ceiling will get fixed one day. I hardly notice it unless I'm in bed with my eyes open. I am gnawing on a misplaced resentment. Ava is what's keeping me up, not the damn ceiling.

I make myself a cup of tea and go into my study to think. Something about Ava's life, her feeling of displacement, keeps nagging at me. When I was a child, I felt so different from my mother and my father that for years I wondered if the hospital where I was born had sent me home with the wrong parents. It was my way of struggling to establish my own identity. Ava's quest for identity is more challenging, her sense of displacement more profound. So profound that when she was an infant, she could only feel it, not name it. As though she knew by instinct that the family who adopted her was not her own. The way children with body dysphoria—boys trapped in girl's bodies, girls trapped in boy's bodies—know from an early age they are not the gender they were assigned at birth.

I'm assuming that Dan and Sharon love Ava, however imperfectly, as much as they would have loved a biological child. Perhaps there is no love strong enough to overcome Ava's feeling that she doesn't belong. Or quench her persistent longing to find her birth parents and unravel the mystery of why they didn't keep her.

This much I know. Teenagers need confirmation. They need caring adults to verify that it's all right to feel sad or angry or any of the multitude of emotions they have. They are in the midst of constant change. Their bodies, their minds, everything is in flux. They are at the mercy of overactive hormones and hyperactive emotions. Every perceived slight, every failure, every rejection feels like the end of the world. Ben Gomez was barely past his teenage years. There were accessible solutions to his problems. He had people on his side, including me. But he couldn't see his way out. Couldn't accept help. Couldn't tell the truth about the depth of his suffering. Put on his cop mask and kept it on until life got unbearable.

"Stop it." The sound of my own voice in the nighttime silence scares me. I can't go down this rabbit hole for the millionth time, raking myself over the coals about what I should or shouldn't have done for Ben.

Ava has asked for my help. She's trying, at least I think she is, to expose secrets, not hide them. What if I'm wrong? What if she's right and no one believes her? What would she do then? And do I want to take that chance? A telephone call. That's all she's asked for. It's a simple request. Why am I trying to make it more complicated than it is?

7

"*Thank you for calling Medical Transcription Services of Northern California. Our office hours are nine to five, Monday through Friday. At the tone, please leave a message of any length. We will call you back as soon as we are able.*"

For a second, to guarantee a callback, I'm tempted to leave a message pretending to be looking for help transcribing clinical notes. "My name is Dr. Dot Meyerhoff. I'm a clinical psychologist. Ava Sower has contacted me for assistance. She would like to set up an in-person meeting with Iliana Ester Ortega. Please call back as soon as possible. Thank you."

I put my phone on the counter and head for the living room to join Frank. Reading the Sunday papers together is part of our tradition. Traditions are good for relationships; they anchor who we are—this is us, this is what we do as a couple. Too many of the cops I see have distant relationships with their families. They rarely do things together. They know nothing about one another's lives or dreams. Everything revolves around the job.

My phone vibrates as soon as I settle in my reading chair. Frank looks annoyed, signals for me to let it go to voicemail. It's an unknown caller, someone not in my contact list. Feeling hypocritical about letting work interfere with our morning, I answer anyhow. A woman's voice, so soft I can barely hear her, asks for me. I identify myself.

"Is something wrong with Ava?"

"Who am I speaking to?"

"Iliana Ortega. You called me a few minutes ago. Is Ava all right? Why is she seeing a psychologist?"

"Ava and her family have approached me. I'm a psychologist, but I'm also a family friend."

"Approached you why?"

"She has some questions and concerns about her adoption."

"I've already given her all the information I have about her health history. I have nothing to add."

"Ava has a lot of questions, not just about her health history. She would like to meet you in person. She asked me to call you to see if I could understand your hesitation about meeting her and, perhaps, influence you to change your mind." I'm being so careful, so formal, I feel like my tongue is sticking to my mouth.

"I have already told Ava we cannot meet. I'm sorry. You're a psychologist, I'm sure you are aware that there are some things a child shouldn't know. Questions that are better left unanswered."

"Ava's eighteen, she's not a child. In fact, she's a very determined young woman. Here's the problem. With so many unanswered questions, she's filling in the gaps in her understanding with wild speculations. Whatever she's imagining is probably worse than the truth."

There's silence on the other end.

"Is there something I could do to make it easier for the two of you to meet? Perhaps you and I could meet first to talk about how best to tell Ava what she wants to know? I'm guessing that it's complicated."

"Yes, it is complicated. And thank you but, no, I don't need help. I have my own resources."

"From what you've said so far, it sounds like you are trying to protect Ava, not avoid her. Am I correct?"

"What Ava wants to know could be more hurtful than not knowing."

"The thing Ava wants most to know is why she was put up for adoption. She hasn't said this directly, but I think she believes she was unloved. Unwanted." Iliana inhales, almost a gasp. "Unfortunately, in your efforts to protect her by not giving her the details of her adoption, she's created a different story, one that's easier to live with. Something you may have said or implied has her believing she was stolen, not placed for adoption. She has accused her adoptive parents of knowingly buying her from a baby trafficker. This has led to a great deal of conflict in the family. As a result, Ava is no longer living at home. She's living with her godmother, who is the person who asked for my help."

Iliana says something to herself or someone else in Spanish. I wait.

"Sorry. I was talking to someone in my house. The last thing I want to do is to create trouble for Ava or her parents."

"If you agree to meet with her, answer some of her questions, that would go a long way to avoiding more trouble."

"I'll think about it, but for right now, my answer is still no." She disconnects.

8

A week passes with no word from Iliana, no critical incidents, no new hires to interview, and no new assignments from the chief. Things are so quiet, it's almost scary. Frank and I are hanging out in the kitchen, having a leisurely late-morning brunch at the counter. It's a lovely day, clear skies, temperature in the 70s. The perfect day for a hike in the hills. My cell goes off. It's Fran. She doesn't sound happy. She hasn't sounded happy all week.

"Cody showed up this morning at seven thirty with two of Ava's friends, Astra and Marisa. Can you believe it? No warning, no phone call, nothing, they just knocked on the door. Ava was a happy girl. I know she misses her friends. Anyhow, that bunch has gone off to San Francisco."

"Excellent. You have the house to yourself for a few hours."

Her voice drops. "Don't I wish. Ava's mother, Sharon, was with them. Didn't ask if it was okay with me, just told the kids to have fun in the city and plopped down on my sofa. She's a hot mess."

"Good luck, sounds like you're going to do a lot of listening."

"She didn't come here to talk to me. She wants to talk to you about Ava. That's why I'm calling."

Frank isn't happy about my going to Fran's. I assure him I'll be back in a few hours, plenty of time left to take a walk. He mutters something about it being Saturday, don't I get the weekend off? I remind him this isn't work, Fran is a friend.

Sharon Sower is a beautiful woman. Pale skin, light eyes, and shoulder-length blond hair swept back at the sides. She's sitting on the couch in Fran's living room dressed in patterned tights and an oversized t-shirt. Her multicolored eye shadow shimmers like an oil slick. She reaches to shake my hand. Her grip is strong. I take a seat opposite her, Fran's coffee table between us.

"Fran and Dan both speak highly of you. I'm so grateful for your work with Ava."

My work with Ava? She's talking like I've signed a contract.

"I was hoping to talk to Ava this morning, but she and the kids were eager to get going. Ava looked good, didn't she, Fran? Capri pants and a blouse. She usually wears those horrible jeans that look like they came from the giveaway box at church." There's a nervous edge to Sharon's chattiness. "They're going to San Francisco. I used to take Ava to the Academy of Sciences in Golden Gate Park. Then to the Japanese tea garden. We live over on the coast in Moss Point now. I guess you know that. I work with my husband. He's in construction. I manage the office, do the books, the scheduling, pay the subs, that kind of thing."

"How can I help, Sharon? Fran said you wanted to talk to me."

Her upbeat demeanor, brittle as glass, splinters on contact with my question.

"That's just it. I don't know how you can help. It's like I don't know my daughter anymore. She won't talk to me. She doesn't want me to touch her. I know how much she wanted to find out about her adoption. I expected it. All adoptive parents do. Dan didn't want her to look, but I knew she would. I just wanted her to wait until she was more mature. Then I find out she's been looking all along, on the internet and stuff. She never used to lie. That made Dan crazy angry and scared."

Words tumble out of her mouth like escaping prisoners running for their lives.

"I'm sorry, I'm babbling. I talk a lot when I'm nervous. Drives Dan crazy. The worst part is what she said her birth mother told her, that she was stolen, and we bought her from a baby trafficker. We would never do such a thing." Sharon dabs at her eyes, leaving a smudge of mascara. "Am I making any sense?"

It's still not clear what she wants from me. If I don't know what she wants, I won't know what to give. Or if to give it.

"Ava was a colicky baby, didn't want to be held. She cried all the time. There was nothing I could do to comfort her. I was desperate. I tried to find her social worker. I thought if I knew something about her health history or more about her birth parents it would help. I didn't try very hard or for very long. I was too busy and too tired."

I get it. She has a story to tell and she needs me to listen. Nothing else will make sense until she's laid it all out.

"Everything happened so quickly that we hardly had time to get ready. You remember, don't you, Fran?" Fran nods. "After a few months, Ava settled down and I tried again to find the social worker who handled her adoption. But when I called the adoption agency where she had said she worked, she wasn't there. In fact, they'd never heard of her."

I remember Ava saying her mother gave her the social worker's name when she turned eighteen. If Sharon knew it was a phony name, why did she pass it on to Ava?

"That scared me that they never heard of her. It didn't seem right. I wanted to know more, but I was terrified of losing Ava. I didn't want to rock the boat. We'd been waiting for so long to adopt, I was already in my thirties, afraid if I asked too many questions, someone would take her away." She puts her hands on her chest. "Just saying that makes me nervous."

"So you never knew anything about her birth parents?"

"No. The social worker gave us the papers we needed. Said everything was A-okay." She fans her face with her hand. Asks Fran for a glass of water. "Is my makeup smeared? I don't usually wear makeup, just lipstick, but my friend Marlene, Cody's mother, told me I should dress up a little to meet you. You're a doctor, you'd probably be wearing a skirt and high heels. I'll tell her you were wearing jeans and sneakers. Like a regular person."

We laugh. It's easy for women to connect over clothes.

"It's because of Marlene and Lonny that we moved to the coast—so we could raise our kids together. Every child should have a family. Especially only children. Marlene and Lonny are like Ava's play aunt and uncle. Cody's her play brother, although I think he likes her more than that."

Fran sets a glass of water on the table in front of Sharon. She drinks it down in one long swallow, wipes the water ring off the table with her hand, and asks Fran for a coaster before she puts the glass down. "I needed that. Thanks. Where was I? I was telling you about Moss Point. It's a nice place to raise a child. Better than Kenilworth and Silicon Valley where everybody is chasing money. Do you have children, Doctor?"

"No."

She looks at me with part envy, part pity.

"All I ever wanted to be, beside Dan's wife, is a mother. I don't have a lot of education. I graduated from high school and got my LVN. Then I met Dan and we tried to get pregnant. We tried and we tried for ten years. Spent all kinds of money we didn't have on doctors. I had to stop working. The doctors told me taking care of old people, turning them in their beds, lifting heavy stuff, was too stressful. I was sad to leave. I liked helping old people." She looks at me. "Am I telling you what you want to know? I feel like I'm just running on. I've never talked to a psychologist before. Maybe I should have." She laughs at her own joke.

"How did you and Dan first meet the social worker who handled Ava's adoption?"

"Dan found her. Cops know a lot of people." She leans across the coffee table and touches me on the knee. "Being Ava's mother is who I am, who I've been for eighteen years. Much as I want her to be happy, the truth is I don't want to share her. I'm afraid her birth mother is going to turn her against me, against us. I feel like it's already started."

Fran leans in, touches Sharon on the arm. "Ava's told me over and over, this is not about rejecting you, it's about finding her roots."

"That's not how it feels. It doesn't matter what I say, Ava believes that woman, not me."

Fran moves to the couch, puts her arm around Sharon's shoulders, and lets her cry.

It's close to four o'clock by the time Cody, Ava, Astra, and Marisa get back from the city in a gigantic truck with huge tires and a loud muffler. Long after I promised Frank I would be home. He texted me about two hours ago. Tired of waiting, he was going to hike by himself.

Marisa is even skinnier than Ava. She's wearing shorts and a crop top. Nobody wears shorts in San Francisco in the summer except tourists. Marisa reaches out to shake my hand. Her fingernails are painted blue, and she's wearing a ring on every finger and a half-dozen woven bracelets on each hand. She has multicolored streaks in her long light brown hair. Astra wears glasses. Her reddish hair is buzzed short on one side and hangs loose on the other. No streaks. Her mother is a counselor. She's glad Ava is talking to me because her mother thinks Ava's family needs therapy. Marisa interrupts to announce that her mother has a GED and she's also happy I'm helping Ava because Ava could be carrying some nasty-ass mutant genes. What if she got pregnant? She looks at Cody, who turns three shades of purple.

"Stop it," Ava says. "I am not pregnant. Holy crap, Marisa."

"I told you about my aunt who adopted . . ."

"Enough." Fran stands. "Why don't you girls wait in the truck?"

Marisa shrugs and walks away. Astra says it was nice to meet me, and Cody just stands there watching Ava with big eyes, clearly smitten. He's small for his age. His face and neck are marked with adolescent acne. He's wearing jeans and a dark blue t-shirt printed with a large anchor and the words *Wilson's Boatyard*. His dark hair sticks out at angles under a backward baseball cap emblazoned with a miniaturized boatyard logo.

"Hi, Cody," I say. "I'm Dot Meyerhoff."

I lean over to shake his hand. Shaking hands with adults is evidently not something he does very often. My grip is far stronger than his. He murmurs something I take to be "nice to meet you."

"I'm looking at your hat. Is that where you work, Wilson's Boatyard?"

"It's my father's boatyard. Do you have a boat? Do you like to fish?"

I shake my head on both counts.

"My dad could take you out. He has half-day and one-day trips. My mother will pack you a lunch. He's the best. Knows where the fish are." He digs in his back pocket and pulls out a wrinkled brochure.

"Cody, stop." Ava scowls. "She already said she doesn't want to go fishing. Go wait in the truck with Marisa and Astra. Please."

"Nice to meet you, Cody," I say, taking the brochure. "Sounds like you're really proud of your dad."

Ava glares at me as if I have turned Cody's love for his father into a rebuke of her own contentious relationship with Dan. Then she looks at Sharon. "Have you been crying, Mom?"

Sharon smiles. "Just a little. You know me, I cry at TV commercials. I was telling the doctor about when you were a little baby."

Ava rolls her eyes. "Here," she says. "I bought you some almond cookies." She hands Sharon a brown paper bag, butter stains marking the outside.

"I love almond cookies. Thank you, sweetie, that was so thoughtful of you."

"We ate lunch in Chinatown. They have all these yucky roast pigs and ducks hanging in the windows. It was gross. I had egg foo young."

She looks at Cody and taps her watch, a giant thing that probably tracks all her bodily functions. Frank wanted to buy me one for my birthday, but I told him they were too big and too complicated. Plus, the only function I'd ever use was the one that called 911 if I fell over.

"You guys better get going or you'll run into traffic," she says.

Sharon gets up, thanks Fran and me for a wonderful afternoon. She envelops Ava in a hug, her arms covering most of Ava's back. Ava hesitates for a moment, then gives in. Puts her arms around her mother and pats her on the back like she's comforting a child.

We wave goodbye from the driveway. Sharon sends air-kisses. Cody leaves a little rubber on the road to emphasize his masculinity. Marisa and Astra are bent over their phones.

"Nice of you to buy your mom a present," I say as we walk back toward the house. Then, "I called your birth mother."

Ava's eyes widen. She isn't wearing a touch of makeup, no liner, no mascara, yet her eyes stand out in the dusky light.

"You called her? What did she say?" Ava starts hopping back and forth, left foot to right and back again like some external force has taken control of her body.

"Whoa, Betsy," Fran says. "Slow down, I got neighbors. I don't want them thinking I've opened a boarding home for crazy girls." We go inside.

"Sorry." Ava stops moving. "What did she say?"

"She said she'd think about it, but for now no."

"Did you tell her I'll kill myself if she won't meet me?"

"I did not. I told you I wouldn't lie for you."

"Kill yourself? Oh my God." Fran is shaking her head, her hands on her hips. "You don't really mean that, do you?" Her face is whiter than the shirt she is wearing. "She's not serious, is she, Dot? People who threaten suicide never do it, right? They're just looking for attention."

This is a common myth. The fact is that people who kill themselves have often hinted at it multiple times.

"Put yourself in Iliana's place, Ava," I say. "How would you feel if the daughter you gave away called you up out of the blue eighteen years later asking to meet you?"

"I'd be doing a happy dance. I couldn't wait to meet her."

"That's ridiculous, Ava." The color is coming back to Fran's face. "You have no idea about her circumstances. I can think of sixty-four reasons off the top of my head why she's not jumping for joy because you called. She's dying of cancer. Maybe she's married with six children and wants to tell everyone in her family, including her husband, face-to-face, the biggest secret of her life. But her kids are at camp and her husband is on a business trip to Dubai."

Ava breaks into a smile despite herself. "You read too many books, Aunt Fran."

"I have a lot of faults, Ava girl. Reading isn't one of them. As far as I'm concerned, you don't read enough. The result being that you suffer from a lack of imagination and empathy. Both of which you get from reading."

"You've waited almost eighteen years, Ava," I say. "I think you can wait a little longer."

"You both think contacting my birth mother is a bad idea, don't you?"

"I don't know if it's a good idea or not," I say. "All I know is that whatever happens, you're the one who has to live with the consequences, not me. Not Fran."

"That's my point. Don't you get it? I'm nothing but the consequence of other people's decisions. Iliana was the one who decided not to keep me. Now she gets to decide if, when, and where we can meet. All I ever get to do is wait. It's not fair."

"Not fair?" Fran says. "Welcome to my world. I'll tell you what's not fair. It's not fair I was a widow in my thirties. It's not fair BG got killed by some thug who stole thirty dollars worth of crap nobody wanted in the first place." She's tearing up. "Enough of this, I'm going to warm up something to eat. I'm hungry." She stomps toward the kitchen.

"Damn it. I made her cry." Ava looks like she's about to cry herself.

"I think it was the memories that made her sad, not you."

"I love Fran. I don't want to make her cry. I don't want to make anyone cry. I just want to talk to my birth mother. Why is this so hard?" Ava walks into the kitchen. I follow her. "I'm sorry, Aunt Fran. I didn't mean to upset you." She hugs Fran from behind. Fran shrugs her off.

"Wash your face, kid. I'm warming up some vegetable soup from the café. Nothing in here ever had a face, so you can eat it."

"You're just like Sharon, you think the solution to everything is food."

"That's why you're so fat, huh?" She swats at Ava with a dish towel. "Want to join us, Dot?"

I tell her I need to go home. I already messed up my hike with Frank. I promised to make him dinner and take him to the movies.

Ava grips me by the shoulders. "Call me the minute you hear from Iliana. Promise?"

"Absolutely. *If* she calls back, you'll be the first to know."

9

This time, when Fran calls, Frank and I are in the living room. He's been watching a cop show featuring a female officer wearing impossibly high heels as she busts down a door without backup, shoots a gun out of the hand of a tatted-up muscle-bound gangster, kills two of his buddies, then goes home and has fabulous sex with her beyond handsome boyfriend. Total fantasy. I can't watch shows like this without remembering Pepper's bruised face and her terrified eyes.

"Hey, Fran," I say. "What's new?"

"I feel like I'm running a nuthouse. Ava's like a crazy woman. As soon as we get home, she goes to her room to FaceTime her friends or talk to Cody. Sometimes I can hear her crying. I ask if I can help. She doesn't want to talk. Cody's been calling every night. Sometimes more than once. They had a big fight, he told her she needed therapy, she told him to go to hell. The next day, he shows up here with bouquet of half-dead flowers he bought at the gas station on the way over the hill. She wouldn't talk to him. He sat in his car for an hour until I told him to leave, I couldn't have him sleeping in my driveway. Three days later, I hear her talking to him on the phone, laughing hysterically, like nothing happened.

"She can treat him like crap and he comes back for more. I asked her if he's such a pain, why do you hang out with him? She said the boys at her high school only liked blond girls with blue eyes. If she needed a date for something, Cody was always available. Partly because he's such a dork—her words, not mine—none of the girls in town will go out with him. But then she said this really touching thing. They grew up together. She feels like his sister. He knows her better than anyone and he doesn't judge her. When she's with him, she can be herself." Fran sighs into the phone.

"Sorry to be such a motormouth. I'm going stir-crazy locked up with this crazy girl day and night, at home and at work. Not only that, Sharon calls every other day asking if Ava's heard from her birth mother."

"Why is she asking you?"

"She's too afraid to ask Ava. Doesn't want to pry. I don't know how much more of this I can take, Dot. I'm getting really tired of being in the middle."

10

The next Saturday is unseasonably hot. It's as though someone flipped a switch on California's natural air-conditioning. There isn't a drop of cool wind. Frank is out back, watering the garden. As soon as he's done, we're heading over the hill to the coast to find some cool air, take a hike on the bluffs overlooking the ocean.

The winding road to the coast is crowded with like-minded folks wanting to escape the heat. We crawl along at ten miles an hour, grateful for the A/C. Frank is telling me about his latest photography project and the possibility he'll need a new, very expensive camera. He's not looking for my approval. It was Frank's suggestion that we keep our money separate. He has his account, I have mine, and we share one credit card for household expenses. I thought it was a great idea. Only my former therapist, Dr. Philipp Rogoff, questioned the reluctance to mix our finances. He wondered if we were getting married on the installment plan, one cautious step at a time, and if this wasn't equivalent to a vote of no-confidence in our future? Just the opposite, I assured him; it was an expression of how much we trusted each other.

We park the car. The ocean is calm and sparkly, the beach

below nearly deserted, save for a few families exploring the tide pools and several very happy dogs who are plunging in and out of the water chasing one another. A dozen or more surfers in black wet suits bobble on the smooth surface of the water waiting for a wave. I put my cell phone in my pocket. Frank straps on a belly pack with some water and a few protein bars. We are hiking a single-track dirt trail that winds through a community of native plants, all of them in bloom: beach burr, coyote bush, yellow lupin, and fern. Tough, low-to-the-ground plants that have adapted to the wind, waves, and salt spray. A runner passes us going the opposite direction. We step aside. His shirt is soaked with sweat, he has earbuds playing, and his eyes are focused on the trail. There are plenty of rocks and roots to stumble over.

"What's the point?" Frank says, looking after the runner. "He might as well be in the gym on a treadmill; he can't hear the waves and he's missing all this gorgeous color."

My phone vibrates with a text. It's from Iliana. I motion for Frank to keep walking.

The wind is picking up off the ocean. I step aside again to let a hiker and her dog pass. The dog is a wiggly mixed breed eager for me to pet him and just as eager to keep going. I balance on the edge of the path, mindful of the sign behind me warning walkers to stay on the trail, not to disturb the delicately planted dunes. Frank turns to check on me. I wave. He waves back and keeps walking. The sun is bright. I squint to read Iliana's text.

Can we talk in person? Just U and me. Tomorrow, Sunday. 1:00 p.m.

"Tomorrow? At her house? I'm coming with you." Frank and I are on our way home, crawling along at five miles per hour. Part of a crowd of tired, wind-burned hungry hikers with sand in our boots. "She could be dangerous."

"She doesn't sound dangerous, she sounds scared."

"You know this how? From the sound of her voice? I don't have to come in. I'll wait at the curb."

"I'm in the mood for pizza. How about you? We can phone ahead and pick one up at Tony's-To-Go."

"You're changing the subject. When are you going to tell Ava about this meeting?"

"I don't know. Here's the problem. I promised Ava I'd tell her the minute I heard from Iliana. Number one, I wasn't really expecting to hear from Iliana again. Number two, I didn't anticipate she would take me up on my suggestion that she and I get together before she meets Ava. She's trying to hide something she believes Ava is better off not knowing." Frank looks at me. "Don't ask me what that is, I haven't got a clue."

"So what are you going to tell Ava?"

"I've painted myself into a corner. If I don't tell her, Ava will be pissed at me for breaking my promise. If I do tell her, she'll be badgering me every second to take her along."

Somebody behind us leans on their horn, starting a chain reaction of horn-blowing. Frank mutters under his breath and looks at his phone trying to get a traffic report. If there's a road accident ahead, we could be stuck here for hours.

I close my eyes. I'm tired and I need to think this through. On the one hand, I'm surprised and relieved that Iliana wants to meet me. I haven't a clue about what she's been thinking all these years. When and if she meets Ava, it's going to be thorny. Ava's feelings are a tangle. Longing mixed with resentment mixed with the countless stories I imagine she's made up about her birth parents. She and Iliana can't just sort things out on their own. It's too complicated. Ava's angry and in a hurry. Iliana is scared and feeling pressured. It's a dangerous combination.

"Forget the pizza," I say to Frank. "I need to go home, take a shower, and talk to Ava. If I break my promise or lie to her, I'll throw what little trust she has in me right out the window."

"So call her on the phone."

"No way. This is going to be a difficult conversation. I need to do it in person."

It's 7:00 p.m. Fran is in her bathrobe, drinking a glass of beer and reading a book while Ava, in baggy flannel pajama bottoms and an oversized t-shirt, scrolls on her phone. They both look surprised to see me.

"I need to talk to you, Ava. Can we go to your room?"

"You can say whatever you want in front of Aunt Fran." She looks frightened. Her eyes are wide. She's sitting cross-legged on the floor, her back against the couch. She tucks her phone under one leg.

Fran closes her book. "Not a problem. I'm at the end of the chapter."

I sit on an upholstered chair, facing them both.

"I promised to tell you if I heard from your birth mother."

Without a word, Ava unfurls her legs, places her hands on her chest, fingers crossed, and closes her eyes. She moves with purpose, like she's following a familiar childhood ritual. Praying, wishing on a star, throwing a coin in a fountain, blowing out her birthday candles.

Fran gives me a "what's the holdup?" look.

"I'm going to meet Iliana tomorrow at her house in San Francisco. Just me and her." Ava's eyes pop open. Her arms drop to her sides. "*Just* me and her, Ava. You can't come. I'm sorry."

"Why not?" Her eyes bulge with tears.

"Your birth mother doesn't want to meet you. Let me say that differently. It's more like she can't meet you. Is afraid to meet you. I don't truly understand why she's afraid or what she's afraid of. I hope by talking to her tomorrow, I'll understand more."

Ava turns to Fran. "I told you. She hates me."

"I don't think she hates you, Ava," I say. "She didn't give me that impression at all. In fact, to be perfectly frank, I believe she's trying to protect you."

"Protect me from what?" Ava is scowling. "I don't need her protection."

"You don't know that. And neither do I."

11

On Sunday, I dress to meet Ava's birth mother like I'm going for a job interview, in slacks and a silk shirt. It's going to be hot again for the umpteenth day in a row. I've stopped arguing with Frank about driving me to San Francisco after he suggested we finish the day by going to our favorite North Beach restaurant. He thinks I'll need to decompress with a good Italian wine and handmade pasta. He whistles when I come down the stairs. He's wearing jeans, a t-shirt, and a sports jacket. I ask him if he's packing a gun and bringing his bulletproof vest.

Ava argued with me for ten minutes last night, pleading to come with me today. Accused me of horning in where I wasn't wanted, colluding with Dan and Sharon, and a dozen sins and ethical violations that would result in losing my license to practice psychology because I wasn't fit to counsel a dog. Then she stormed off to her room. Fran nearly had a fit. Wanted to make her apologize for being rude and acting like a spoiled child. It took another ten minutes to calm Fran down. Ava's not angry at me, I told her. Under all her anger, there's a sad, frightened girl who is trying to find her place in the world.

We cruise north on 280, just as the fog is retreating over the coastal mountains, revealing a cloudless blue sky. The

Crystal Springs Reservoir to our left is glittering in the afternoon sun. As soon as Frank turns onto Nineteenth Avenue, the sun takes a curtain call behind a blanket of fog. Shoppers are bundled in jackets and long scarves, their heads bent against a cold wind blowing in from the Pacific Ocean. A streetcar slices the broad avenue in two, passing San Francisco State and the sprawling Stonestown Mall, then veering off to the right near the eucalyptus-filled entrance to the Stern Grove concert venue. After that—save for the occasional garish hot pink house—the street is lined with ash-colored two-story homes. Faded beauties with torn window coverings and the occasional display of faded plastic flowers haphazardly stuck in window boxes with peeling paint. No stores, no shops, no parks. Too much concrete, too little greenery. And so many security gates I'm willing to concede that Frank was right to insist on coming with me.

We turn up a steep hill and everything changes again. The higher we go, the more prosperous the houses. Even the sky is brighter. Siri tells us to slow down, the destination is on our right. Frank pulls to the curb in front of a small craftsman-style house, pale green stucco with dark brown shutters. There are wide steps leading to the front door, which is covered by an ornate security screen. I look around. Not only is it the smallest house on the street, it's the only one with a covered door.

"Here you go," Frank says. "Got your phone? I'll be right here if you need me." I don't move. "You sure you don't want me to come in with you?"

"Perfectly sure. Thanks anyway." I lean over, give him a kiss, and hand him my cell phone. "Hang on to this. I don't want to be interrupted."

He gives it back. "Put it on silent, but keep it, just in case."

A neighbor comes out her front door walking a mangy little Chihuahua mix. She looks us over and keeps walking.

"Now or never," Frank says.

I get out of the car. The front windows are covered with drapes as if the house is sleeping or the occupants are away. A drape moves, then drops back. I walk up the steps until I'm standing on a doormat that says "welcome" in five different languages. I ring the doorbell. The front door opens behind the ornate scrolls of the security screen. The only thing I see is a shadow. A woman's soft voice asks if she can help me. For a second, I think I'm at the wrong house.

"My name is Dr. Dot Meyerhoff. I'm looking for Iliana Ester Ortega. She's expecting me."

"Everything okay up there, Iliana?" The dog walker is coming up the street again. Her eyes are on Frank.

"Fine, thank you, Mrs. Davis." The soft voice is now loud enough to reach the woman on the sidewalk. The door opens farther, then the security screen swings wide, and I am invited in.

12

Iliana Ester Ortega is delicate, small boned, with springy black hair gathered in a large comb. Her smooth skin is like Ava's, a pale, tea-colored shade of brown. She's wearing jeans, a loose sweatshirt, and espadrilles that tie around her ankles. No makeup, no jewelry. There's a tremor under her right eye. Her chest is pulsing with short, rapid breaths. She looks past me, over my shoulder.

"Who is the man in the car?"

"My husband, Frank. He drove me here."

"I can't ask him in. I'm sorry."

"No problem. He's fine waiting in the car."

She closes the screen, latches it, then locks the inner door. For a long minute, we stare at each other, mute and unmoving.

Ahead of me is a stairway to the second floor and a hallway to the back of the house. To my left, a wide arched doorway opens into a living room. Beyond it I can see a glassed-in study with a long desk overlooking a garden.

Iliana motions me inside, points to a leather love seat, and gestures for me to sit.

"¿Qué pasa? ¿Quién está?" A voice comes from upstairs.

"It's okay, Mother," she answers. I see now that her eyes are dark brown and almond-shaped like Ava's, fringed with those same dark lashes. "It's my daughter's friend."

Iliana excuses herself and leaves the room. She moves like a feral cat, nervous, guarded. As if one wrong word from me and she'd run off or turn on me and bare her teeth.

There's a whirring sound from the staircase as Iliana's mother descends in a mechanized chairlift. She is a wizened creature, her eyes and mouth buried in folds of skin. With Iliana's help, she boosts herself from the chair to a walker, then glides into the living room, the tennis balls affixed to the legs of her walker making soft, scratchy sounds on the hardwood floor.

"This is my mother, Marisol. She doesn't speak much English, but she understands more than you think."

Marisol stares at me then settles herself in an oversized upholstered chair. Iliana rearranges some pill bottles on a table next to the chair and pushes a box of tissues closer. The words they exchange are soft and in Spanish. Once her mother is settled, Iliana chooses a chair for herself, a white wicker rocker, and positions it so she is facing me. She looks young despite tiny glints of silver in her hair. She lifts her eyebrows. Two perfectly arched dark brown crescents. "Thank you for coming here today. Welcome to my home."

There's a pot of something hot and a plate of powdered sugar cookies on the coffee table, along with three tiny cups and a stack of embroidered napkins. "My mother made Mexican chocolate." Iliana pours us each a small cup. Her hands are trembling.

I sit on the edge of the couch holding the miniature cup in my hands. I don't know what I was expecting, who I was expecting, but it wasn't this tiny woman with her tidy house and her cautious, formal manners. I take a sip.

"Delicious," I say. "Gracias, señora." Marisol smiles. Looks at Iliana who is looking anywhere but at me.

"I see what looks like an office and beyond it a garden. Ava says you are a medical transcriptionist. Do you work from home?" It's a simple, neutral question meant to jump-start a conversation.

"I am a medical transcriptionist. And I sometimes do translation work. And I work from home." Her answers are in perfect order, mirroring my questions. She runs a hand through her hair, wrapping a springy coil around the fingers of her left hand. She's not wearing a wedding ring. She sips her chocolate and puts the cup down.

"Thank you again for agreeing to come here. I don't go out much. My mother and I stay mostly to ourselves. Which is why it was a shock when Ava contacted me. I didn't expect it. To be truthful, I didn't want it and I've tried hard to avoid it. I've never looked for her and I've never wanted her to look for me."

The severity of her words is at odds with her soft eyes and the minute quiver around her mouth.

"My mother and I understand that Ava has questions about herself and how she came to be adopted. This is normal. Unfortunately, what she wants to know is not. I don't think it's beneficial for her to know the details and I don't want to revisit it for my own well-being." She sounds rehearsed, precise, a teacher on the last day of school cutting to the heart of a complicated theory she wants to imprint on her soon-to-disappear students. "My reason for asking to meet with you is that I hope if you know the reasons behind my reluctance to meet Ava, you, as a psychologist, will be able to explain to her why it is in her best interest to simply move on."

Having delivered the heart of her message, Iliana's hands lie loosely on her lap, and her slender shoulders relax into a gentle curve. She's established her bottom line and seems slightly sad for having done so.

"May I ask you a question?" she says before I have a chance to speak. "Has Ava had a bad life?"

"A bad life? I don't think so. As I mentioned, I'm a friend of Ava's godmother. She was the one who asked for my help. Frankly, I don't know much about Ava's history or her family. Just that she desperately wants, needs, to meet you."

"Just as well. The less you know . . ." She doesn't finish her sentence.

"To be clear, Ava doesn't want anything material from you or your mother. She's not looking for money. You might say she's having an identity crisis. She's struggling to figure out who she is. This is normal for someone her age. An essential part of figuring out who she is is learning the reason you and her birth father put her up for adoption. Right now, as I said on the phone, she's filling in the gaps with her imagination. As a teenager, her imagination tends to be a bit dramatic." Iliana is staring into her half-empty cup. "She's accused her adoptive parents of buying her from a trafficker. I'm presuming she's misinterpreted or is misrepresenting something you said to her."

Iliana puts her cup on the coffee table, folds her hands in her lap, and waits for me to continue.

"Psychologically speaking, being abducted may be easier for her to accept than believing what she fears more than anything, that she was placed for adoption because she wasn't loved."

Iliana raises her hand, signaling me to stop talking. For a second I think I have said too much, too fast, and she's going to spring out of her seat and order me out of the house. She walks to the window, moves the drapes aside, and stands there, her eyes fixed on the street. Marisol follows her every move.

I look around. The living room is simply furnished in gray and white with splashes of color from pillows and striped cotton blankets. There are no toys, no children's books, no baby monitors, nothing to suggest children live here or come to visit with their messes and sticky fingers. I see a framed diploma on her office wall and a shelf of thick medical texts arranged by the color of their covers. File folders are neatly stacked in a pile, their edges aligned. Nothing in this house is out of place.

Iliana returns to her seat, her footsteps padding softly across the floor.

"I hope I haven't said anything to offend you or your mother."

"You haven't offended me. I just needed to move, release some tension."

"I know this isn't an easy conversation for you to have."

"Of course. I knew it would be difficult. To you it's a story, an interesting one perhaps. To me it's so much more."

"I don't mean to minimize anything you've experienced, Iliana. If I have, I apologize. I don't want to cause you any distress. I'm only here because I believe Ava deserves to know the circumstances of her adoption. You say it is in her best interests to move on. She's living with a mystery. I don't think she can move on until she solves it." Iliana looks at her hands, neatly folded in her lap. Rubs at something on her thumb. "And because you asked me to come."

Iliana continues to stare at her hands. She was the one who called this meeting, not me. Has she changed her mind? Have I come here for nothing? And if I have, what will I tell Ava? A silent minute crawls by. I'm not going to beg Iliana to talk, if that's what she's waiting for. Her head is down. She folds and unfolds her fingers like she's never seen them before. Marisol whispers something in Spanish. Iliana raises her eyes and looks at me.

"If I tell you what you think Ava wants to know, will that satisfy her curiosity?"

Curiosity doesn't come close to what I think Ava is feeling. "I think so. I can't guarantee it, of course. I do think she will be better off knowing who she came from." Iliana's eyes darken. "Let me ask you this, Iliana, what's the worst possible thing that could happen to you or Ava if you reveal the circumstances of her adoption?"

She smiles, a tiny prick of a smile, as if smiling is against her will. "My therapist asked me the same question."

A therapist? That must be the resource she mentioned on the phone. "What did you say in response?"

"That I didn't know. I hadn't thought about it because I never imagined I would have to, never imagined seeing my baby again."

Her baby? Two such ordinary words spoken with painful simplicity. Short but weighed down with sadness. A choker chain linked to her heart. Sorrow crowds my chest.

"I don't take what you're going through lightly, Iliana. I can't experience it the way you do, but I truly appreciate that Ava's showing up, literally out of nowhere, has been enormously disruptive. How it's forced you to confront painful memories and bear the emotions that go with them."

A small pulse on Iliana's right cheek starts beating. Her hands close into fists.

"I've brought you a photo of Ava. It's her high school graduation picture. A typical photo from the waist up." I asked Ava to give me the photo, not sure if I would use it or not. I'm worried that showing Iliana Ava's picture is tantamount to pulling a cheap emotional stunt, a predictable tearjerker. I want to make Ava real for Iliana. The way she's become real for me. Iliana is holding on to a distant memory, an unembodied ache, not a flesh-and-blood young woman with complex needs and a wide-open future. I open my purse and take out a small envelope. "Would you like to see it?"

Marisol again says something to Iliana in Spanish. Iliana thinks for a minute, opens her fists, splays her fingers to release the tension, and reaches for the envelope. She opens the flap and pulls the small photo toward her. Her eyes are closed. I can hear her breathing.

Marisol hisses at her. "Míralo."

Iliana opens her eyes. She holds the picture by its edges, staring at it with such intensity I expect it to burst into flames. "She's beautiful."

"She is," I say. "Very beautiful and vibrant."

Iliana gives the photo to Marisol. "Mi nieta," Marisol says. She's holding Iliana's hand. There are tears running down Marisol's face. Iliana wipes them away with a tissue, then dabs at her own eyes before walking back to her chair. She puts the photo in the envelope and hands it to me.

"No. Please keep it. It's for you. Ava wanted you to have it."

She holds it to her chest for a second, then places it on the table.

"Is she tall?"

"No, about your height."

"And her hair, does she always wear it like in the picture? Swept up with corkscrew curls?"

"No, not like in the picture. I think she had it done up especially for the occasion. Mostly it's down around her head, like a cloud of cotton candy." I put my hands out to illustrate. "Sometimes she puts it in a scrunchie."

Marisol says something in Spanish.

"My mother wants to know the color of her skin. Is it dark or light?"

"She's light skinned, like you are. Maybe a bit lighter."

"Her father was Caucasian." Iliana exhales loudly, as if, without intending to, she has taken the first perilous step down a dark path to an even darker truth. "Can I get you something? More hot chocolate? My mother and I don't drink so I can't offer you wine. Would you like to take something to your husband? Some water perhaps?"

She's stalling. Testing the water, sticking one toe in at a time.

"No, we're both fine. May I ask, how did you and Ava's father meet?" To me this is an innocuous question. Another way to get the conversation going.

"I'd rather not say."

"I'm sorry. Was that the wrong question to ask?"

"It was irrelevant. What you really want to know is if the man who got me pregnant was my boyfriend. He was not." Her face hardens. She's challenging me to be more direct. But if I am, she's going to retreat. The more I pursue, the more she'll withdraw. Either way, direct or indirect, I'm not getting any closer to persuading her to meet Ava face-to-face.

"This story Ava is telling about being stolen. Any notion where she got this idea?"

"She wasn't stolen, she was taken."

Taken? Are we playing word games? Taken with permission? Without? "By whom was she taken?"

"A social worker. I told myself it was for the best. I was too young to be a mother. We were poor. There was no money to raise a child."

"And the father? Did he agree to the adoption?"

"He didn't know I was pregnant."

"You said you were too young to be a mother. How old were you?"

The pulse on her cheek is now the size of a small beating heart. She looks at me; her eyes are hard, defiant, like a prisoner facing her interrogator. "Thirteen. I was thirteen." She waits for my reaction. I am shocked, but not surprised. "Aren't you going to ask me if the sex was consensual? It was not. I was raped."

13

As soon as I get my breath back, I reach for her hand. "Oh, Iliana, I am so sorry." She pulls away.

Marisol makes a noise. Iliana raises her hand to silence her. The room goes quiet with the relief that comes from releasing a long-held terrible secret. A secret hidden behind the precise neatness of Iliana's carefully contained life with its security screens and drawn drapes.

"Now I have a question for you, Doctor. How would it help Ava to know that she is a reminder of the worst moment of my life? The carrier of her father's criminal genes? A child cannot love herself unless she believes she was created from love. How can I tell her she is the child of a rape? It would destroy her."

"Iliana, you have nothing to be ashamed of. You were a child yourself. Ava will understand."

"You're wrong. These days, girls Ava's age keep their babies. Go to school with them. Show them off with pride. Ava will hate me even more."

"Es mi culpa, es mi culpa." Marisol's voice bounces off the walls like a trapped bird looking for a way out. "Es mi culpa."

"No, Mami, no es tu culpa."

Iliana's voice is sharp at the edges yet weary. The way a person sounds when they've repeated something over and over.

"My mother blames herself. We had so little money, my father was dead, and she was working seven days a week as a hotel maid. She needed me to babysit for extra cash."

"Babysitting was when you were raped?"

She takes a long breath. A skydiver about to leap into thin air. "I was babysitting for a white family, watching their child while they had a party. The father drove me home. He stopped where it was very dark. I didn't know where we were. First he said he wanted a kiss. I was too scared to say no. Then he started to touch me. He smelled like beer. He kept saying how pretty I was. That he thought I liked him. I pushed him away, but he was too strong. I should have tried harder."

Iliana is fiddling with a piece of loose wicker on the arm of her chair as she talks.

"I was afraid he might put me out of the car in the middle of nowhere. Or kill me. He told me he was a police officer. If I told anyone what happened, he would have me and my whole family deported back to Mexico. Then he shoved twenty dollars at me and drove me home."

"I am so sorry this happened to you."

"You see. I even hurt you with my story. Imagine what it will do to Ava. I don't want her pity or yours."

"Of course, you don't. Neither would I."

A soft silence falls between us. Iliana shifts in her chair. She takes Ava's picture from the envelope and strokes it with her finger. She allows herself a single tear, then puts the photo away.

"I don't know Ava well," I say. "But I know her better than you do. She wouldn't pity you. She's feisty. She'd be angry. Not at you, at the man who raped you."

"If that's how she is, then she'll be disappointed in me for not fighting back. She'll want to know if I told anyone. I did not. I was a poor little brown girl in a house full of rich white people. Who would have believed me? I almost didn't believe it myself. I told myself I fell asleep and had a bad dream, that is until I started having morning sickness. That's when I told Marisol what happened. She took me to the police department. At first the officer was nice, asked me a lot of questions, but when I said the man who raped me was a policeman, everything changed. The officer got mad, accused me of lying, trying to get money from a rich white guy. He told my mother she should get my 'beaner boyfriend'"—she places air quotes around the slur— "to pay child support, unless he'd already gone back to Mexico."

I know cops. I know how they can be with their rough voices and hard eyes. And for some, how easily their loyalty to each other can overwhelm their pledge of service to the community.

"I stopped going to school. I was embarrassed to be pregnant. And I wouldn't leave the house because I was afraid of running into the man who raped me. My mother knew someone who knew someone who knew a social worker who would help girls like me. It took every bit of cash we had plus some we borrowed. That's when we left Moss Point and moved to San Francisco because my mother had a friend here who could get her a job." She pauses, waiting for me to say something. "See what I mean? I let him rape me. I let someone take my baby. I let the police treat me like dirt."

"You were a child. You were powerless. None of this was your fault."

"Look around, look at my gates, my drapes. You say Ava is feisty. How is it going to help her to know her mother is scared of her own shadow?"

"I need to say something, Iliana, with all due respect to what you've been through. You and Ava are both making up stories about each other. Each of you has a piece of the story, neither of you have the whole picture. She thinks you didn't love her, don't love her. Nothing could be further from the truth, could it?" Iliana doesn't say anything. "You think you know what she wants from you. You haven't seen her for eighteen years. You don't know what she thinks or how she'll react to whatever you tell her. I'm asking you to put aside your concerns and think about what she needs."

"And that is?"

"The truth."

We sit stiffly in another pool of silence.

"The truth is," Iliana says, breaking the standoff, "that all those months of feeling her stretching and kicking inside me, jamming her little feet against my stomach, made Ava as much a part of me as my hand or my heart. When the social worker took her, even knowing it was the right thing, I felt like a part of me had been torn away. I wanted to take her back, but my arms weren't long enough to reach her."

Iliana's watery eyes are glossy in the fading light. She's been assaulted twice. First by the man who crushed her child's body. Then battered by a system bent with bias.

"I still feel like a mother. When people ask me if I have children, I don't know what to say. I gave birth once. Doesn't that make me a mother?"

I have no words to answer her question.

"Ava must never think any of this was her fault."

"Of course not."

"Never."

"I understand."

She and Marisol exchange another of their coded glances.

"Thank you for coming today. It's a relief knowing that Ava has you in her life for guidance and for support." She stands.

"This wasn't easy for you or your mother, Iliana, I know that.

But now, having told me, a literal stranger, what happened to you, it will be easier for you to meet Ava."

Anger flashes across Iliana's face. "This was not a dress rehearsal, Doctor." Her voice is hard. "I haven't agreed to meet Ava."

"I'm confused. I thought the purpose of our meeting was to talk about how best to tell Ava what she wants to know, so that it would go well when the two of you meet."

"I never agreed to that."

"Then why did you ask me to come here today?"

"So you can explain to Ava the reasons I can't meet with her. She'll be disappointed, no doubt. It's reassuring to me that you'll be there to comfort her."

"You're making a mistake. It will be easier the next time."

"No, it won't. It will never be easier." She frowns. Her eyebrows throw a dark hood over her eyes. "I have contributed so little to her life. The one thing I can do is protect her from the terrible knowledge of how she was conceived."

"She can take it. She's a spunky kid. I can help her. Her godmother can help her."

"She already feels different because she was adopted. Will she feel any better about herself to learn that her biological father is a rapist and her birth mother is a coward?"

"You're not a coward. Look at how you forged forward in your life. Look at what you did today. I can tell you from personal experience kids whose fathers did bad things can turn out just fine." I flash on my father again, ranting like a crazy man, frightening the neighbors, and irritating the cops who had better things to do than haul him off to the local emergency room for the umpteenth time until he calmed down.

"I wish there was an easier way, Iliana, but there is no way around the truth. You believe the best way to protect Ava from suffering is to shield her from the past. I believe the only way to release her from the past is to tell her everything she wants to know. Gently and kindly, which, even knowing you for a short time, is the only way I think you would ever do it. Please don't make this about you. Make it about Ava. She needs what you needed when you were a child, someone to share her pain, to tell her the truth, and then help her figure out what to do with it."

Marisol applauds. Iliana shushes her. Her cheeks are fiery red. Once again, she reexamines her fingers as though she has never seen then before.

"You would be here with her?"

"If you want me to, of course."

"Before we meet, would you tell her what happened, so that I don't have to?"

"I prefer not to. I think it's better coming from you, but if that's what it takes for you to agree to meet your daughter, then I will."

She fiddles with a fingernail, bites down on her bottom lip.

"I need to think about this."

"Of course," I say. "Take your time."

As desperately as I want her to agree to meet Ava, I see how desperately she needs to assert herself and establish boundaries. Recoup some of the control that has been taken from her.

We stand. I wave goodbye to Marisol. Iliana walks me to the door. We shake hands. She steps outside. To my surprise, she bends forward and gives Frank a little wave.

The minute I get back in the car, Frank asks how it went, am I okay, I seem a little pale. I look at my phone. I have text after text, voice message after voice message, all of them from Ava. I put the phone back on Do Not Disturb and close my eyes.

"Going to keep us both in the dark?"

"Drive, please. I don't want Iliana to think I'm spying on her or wanting to come back inside."

"That rough, huh?"

I don't answer. My head is pounding and my thoughts are jumbled.

Frank pulls into a parking lot and shuts off the engine. "I am your husband, not a freaking Uber driver. Talk to me. I haven't been sitting in this car for over an hour with just myself for company so you can give me the cold shoulder."

"I'm not giving you the cold shoulder. I'm trying to process what just happened with Iliana. It was very painful. I'm not sure I can share it with you."

"Why not?"

"Because it's confidential."

"Baloney. It's not confidential. She's not your patient. You're helping out a friend, remember? No contracts signed, no money's changed hands. You're going to tell Ava and Fran what you learned, aren't you?" I nod. "Well then, how about treating me with as much concern as you have for Fran or Ava and every other wounded creature who comes across your path? I'm your husband, for crap's sake. Don't you trust me?" His face is dark. He's gripping the steering wheel with both hands. "Screw it. Let's go to the restaurant." He starts the car.

I tell him to turn off the engine. I'd rather talk in the car than in the restaurant, which is small with tables close together.

"It's not that I don't trust you, Frank. I trust you implicitly. I need time to process what I just heard. When you have a hard day at work, you get to unwind in the car on the way home. I just had a really tough interview and you want me to start talking about it the second I get in the car? I need to decompress. My head is spinning. I'm not even sure what just happened."

He leans over, his hand on my leg. "Sorry. I get it. Take your time." He hands me a bottle. "Drink some water, it will help. I can wait."

I tilt my seat back, open the bottle, and let the water cool my parched throat. Take a few deep breaths to ground myself and begin.

"She was assaulted as a child when she was babysitting."

Frank whistles through his teeth.

"On the one hand, she is smart, organized, successful, and on the other, seriously traumatized and projecting all her fears onto Ava. I thought she wanted my help. She's dying to meet Ava yet trying her best to hide it, not just from me, but from herself. If I was a bookie and you asked me what the odds are Iliana will agree to meeting Ava, I'd tell you to buy a lottery ticket because your chances of winning are better."

Frank kisses me on the cheek. "Sorry for being pushy. But in a way it's your fault for inviting Ava and Fran over for dinner. I feel involved, like I have a personal stake in what's going on."

This is unusual for Frank, who has repeatedly asked me not to involve him in my work. I'm surprised and touched to hear it. There have been times in the past when I've come danger-ously close to dragging him into the headlines for all the wrong reasons. He starts the car.

"I don't know how you do it, Dot," he says as he pulls out of the parking lot. "I couldn't be a psychologist for all the money in the world. Remodeling isn't a walk in the park, but no matter how hard it gets, it will always be easier to fix houses than people."

14

I haul myself through the next morning, still full of pinot noir, focaccia, and Da Flora's handmade lemon pepper pasta. I eat lunch in my office. I call Fran to ask if I can come to the café after closing time. She tells me the sooner, the better. Ava's been so jumpy over the weekend knowing I'm meeting with Iliana that even a visit from Cody and Marisa couldn't settle her down. At four o'clock, my phone buzzes with a text from Iliana asking me to call her. She answers on the first ring.

"I didn't sleep all night thinking about our conversation. Marisol and I talked for hours. What she wants more than anything in this world is to meet her granddaughter before she dies. I owe her at least that much, probably more. Her life has been difficult."

"This has to be your decision, Iliana, yours alone."

"I also talked to my therapist. She suggested that if Ava and I were to meet, I should set some conditions first. She called them ground rules."

"Sounds reasonable."

"You need to tell Ava about the rape before we meet. I can't go through it again."

"Okay."

"You must make her promise not to ask me any questions about what happened."

"I can't make her promise that or guarantee she'll keep her promise."

"Then I can't . . ."

I cut her off. "I'll do my best, Iliana. That's all I can do."

She takes a deep breath. "You'll make her understand that what happened to me is not her fault nor her concern. And finally, you must promise to come with her. Can you do that?"

"Absolutely," I say. "That is a promise I can keep."

"Talk to Ava. If she agrees to these conditions, I will meet with her."

She disconnects. It takes me a few minutes to calm down I'm so excited. Then I text Frank with a thumbs-up emoji.

Fran unlocks the café door and lets me in. The smell of coffee and bacon has changed to the nose-rattling smell of cleaning products. Fran guides me through a maze of still-wet spots on the floor.

"I didn't tell her you were coming. She'd be a hot mess if I did, spilling stuff, mixing up orders. She's in the kitchen helping Eddie with the cleanup. Want some leftover coffee cake? It's all I have."

I decline and head for a table in the back.

"Ava." Fran's voice rises over the kitchen clatter. "Someone here to see you."

Ava comes out of the kitchen, her face shiny with sweat. The second she sees me she blanches, walks across the room like a prisoner on execution day, and takes a chair facing me. Fran heads to the kitchen.

"She doesn't want to meet me, does she?"

"She *does* want to meet you."

Ava pumps her fist in the air. "Yessss!" She drags the *s* sound out like a long tail. "When? Where? OMG, what's she like? Is she nice? Is she pretty?" She starts to get up. "I'm going to tell Fran." I stop her.

"Best not to involve Fran just yet, there are some things we need to talk about."

Ava gives me a funny look and settles in her chair. Her eyebrows, so like Iliana's, come together in a frown. "Okay." She folds her small hands on top of the table like a good student.

Suddenly, I'm at a loss for words. I don't know where to start. How do I tell Ava her birth mother's story when it was hard for me, an adult, to hear it? Do I start with the rape? Or the police betrayal? Or the years of fear and hiding? Or Iliana's broken heart and broken life?

Ava stares at me, her eyes brimming with dread. It may not be the best way to start, but I decide to begin with her worst fear—that she was and still is not lovable.

"As you know, your birth mother has been reluctant to meet you." Ava gives me a "tell me something I don't know" look. "Do you know what a paradox is?" She says she's not sure. "It's two statements that don't seem to go together. Iliana has resisted meeting you not because she doesn't love you, but because she does. That's the paradox. She's trying to protect you."

Ava looks confused. "Protect me from what?"

"There are things about her life and about yours that she believes you are better off not knowing."

"Things like what? She can tell me anything. I'm not a child."

"When Iliana was a young girl, she was babysitting for a little boy while his parents had a party. After the party, the boy's father drove her home. On the way home, he raped her. That's when she became pregnant with you. She was only thirteen."

Ava's face is still. Not a twitch, not a tic.

"So the reason she didn't keep me is because she was raped?"

Her lack of compassion knocks me back. I've been dreading this conversation, fearful of unloading this enormous, damaging secret on Ava shoulders, expecting shock, tears, something more. I might as well have told her what I had for breakfast this morning. This is what I have underestimated and what Iliana doesn't understand. What matters most to Ava isn't her birth mother's trauma, but the indelible stain of rejection that follows her everywhere like a birthmark. Contaminating her view of herself, her relationships, and her ability to trust.

"She gave you up because she didn't have the means to take care of you. She thought she was doing the right thing by relinquishing you for adoption."

"She didn't give me up, she said I was taken."

"What she said to me was that she gave you up."

"You sure?" Ava pushes away from the table, the chair legs squeal against the floor. She folds her arms across her chest. Clamps her lips together.

This is not the story she wants to hear. She wants to hear that Iliana, a child herself, jumped from her hospital bed, hours after giving birth, to fight off the enemy, holding Ava in one hand and a sword in the other.

"I'm sorry, Ava. I know that wasn't what you wanted to hear."

"Whatever," she says from between pressed lips. "I don't get it. The only reason Iliana didn't want to meet me is because she was raped?"

"Your birth mother thinks, rightly or wrongly, that a child cannot love herself unless she believes she was created from love. She didn't want you to know that you are a child of rape out of concern that it would damage you. As I said, she is trying to protect you. I think she has always been trying to protect you."

"She thinks that because she was raped, I'm damaged? I'm not damaged. I'm normal. Do you think I'm damaged?"

There's a rumble from the kitchen, a clatter of metal pans being dropped on the floor, followed by the muffled sound of Fran and Eddie bickering.

"What I think isn't important. It's what you think. What you feel."

"What I feel is hurt and angry because my parents gave me away, not because of how they got me." She pauses. "What about my father?"

"She didn't say much about him. Only that he was Caucasian. She's not even sure he knew she was pregnant."

"Okay then." She scratches her head, rearranges the fluffy puffs of shiny dark hair. "So when are we meeting?"

"That depends. She has some conditions you need to agree to."

"Conditions?"

"We've already covered the first one, that I tell you about the rape, so she doesn't have to. She is still traumatized by what happened and doesn't want to talk about it or have to answer any questions about it. She lives a very private, restricted life."

"I guess I screwed that up when I called."

"Yes, in a way. She's not blaming you. It's just that she doesn't deal well with unexpected things or people. She wouldn't let Frank in the house, maybe because she's uncomfortable around men. She was thirteen, Ava. You need to remember that. The man who raped her took control of her life away from her. Now she overcontrols to compensate."

"What's she like?"

"She's sweet, kind of fragile, tough when she needs to be."

"Do we look alike?"

"Yes, you look a lot alike. She's small, has dark eyes and hair like yours. I also met your grandmother. She doesn't speak much English. I think you'll like her. She's eager to meet you."

"More eager than my birth mother?"

"Less afraid."

"You said there were other conditions."

"Iliana wants you to understand that what happened to her is not your fault or your concern."

"Okay. No problem."

"The third condition involves me. Iliana wants me to come with you when you meet. I'm willing to do that. No matter how much you want to meet her and how much she wants to meet you, it's going to be a difficult conversation. Are you okay with my being there? You might want to talk to Sharon and Dan about it."

"I don't need their permission."

"Not for their permission, but rather as a courtesy. Let them know what's going on."

She shrugs. "No need. It's all good." There's another crash from the kitchen, metal on metal. "I better get going. Sounds like they need help with the cleanup. They're like my parents, those two, always fighting." She turns toward the kitchen and then back to me.

"Thanks, Dr. Meyerhoff. I totally appreciate what you've done for me. Don't worry about me going postal or anything. I get that Iliana is delicate, maybe a little mental. So is Sharon. I'm used to it. I'm stoked that I'm going to meet her and I'm glad you're coming with me. I still want to know who my father is, but I'm not going to shove her up against a wall and demand that she tell me his name. I can handle this. You'll see. It'll be fine. I'll be fine."

15

We've arranged to meet on Saturday. It is a crisp, clear, fogless morning. Ava is waiting for me on Fran's front stoop. As soon as she sees me, she hoists her backpack and heads for my car, moving so fast her feet barely touch the ground. Fran opens the front door, still in her bathrobe.

"Hold on, Ava." Ava stops in her tracks. "Not getting away without a hug. I'll be thinking about you. Got my fingers crossed this goes well."

They hug. Ava gets in the car as Fran leans in to talk to me. "Cleans up good, doesn't she? After I talked her out of being her so-called authentic self in torn jeans and a sweatshirt." Ava is wearing a long-sleeved cotton shirt and jeans without holes. "Remember what I said, kid. Don't expect too much. Don't accept too little. Above all, be kind."

I pull out of the driveway and head uphill to the freeway. Ava's staring out the window, gripping her backpack like it has legs and might run away. Twenty minutes pass in silence. Silence can be a useful tool in therapy, a way to allow space for emotions to surface. This silence feels like a power struggle, a who-goes-first contest. Somewhere around San Mateo I've reached my limit.

"Nervous?" I say.

"A little."

"Want to talk about it?" She shakes her head. "Perfectly understandable. I'd be nervous if I were you."

"Why would you be nervous?"

"For a million reasons."

"Like what?"

"Because I wouldn't know what's going to happen. Because I have high hopes and I'm scared I'll be disappointed. Because I'm worried I'll say something wrong and disappoint my birth mother. Any of that sound familiar?"

"I don't want to talk about it. Talking will only make me more nervous. I need to chill." She pulls out her earbuds, leans against the door, and disappears into an alternate universe of music. She stays there until I pull up in front of Iliana's house and tap her on the shoulder.

"We're here."

She looks up at the house. The security gate is still pulled over the front door, but the drapes are open. Ava doesn't move.

"Ready?"

She jams her earbuds in her pack. Flips the visor down, stares at herself in the mirror, then flips it back up.

"What if she hates me?"

"She is not going to hate you, Ava."

"She's only seeing me because you made her."

"I didn't make her. She wants to see you. She just needed time and support."

"I'm scared."

"Of course you're scared."

"You'll stay the whole time?"

I nod.

She flips the visor down again, tries to smooth her unruly curls.

"Do you have a rubber band or a scrunchie?"

A shadow moves behind the living room window.

"You look fine, Ava. Time to go."

Iliana opens the door before we can ring the bell, then pulls back the security screen. Her hair is loose and springy. She's wearing jeans, a colorful top, big hoop earrings, and the espadrilles she wore before. Her lips are glossy, her cheeks pink with blusher. The resemblance between her and Ava is striking, both of them small and compact with dark eyes, billowing dark hair, and caramel-colored skin. They stand, staring at each other, motionless, like flies trapped in amber.

Iliana is the first to break the silence. "Come in, please. Welcome." She guides us into the living room. Marisol is seated in a wheelchair, wearing an embroidered flower shawl around her shoulders. Her long gray hair is slicked back and braided. She stares at Ava, an unearthly specimen dropped out of nowhere from a place no one knew existed.

"This is my mother, Marisol. She doesn't speak English, but she understands more than she lets on. Please"—she points to the couch—"have a seat."

Ava and I sit. Iliana pulls her wicker rocker closer. Once again there are cookies and Mexican chocolate on the coffee table. Ava's eyes dart around the room, looking everywhere but at Iliana. Marisol says something.

"So sorry, my mother made Mexican chocolate and cookies. Would you like some?"

Ava declines, her voice so soft I can barely hear her. Her left leg is jiggling hard against the couch. It takes me a few seconds to realize we're not having an earthquake, it's her leg that's making the couch shake.

"Thank you for coming, Ava. It is a blessing to meet you at last."

Ava stutters. Starts to speak and stops. Iliana's blessing has confused her. Stolen her words. "Absolutely. Same to you too."

"Chocolate, Doctor?" Iliana hands me a cup. I take it because I don't know what else to do. She pours another for Marisol and one for herself. "May I pour one for you, Ava? Perhaps you've changed your mind."

"Okay." Ava reaches for the cup with a trembling hand. Their fingers touch and Ava drops her cup. The chocolate puddles around the broken pieces in rebuke. Ava looks like she's about to cry. Iliana reaches for her, then freezes. Marisol murmurs something in the background.

"No problem, Ava. Please don't worry. We have plenty of these cups. They come from Mexico. They are very cheap." Iliana goes to the kitchen for a towel and another cup. Ava turns to me mouthing the words *I want to leave* and starts to rise.

"I am your abuela," Marisol says. "Grandmother." She smiles; her teeth are capped with gold. "You are beautiful. Muy bonita. ¿Habla español?"

Ava looks panicked. I gesture for her to sit down.

"No. Sorry, ma'am. No Spanish."

"Like to learn? I'll teach. Iliana will teach. Is easy."

Iliana comes back into the room with a towel and another cup. She mops the table and places a filled cup in front of Ava. "See, no harm done." She raises her cup in the air. "Shall we start again? I am happy to meet you. Welcome to my home." She points her cup at Ava, then at me, before taking a sip. "So, now, please, tell me about yourself. I want to know all about you."

Ava flicks her eyes at me then back to Iliana. She sets the tiny cup back on the table. Her hands are trembling. "I'm eighteen. I guess you know that. I just graduated from high school. I live with Sharon and Dan Sower in Moss Point by the ocean.

My father used to be a cop, now he's in construction and my mother's a stay-at-home mom. This summer I'm living with my godmother, Fran, and working in her café. I'll be going to community college in the fall. I have to pick a major. Probably literature or psychology." She skids to a stop.

"And the family who adopted you, they have been a good family?"

Ava nods.

"I am glad to know this. Would it be okay if you told me more about them, what your family life was like?"

"Why do you have those gates on your front door?" Ava's question sails in at an unexpected angle.

Iliana stiffens, clearly taken off guard. "I feel more comfortable with a gate over my door."

"Why?"

"That's a very personal question, Ava," I say. She's going off script. Behind her nervousness, a mountain of resentment is starting to shake loose, a rock here, a rock there, soon a landslide. I throw down a decoy question to dilute the tension. "Ava, maybe start with something about Iliana's transcription service or her work translating. I, for one, am curious. What kinds of documents do you translate?"

"Medical reports mostly." Iliana is talking to me but looking at Ava. "The end-of-year prospectus for an investment firm."

"Why did you give me away?" Ava's chin juts forward, defying me to stop her.

"Iliana, you don't have to answer that." I put my hand on Ava's arm. "We had an agreement, Ava. If you don't stop this right now, we have to leave."

"Please don't." Iliana's lips knot together. She shuts her eyes and starts to make little tapping motions on her thighs. It's a grounding technique. I use it myself with clients. After an endless minute, she opens her eyes and turns back to me. "Not to worry, Doctor. I'm fine. Now that Ava's here, I don't want her to go. I'm nervous, but I don't feel as frightened as I imagined I would. I'd like to try to answer her question." She turns back to Ava.

"You asked why I gave you away. As I said before, I didn't give you away. You were taken, not stolen, taken."

"Who took me?"

"Do you remember being thirteen? When all you think about is being popular with your friends? Could you have raised a child when you were thirteen?" She doesn't wait for Ava to answer. "There was so much I didn't know and I had so much shame. When this social worker came into my hospital room, she said she had a white family with a nice house, but I had to make a decision right away. I didn't think about your feelings. I didn't think about what it would be like to believe you weren't loved. To look different from everyone in your family. I thought I was protecting you."

Ava and Iliana lock eyes, as if there is no one else in the room.

"How did you know I was safe? Did you try to look for me? Did you ever wonder if I was okay? If I was happy?"

"Only every day. Every second of every hour. Every girl I saw that would have been your age made me sad but also happy, because I hoped you were living a better life than I could have given you."

"Why did you name me Ava?"

"I didn't. I named you Carmela Sabrina Ortega. You were a beautiful baby. You deserved a beautiful name." Iliana dips her head. Rubs her fingers across her forehead. "Can you understand that I thought I was doing the right thing for you, not for me?"

"Carmela Sabrina? My real name is Carmela Sabrina?" Ava

looks at me; her eyes are wide and her cheeks pink with excitement, like a child who has just received an amazing, unexpected gift. "That's the most beautiful name I ever heard. It's musical, makes me think of birdsong or water running over rocks. I love it."

Iliana and Marisol smile. The tension in the room drops several degrees. For a moment, everyone is joyful.

"Can I ask you about my biological father?" Ava says. The tension comes roaring back like a mad dog. "Dr. Meyerhoff told me what he did to you. Did he also make you give me away?"

"No. It was my decision," Iliana says. "He had nothing to do with it. I don't believe he even knew I was pregnant." She smiles. "Forget about him, please. Look at you, you're beautiful. It's a miracle and a mystery that something as beautiful as you are came from something so ugly."

"I'd like to meet him. Could I?"

The color flushes from Iliana's face. "That's not possible. I don't know who he is or where he is. I hope never to see him again. He's the reason I have a security screen on my door."

"You were babysitting. You must know his name."

I put my arm on Ava's. She shakes it off.

"My therapist says it's very common to not be able to remember certain parts of a trauma. It's how the brain protects itself. I do remember the baby. It was a boy. He was about a year old and cried a lot. They dressed him like a little cowboy. His name was Cody."

Ava gasps. Her mouth bobs open like a stranded fish.

"What's wrong?" Iliana asks.

"Ava has a very good friend named Cody," I say. "There must be lots of boys in Moss Point named Cody. It's a popular name." I put my arm around Ava's shoulder. This time she lets it rest. Her shirt is sweaty and I can feel her trembling.

Marisol says something in Spanish. "My mother says not to forget I told the police that the man who raped me was a police officer. They didn't believe me. Thought my boyfriend got me pregnant and I was trying to get money from a rich white guy. Is your friend's father a police officer?"

"No. He runs a boatyard." Ava's voice is hardly louder than a whisper.

"So it can't be the same man." Iliana puts her hands over her heart. "I am relieved. The last thing I would want is for what happened to me to hurt you even more than it has." She sighs. "Perhaps we could use a break. Would you like to see my garden? It's where I spend a lot of time." She stands.

Ava's voice breaks. "I'm sorry you were raped. I should have said that before."

Iliana freezes. Turns slowly and sits again.

"Thank you, Ava. That means a lot coming from you. I hate what those ten or fifteen horrible minutes have done to my life. But now that you're here . . . I can't say I'm happy that it happened, that would be a lie. But I see that good things can come from bad. For years, Marisol has wanted me to find you and I've resisted. I thank you both for making sure I didn't throw away this opportunity." She smiles. "So any more questions? Just ask. I don't want there to be secrets between us."

Ava announces that, for now, the only question she has is, Where is the garden?

Like everything else in Iliana's house, the garden is small but neat. The flower beds are edged straight as pins. Pale yellow primroses line the paths. Each plant is pruned and dead-headed to perfection. Fruit trees are gracefully espaliered against a wooden fence. Iliana knows the botanical name of each plant and all its varieties. Ava is hanging on to her every word.

After a tour of the garden, we see the rest of the house, every room as colorful and as neat as the one before it. Then we head into the open and airy kitchen. The walls are covered with open shelving. Ornate metal dish racks are filled with hand-painted pottery. There are straw baskets on the counter and racks of dried chilis hanging from the ceiling. Iliana refers to it as a little bit of Mexico that makes Marisol happy now that she is too old to travel to her home country.

And then it's time to leave. We stand by the front door. The gate is open and the street is flooded by fog. Ava and Iliana are holding hands, their fingers lightly, shyly, twined together.

"I hope we stay in touch, Ava," Iliana says. "Now that we've finally met, I don't want to lose you. There's still so much I want to know about you and your life. But I don't want to upset your adoptive parents, so please say no if staying in touch would make you or them uncomfortable. Maybe even ask them if it's okay before you decide."

"I don't have to ask anyone's permission to stay in touch with you. You're my mother."

Iliana pats her heart with one hand. "I hope that now you understand why I didn't want to burden you. What happened to me is mine to deal with. It's in the past. There's nothing I can do to change it and it's certainly not yours to carry. Promise me you'll let it go."

"I promise. Cross my heart, hope to die." Ava raises one hand as if she's about to testify in court.

Iliana lets go of Ava's hand to shake mine and thank me, not just for coming, but for being someone Ava can talk to because she now understands, more than she did before, how difficult this has been for Ava.

"Goodbye, for now, Ava. I'm so glad you found me."

"Me too," Ava says. "Supermega over-the-top glad." She takes a step toward the car and then turns back to Iliana. "Do me a favor?"

"Anything," Iliana says. "Just ask."

"From now on, please call me Carmela."

16

"Thank you, thank you, thank you." Ava tries to hug me as I'm driving, causing me to narrowly miss running up on the curb and careening into some bushes. "Isn't she amazing? Greater than I ever thought. Think about what she's been through and what she's done. Put herself through college, has her own business and her own house. And she's so pretty." She digs in her backpack for her phone. "I am going to text Fran and Marisa and Cody. OMG Cody. Wasn't that beyond weird when she said that baby's name was Cody? I almost barfed. Maybe I shouldn't tell him. He'll go mental. Another Cody in Moss Point? I know what he'll do, he'll try to find that other Cody and pretend to do smack to his father. He acts like a tough guy but he's really a wimp. He'll get in trouble and I'll have to help him out."

She bends to her phone, starts tapping out text messages. Ava and her birth mother have connected in a big way. It's what Ava wanted and all Iliana has longed for. I'm the one who negotiated it. I'm the one who made it happen. I should be elated. Instead, I feel a gnawing irritation under my ribs, like I've swallowed something scratchy. The driver in a fancy sports car behind me leans on the horn, then passes me on the left and cuts back into my lane so sharply I jam on my brakes, jolting Ava out of her cyberworld. Her phone goes flying. She gives me a look that could only be described as unfriendly. *Well, back at you, girl*, I think. I'm not feeling very friendly myself at this moment. *You violated the conditions of our meeting after promising to agree to them. You made me look like I lied.* She picks her phone up off the floor of the car.

"Hold up," I say. "I have a question for you. When are you going to tell Sharon and Dan that you met your birth mother?"

"I'm not. I don't want to talk to them. I don't even want to be in the same room with them. They're horrible. They had to know she was raped. That's why they didn't want me to look for her or my biological father."

"You don't know that for certain."

"Yes, I do. My social worker lost her license for doing illegal adoptions. What else could it mean? She took a baby from a rape victim without her permission. That's why they took her license away."

"Even if that were true and, again, you don't know that for sure, that doesn't mean your parents knew. Maybe the social worker lied to them."

Her phone vibrates with a text. It's from Cody. She tells me she has to call him back because he's going bug nuts waiting to hear from her.

"Tell him you'll talk to him when you get back to Kenilworth."

"He can't wait. He's such a baby. I won't be long."

I keep driving, heading south on 280, out of the fog toward the sunshine. Ava, drunk on her newfound maternal love, launches nonstop into a detailed description of Iliana, Marisol, the house, the garden, the chocolate.

"You wouldn't believe how nice she was, Cody. She's not even angry at the guy who raped her. If somebody raped me, I'd want to claw his eyes out. I wouldn't stop at anything until

I found him and sent him to jail." She pauses. "I know he's my father. He's still a creep. He didn't stick around, didn't give her any money, nothing. She had the courage to go to the police, but they didn't believe her." Cody says something in response. Ava listens for a second and rolls her eyes. "Because, Cody, she's Mexican. Get it? They would have believed her if she was white." She looks disgusted. "I gotta go. I'll call you later."

Right on time, a memory raises its ugly head. My father, his face distorted with fury, is telling me that working with the police, the state-sponsored minions of an authoritarian regime, is tantamount to consorting with the enemy. He comes back from the dead with every egregious police act, every scandal. I shout at his memory. Tell him that there are bad apples in every profession. That most of the cops I know are decent, hardworking people doing their best in an almost impossible job. Sometimes he shouts back that I'm a fool.

Ava asks if I'm talking to her.

"I'm right, aren't I? If somebody's white daughter in Moss Point got raped, the cops would be falling all over themselves to find the person who did it. My mother deserved to be believed."

"Yes, she did," I say.

"Still does." Ava's face has gone surly. "It can't be that hard."

"What can't be that hard?"

"Moss Point is a small town. Should be easy to find that other Cody. He'll be just a little older than me. When we find him, we'll find his father."

"If there was another Cody in Moss Point, wouldn't you know him?"

"Not necessarily. Maybe his family moved when I was a baby. Some people don't like the fog or the commute over the hill. I could ask Dan or Lonny. They know everybody in town."

"Hold on, Ava. Iliana was perfectly clear that this isn't your concern."

"She only said that because she's trying to protect me. Just like you. That man, whoever he is, deserves to be punished. He ruined her life and mine."

"Your life hasn't been ruined. That's an exaggeration." She gives me a "who are you to decide that?" look.

"It could have been different," she says.

"And it could have been worse. Way worse. Look, I get it. You've met your birth mother, you know what happened to her and you want to help. But finding the man who assaulted her is not a good idea. You don't want Cody to look for him. Why is it different for you? Finding him is not going to help Iliana or change her life. Meeting you is what has changed her life. You're what's important to her, not him."

"So I won't tell her, not until I find him."

"Ava, you don't have to prove anything to Iliana or yourself. What you've done already is extraordinary. Other girls would have given up their search, but you persisted. That says volumes about who you are, what you're capable of. Iliana is overjoyed that you're in her life again. That's all she wants. She's not asking you for anything more."

"I'm not doing it for her. I'm doing it for me. He's my birth father. I want to tell him what I think about him. He needs to go to jail."

"If Iliana had wanted to pursue him, she could have gone to the police herself when she got older."

"She tried once. Didn't work out too well, did it?"

"That was eighteen years ago, Ava. Things have changed for the better."

"Maybe. Maybe not."

"Please don't attempt to find this man on your own. It may

not be safe." I turn up the A/C. The scratchy feeling under my ribs is growing hotter and bigger. "What is it with you? Iliana doesn't want you to get involved with what happened to her. She asked you to promise to let it go. And you did. You said, and I quote, 'I promise. Cross my heart, hope to die.' What kind of promise is that if you take it back when you feel like it? You need to respect her request. If you can't, if you won't, I'm going to be very disappointed. I've gone way out of my way to help you. If I can't trust you, I can't help you."

For a moment she looks worried. "Now you're protecting me. I'm not a baby."

"It's not a matter of protection, it's a matter of common sense. This man could be dangerous. Being his daughter doesn't offer you protection."

"I didn't say it did."

"You just met Iliana. Why risk making her angry?"

"She won't be angry, she'll be happy. Megahappy." Ava looks at my face. "Whatever. If you don't want me to look for him, I won't." She digs around for her earbuds. The only sounds I hear for the rest of the ride are her fingers tapping away at warp speed. And the little drip, drip, drip of my growing concerns.

17

I head back to work on Monday still feeling wrung out and a little irritated with Ava. Frank and I have had several conversations over the weekend. He's encouraging me to pull back. I've done what Fran and Ava asked me to do. He thinks it's time for me to move on. I'm half in agreement. Ava is not my client. Her needs as a stormy adolescent are beyond my professional competence, not to mention my patience. Frank thinks Ava's problems are taking up too much of my time. He doesn't say it in so many words, but I interpret this to mean time I should be sharing with him. Time when I should be fully present, not preoccupied with Fran, Ava, or Iliana.

First thing on my schedule this morning is a debriefing at the KPD for the animal services unit. A small team of dedicated officers who are repeatedly traumatized by animal cruelty and the sad fate of animals who are being euthanized because they are unadoptable. No happy reconciliations for these poor creatures. On my way into headquarters, I bend to pet an old Irish setter who has been abandoned by his owner, left to wander the streets, raiding trash cans for food and sleeping on heat grates. Too weak to stand, he licks my hand, grateful for the tiny scrap of attention.

* * *

The scratchy, scorchy thing in my stomach twists around, taking me back to my conversation with Ava during the ride home from Iliana's. How quickly Ava's gratitude for my help turned into a pout. She was very clear. She wants what she wants. And what she wants is to find her birth father, no matter the consequences to her or the damage to her relationship with Iliana or me. I stew about this through three preemployment screenings, two counseling appointments, and a field training meeting to assess the progress of three rookies, fresh out of the academy.

I review my thoughts again with Frank over dinner. By the time we go to bed, I am determined to tell Ava that from now on, she's on her own.

The next day, I head to the café for a late lunch. I'm planning on sitting Ava down and having a serious conversation. This is getting out of control. If she persists in looking for her birth father, I am not going to support her or help her. Fran is wiping down the counter. There are only a few customers left. The minute she sees me, she starts in.

"Ava has multiple personalities. First, she was all happy and excited about meeting Iliana. Went on for ten minutes raving about how Iliana's so beautiful, so nice, just like an angel. Next minute, she's furious with Sharon and Dan and back to the theory that they stole her from this helpless girl. Now she's pulling on her Wonder Woman vest and swearing to hunt down Iliana's rapist and send him to prison. What am I going to do with her?"

"What do you want to do?"

"Why do you shrinks always answer a question with a question? I don't know what I want to do, that's why I'm asking you. I feel like I should do something. I told her to call her parents.

She said you told her the same thing. Then she told me to chill out, she'd call when she was ready and not before. I told her she has no right to be nasty to me or anyone else. Especially when she's living in my house, eating my food, and working in my café. Plus, I am not going to stand by and watch her hurt the only parents she's ever known."

I look around the restaurant. No Ava. "Where is she?"

"Out in the back talking to Cody. On my time. She said it was an emergency. That she'd only be a minute. That was fifteen minutes ago. Would you check on her, please? I got a restaurant to run."

I walk through the kitchen. Eddie is half in, half out of a giant refrigerator. Moving stuff around, making a lot of noise. I edge past him, my heels catching in the drain holes on a rubber mat.

"Just in time, Doc." He slams the refrigerator door shut. "I got to talk to you. Ava told me the whole story. I don't know what to do."

"What to do about what?"

Before he can answer, there's yelling and something crashes in the backyard. Eddie pushes open the screen door and I follow. Ava and Cody are standing face-to-face in the middle of the tiny yard. A metal table and two chairs are lying on their sides. A jade plant growing in a rusty coffee can lies broken on the ground in a pile of dirt. Cody's face is red and he looks as if he's been crying. Ava grabs my hand.

"I was trying to calm him down. I told you what he'd do. He wants to look for that other Cody."

"I thought you weren't going to tell him."

She shrugs. "I changed my mind."

"Go back in the restaurant, Ava," I say. "Fran needs you. There are still a few customers." Eddie opens the door for her as she walks back into the kitchen then holds it open for himself.

"Him first, Doc." Eddie points to Cody. "Then me." He slams the door.

Cody appears frozen in place, his feet shoulder-width apart, his hands knotted into fists, like he's ready to fight me.

"You remember me, Cody, don't you? Dr. Meyerhoff. Friend of the family."

He glares at me, the sun in his eyes. Bends over, picks his baseball cap off the ground, shakes off the dirt, and tugs it low over his face.

"Help me clean up this mess, please," I say. He bends over, rights a chair. His movements are stiff, wooden. He places the chair upright on its legs and stops, waiting for me to tell him what to do next, as if he's in a fugue state, unsure of where he is or what he's doing. Just this little bit of movement spills off the adrenaline that's making his eyes bulge and slows his rapid breathing.

"Table next," I say. "Then the plant. Then maybe use that broom to sweep up the dirt."

He helps me with the table. He's not talking, but I can see his breath continuing to slow down. Any minute, all his adrenaline spent, he'll collapse. I grab the broom, hand him a dustpan. He kneels down, balancing himself with one hand on the ground.

I look around. "Not bad. Good enough for government work. Have a seat." I pull out a chair, one facing away from the kitchen where I can see Eddie's bulky form behind the screen door.

"What's going on? You and Ava got into it?"

"I want to help her find the bastard who raped her birth mother." He's talking to me but staring into space.

"You want to help her and she won't let you."

"She thinks she knows everything. Treats me like I'm a moron. I know what I'm doing."

"That must hurt."

He looks at me for the first time since we've been talking. "You're a head doctor. Tell her she's wrong. Make her change her mind."

"Head doctors try to help people solve problems and feel better. We don't tell them what to do or solve their problems for them."

"Well, somebody better tell her what to do or she's going to get hurt." He starts to stand. "I'm going home."

"Are you sure you're okay to drive? You're still pretty upset."

He slams his hands on the table. "Why does everybody treat me like a freaking baby?"

"I'm sorry. I'm just concerned. I see what you're trying to do. You're trying to help, be a good friend. Too bad Ava doesn't understand."

For a moment he looks confused, as if I'm speaking a foreign language. After a second or two, his shoulders relax and he slumps a little, as if my effort at understanding has released some bottled-up fury that has been keeping his spine straight.

"You really like Ava, don't you?" I go on. He examines me with his eyes. Like I'm a bug he's never seen before, trying to decide if I bite. "A lot more than she realizes?" He nods. "That's painful. That really hurts." He jerks his head away, so I can't see his eyes. He hesitates, then gets to his feet. He's gangly, like a puppet with a broken string.

"Thanks for the help. I'm sorry about the mess. It's Ava's fault too," he says and walks out the back gate without another word.

"Don't move." Eddie barges out of the kitchen the second Cody leaves. "Don't say nothing. I heard it all." He sits at the table, his bulk spilling over the sides of the tiny patio chair. "I got a story to tell you that will knock your socks off. Think that kid has trouble? You ain't heard nothing yet."

18

By the time Eddie and I are finished talking and making what looks to him like a plan and to me like jumble of good intentions, all the customers are gone and the restaurant is empty. Ava and Fran are sitting together in a booth, drinking coffee. I pour myself a cup and sit down with them.

"I told Cody to stay out of it, that he'd just make a mess, and he went postal. Started throwing stuff around all because I said he should mind his own business."

"That's not why he went postal, Ava," I say. "He likes you a lot more than you like him. It's breaking his heart."

Ava makes a gagging gesture. "So throwing things is going to make me like him more? He's older than me but acts like a child. I keep telling him we're just friends, maybe even best friends, but he won't listen. At least he's stopped trying to kiss me." She shivers. "I feel sorry for him. I keep encouraging him to get a real girlfriend. He won't listen."

Eddie joins us. He's drinking coffee out of mug. He's trying to hide it, but I can see his hands shake.

"If we're finished talking about Cody's broken heart," Fran says. "I have something to say." She makes a drumroll sound tapping her hands on the table. "From now on, Ava wants everybody to call her Carmela. She insists on it. I don't know what you two are going to do, but I told her she's been Ava all my life and I'm too damn old to change. If I can't call her Ava, the best I can do is 'Hey you.' She doesn't think this is funny."

"It's not funny. Carmela is my name. My birth name. I have every right to be called whatever I want."

Fran raises her hands in surrender. "I still think you're a pain no matter what you call yourself. I'm out of options here. You need more help than I can give you. Time for me to let go and let God. On Sunday, I'm going to church to light a candle for Saint William of Rochester."

"Who's he?" Ava asks.

"The patron saint of adopted children. He was murdered."

"Who murdered him?"

"His adopted son." There's a moment of stunned silence. "It's a joke. Get it everyone?" I smile. Ava squeaks out something that might be a laugh and Eddie looks like he just got the worst news of his life.

"Now I got something to say," Eddie says. "It's no joke." We all turn to look at him. "I've been chewing on it for twenty-four hours trying to figure out how to say it. Sorry, Ava, you're not going to like it."

Ava stiffens. "Just say it."

"You told me about your birth mother and what she said about the pervert who raped her. I appreciate you telling me. I really do. What I got to say in no way means I don't appreciate it . . ."

He's stumbling over his words.

Ava opens her hands. "Just tell me, Eddie. I'm a big girl."

"Remember you asked me because I was a cop, how you could track the guy down and I said I'd think about it?" Ava nods. "Well, I thought about it. I'm pretty sure I know the guy.

We were drinking buddies at KPD. His name was Lonny." Ava chokes on her coffee. "I didn't want to say, but the doc encouraged me. Said I should be honest because people have been lying to you." He looks at me and back at Ava, who is mopping her shirt with a napkin as if she'd spilled indelible ink down the front. Fran leans over and puts her hand on Ava's back.

"He was a real boozehound, this Lonny. Could drink me under the table. One year on the job and he got fired for DUI. Moved over the hill and opened a boatyard. His wife got pregnant, had a baby, and named him Cody."

"Liar." Ava hisses at Eddie with the accuracy of a spitting cobra.

"I know it sounds impossible, but it has to be the same guy. When he had the baby, he sent all us shift buddies a box of cigars with the kid's name, C-O-D-Y, on the cigar band and his photo on the box. Freaking kid looked like Winston Churchill. Last I heard, his wife threw him out and wouldn't take him back until he got sober. Haven't seen the guy in years. If you're trying to get sober, you don't hang out with your old drinking buddies."

"Lonny would never rape anyone. Never." Ava's voice is shrill, on the edge of panic.

"Are you sure about this, Eddie?" Fran says.

"I may be a miserable SOB, Fran, but I wouldn't lie about something like this. Not to Ava."

Ava slumps against Fran, hiding her face with her hands.

"I'm sorry." Eddie raises his voice. "I couldn't keep this to myself. You gotta understand, I'm not accusing Lonny Wilson of rape or anything else. All I'm saying is that he was a cop. A righteous drunk. And he has a kid named Cody." Eddie's face and neck are red. "Ask your father. Him and Lonny were like the Bobbsey Twins. They did everything together, including getting bombed. That's why your father moved to Moss Point, so he and Lonny could sober up together."

"Enough." Fran slaps her hand on the table. "Get out of here, Eddie. Ava and I will close up."

Eddie slumps as he pushes back from the table. I've never seen him so sad. "Sorry to be the bearer of bad news. Wish there was something I could do to make it better." He stands, unties his apron. "You know, kid, you could settle this in a minute. Take a DNA test. It'll be my treat. It's the least I can do."

"I hate him." Ava's eyes are starting to swell.

"Hate who? Eddie, Lonny, or Cody?" Fran tosses Ava a rag. "Start cleaning up, it'll make you feel better."

"Lonny would never rape anyone. Never in a million years. Eddie doesn't know what he's talking about."

I turn to Fran. "Do you know Lonny?"

"A little. He and Dan were close. Same for Marlene and Sharon. Like Eddie said, they did everything together, holidays, vacations—still do as far as I know. Lonny spent a lot of time with Ava and Cody. Sort of like her second father." She purses her lips together. "I'm with Ava. I can't imagine him as a rapist. You know how some guys make you hope you never get caught alone with them in an elevator? I never got those kinds of vibes from Lonny. Never."

"How do I get my DNA tested? How much does it cost?" Ava is wiping down the counter hard enough to take off the finish.

"You need to talk to your parents, Ava."

"Dan slapped me for telling the truth about my adoption. What'll he do to me if I tell him I need to get tested so I can prove his best friend in the world is not my mother's rapist?"

"This is complicated. That's why it's important to slow down, think it through."

"I want a DNA test. Can you get it for me, please, Dr. Meyerhoff?"

"I don't work with DNA. Ask Eddie."

"No. I want you to help me. Not Eddie. Find out for me, please. I'll sneak something of Lonny's out of his house. He won't even know. Like Eddie said, this could all be over in a minute. Hundred percent it won't be Lonny. Then we can look for the real rapist."

"We?" Fran is leaning against the counter as if it's all that's keeping her on her feet. "Who do you think we are, Cagney and Lacey?" The reference to this long-ago TV show goes over Ava's head. "Get back to work, will you? I want to talk to Dr. Meyerhoff. In private." Ava picks up a tray of dirty dishes and heads to the kitchen.

"The sooner we get this over with, the happier I'll be. The stress is not good for me. I feel like a referee at a boxing match. Dan and Sharon in one corner, Ava in another, me in the middle. My doctor says my blood pressure is through the roof. I wish I could make Ava go back home."

"Why can't you?"

"I already tried. Dan doesn't want her back."

"Let me get this straight. You went to the café to announce you were going to quit helping Ava and you didn't do it?" Frank is in the kitchen chopping vegetables and leftover chicken for a dinner of fried rice.

"Fran needs my help. So does Ava; you should have seen her face when Eddie said he knew Lonny."

"And you love to be needed." He dumps the cooked rice into a hot pan, releasing a cloud of onion-flavored steam.

"What if Lonny is her father? Can you imagine how she'll feel? She's known the man all her life, he's like her second father. What about Cody? He's infatuated with Ava. How's he going to react when he finds out she's his half sister?"

ELLEN KIRSCHMAN

"*If* he finds out she's his half sister. You're getting ahead of yourself. This could all be total coincidence. Eddie's a decent guy, but he's killed an awful lot of brain cells with the booze."

"This is a crisis. I understand what you're saying, but it's not the time for me to pull back."

"Ava's a headstrong kid. You're asking for trouble."

"If Eddie's wrong and Lonny had nothing to do with this, then I'll back off."

"So you say."

"Ava's mixed-up, I agree. Given what's happened, of course she is. But she's also determined and plucky. I was like that as a kid. I can identify. God knows what would have happened to me if I hadn't been determined to get away from home, get an education."

"Rivka's a doll. I love her." Frank and my mother have a mutual admiration society. They love cooking together.

"You didn't know her back then. Or my crazy father. Anyhow, what about Iliana? She's been deeply damaged. Doesn't she deserve justice?"

"According to you, she doesn't want justice. She wants to move on." Frank flips the rice, stirs in the chicken and vegetables. "You're the one who told me that what Iliana wants is to get to know Ava and put the rape behind her. From where I'm standing, you are aiding and abetting an eighteen-year-old girl to do exactly what her birth mother has asked her not to do."

"So I should tell Ava she's on her own?"

"You could refer Ava and her parents to a family therapist."

"That would be great if they'd go. Right now, they're not even talking to each other."

Frank spoons the rice mixture into bowls and puts them on the counter. "I couldn't stop Ava even if I wanted to, Frank. She's stubborn. She's going to do what she wants to do. Period."

"And your solution to that is to help her in any way you can?" Frank scowls and hands me a set of wooden chopsticks. I hate it when he scowls. I hate it when he's mad at me. I hate it even more when he's right.

19

The first thing I do the next morning is call Pepper from my private office to ask how and where someone can get a reliable DNA test. She tells me to call Michelle at the RBG DNA laboratory because that's the lab KPD uses. Then she asks if we can meet for coffee this afternoon. It's almost time for her monthly check-in. As always, she doesn't want to meet in my private office because it triggers memories of being kidnapped. It doesn't help to point out how much better she is than she was this time last year. Pepper can be as pigheaded as Ava. I agree to meet at Fran's Café. It will give me a chance to check up on Ava.

Michelle at the RBG DNA lab answers on the third ring. I tell her who I am. She's been working at RBG for ten years, knows a lot of KPD officers. I tell her I'm helping a private client who is trying to establish paternity. Michelle tells me that RBG guarantees a 99.9 percent probability of parentage, but only if my client can submit a clean sample, not one that has been contaminated with someone else's DNA.

I ask her what to do if my client's alleged father doesn't want to submit his DNA for testing.

"Happens all the time in paternity cases," she says. "Not to worry, there are ways to get a discreet paternity sample. By that,

I mean that the alleged father's DNA is being taken without his knowledge or permission. Your client has tons of options for collecting samples; food, tissues, nail clippings, cigarette butts, diabetic test strips, chewing gum, a minimum of sixteen strands of hair with roots attached, a razor blade, a toothbrush, a drinking can, a plastic cup, a drinking straw, an envelope flap, ear wax, and semen."

By the time she gets to the ear wax and semen I'm ready to hang up. Michelle wants to know why my client couldn't just ask her father to cooperate. I tell her the biological mother was raped. She goes silent for a moment. "There's something you need to tell your client. Home paternity tests done in secret have no legal benefit. If she's planning legal action against her father, she would have to petition the court to compel her biological father to submit. Fortunately, there are other ways to determine paternity, such as using DNA from a first-degree relative. Someone who shares fifty percent of their genes with your client's father, like another child or a sibling. But keep in mind the chances of obtaining the 99.9 percent probability of parentage are much better if the biological mother also submits her DNA."

Pepper is already halfway through one of Eddie's enormous salads by the time I sit down. She's in uniform.

"Hey, Pepper. Before we start, can I ask you a question about the statute of limitations?"

"Funny. I was going to ask you the same question," she says. "I want back on the street. And soon. Teenagers are miserable creatures. The slightest thing feels like the end of the world. And the teachers aren't much better. I caught two of them doing the nasty in a supply closet." She spears a chunk of tomato with her fork. "Why do you want to know about the statute of limitations?"

"What is the statute for childhood sexual assault?"

"How old is the victim now?"

I see Ava on the far side of the café waiting on another table. Pepper follows my eyes. "This have something to do with Ava?"

"Her birth mother. She's thirty-two."

Pepper's face wrinkles like I've just put something smelly under her nose. "Bummer. Was she a minor?" I nod. "Then she has until forty to file criminal charges. No cutoff date for civil. And the charges need to be brought in the jurisdiction where the crime occurred."

Her shoulder mike unleashes a cloud of static that only she can understand. She slams a twenty on the table. "Catfight in the girls' room. See you later. Give the change to Ava and tell her to smile more."

Two minutes later, Ava takes Pepper's seat. She asks me if I've found out about DNA. I tell her what I learned from Michelle at the lab.

"I need to remind you, Ava, that Iliana doesn't want to pursue this. She was very clear about it and you promised to let it go. If you pursue this, you break your promise and you risk damaging your relationship. Maybe to the breaking point. Is that what you want to do?"

"She loves me. She'll be okay with it."

"What's more important to you? Finding your birth mother's rapist or testing the strength of your relationship?"

"Why do I have to choose?"

"Because I don't think you can have both."

As soon as I finish my coffee, I go to police headquarters to make my rounds. Things are quiet. No ringing phones in the 911 communications center, no one in the break room, no one in the police garage, no one in the gym. I head upstairs to mahogany row. The door to Chief Jay Pence's office is open. He's leaning back in his chair, staring out the large bay window behind his desk. His office furnishings are dark wood. The paneled walls are hung with framed certificates and letters of commendation. A small table with two chairs and a stack of blue-and-gold coffee mugs embossed with the KPD shield is positioned in a corner. A studio photo of his wife, Jean, dressed as always in white, stands on his desk. I knock on the door frame. He startles, wheels around, and waves me in.

"Sorry, I was zoning out. It's budget time again. Got to figure out how to work smarter with fewer resources."

I assume this includes my salary. It's a discretionary expense he needs to justify to the city council every two years. He's the third chief I've worked with and easily the most unpredictable when it comes to valuing my services. I can go from being on his good side to his bad side in less than an hour without ever knowing what happened. Judging from his smile, today I'm in the clear. I hope to keep it that way.

"What's up, Doc?" He wiggles his hand, mimicking Bugs Bunny with a carrot. Like a behavioral tic, he can't resist miming the old rabbit when he sees me. He stands and stretches. For a man in his fifties, he's in good physical shape, always sharply dressed, his silky white hair gelled into a silver helmet. "What brings you around?"

I've been making rounds since my first day on the job—better than waiting for people to seek me out. It's exactly the kind of effort he fails to notice.

"Do you remember an officer named Lonny Wilson? Worked here around eighteen years ago?"

"I do. We were in the academy together. Haven't seen him in decades. He and Eddie Rimbauer were friends. Drinking buddies. Only Eddie could handle his liquor; at least, he could when he was young and had a functioning liver. Lonny couldn't." Pence walks around his desk to face me. "I haven't thought about Lonny in years." He laughs to himself. "I have lots of stories about Lonny. Probably shouldn't tell you this one, I'll embarrass myself."

He's going to tell me no matter what I say, but he wants me to beg first. "Whatever it is, Chief, I'm sure I've heard worse."

He leans against the edge of his desk, crosses his arms, and looks at the ceiling as if composing the memory requires deep concentration.

"It happened the night we graduated from the academy. Eddie Rimbauer invited a bunch of us rookies out to celebrate. We were total greenhorns. If he'd told me to jump off the Golden Gate Bridge, I would have done it I was so in love with the job. He took us to this sleazy cop bar, ordered a pitcher of beer for each of us, dropped our shiny badges in the pitcher, and made us drink it down until we could get the badge in our teeth. Then he took our pictures."

I try to imagine Pence as a sloppy drunk, a badge in his mouth and his hair in his eyes.

"I was so drunk I had to call Jean to drive me home. But Lonny, he kept right on drinking. Not just that night apparently. About six months after he got off probation, he got fired for drinking on the job. He roughed somebody up and the guy complained he smelled alcohol on Lonny's breath. Cost the city a bunch. That's why I hired you to screen out the potential alcohol abusers."

Pence loves the idea of being a modern police chief. Never mind that he didn't hire me, he inherited me, and he threatens to fire me on a regular basis.

"Why are you asking about Lonny Wilson?"

"I just ran into someone who knows him. I didn't realize he used to work here."

"He was a hard-drinking, hard-driving cop. A real dinosaur. I'm happy to say that now that Eddie Rimbauer's finally retired, the dinosaurs have gone extinct."

20

According to Fran, it was Pepper's idea that Ava go to the Moss Point Sheriff's Department to see if we could find the police report about Iliana's rape. If it happened in Moss Point, it would be their case. Ava isn't happy about talking to the sheriff before getting her DNA tested, but somehow Pepper convinced her it was the right thing to do. She only agreed because I said I would go with her. I only agreed because I was tired of debating with myself and Frank about helping her. Since I didn't seem able to back out when I'd tried, I declared myself in for a dollar, in for a dime.

The trip has made Ava nostalgic. We're driving along the winding two-lane road that loops up and around the coastal range before dropping into the flat farmland that edges the Pacific Ocean. There's hardly any traffic. The heavy cloud cover has scared off all but the most dedicated beachgoers. The fields on either side of the road are covered with snapdragons, Brussels sprouts, artichoke plants, and pumpkins. Cows dot the surrounding hills like scattered pebbles.

"I've only been to the sheriff's department twice in my life. First time in the fifth grade when we were on a field trip. I remember watching the police dogs do tricks. They were the most beautiful, intelligent animals I ever saw. Not like cows, which are dumber than stumps. The second time I went I was in high school. My class was forced to attend a program called DDD: Don't Drive Drunk. They showed us horrible videos of car crashes and smiley prom pictures of dead teenagers. Then they made us go through a fake funeral and write letters to our parents apologizing for dying without saying goodbye. It was gross."

I pull up in front of a small, Spanish-style building, white with a red tile roof, a taqueria on one side, a local winery and tasting room on the other. There's a little black-and-white sign in front of the door that reads "Moss Point Sheriff's Department." We enter through the front door. In the lobby, a large gray-haired woman in a blue uniform is seated at a desk behind a glassed-in counter. She looks too old to be a working cop. I can't tell if she's reading a magazine or taking a nap. I tap on the glass. She looks up. It takes her a second to get her bearings. She stands with some difficulty and walks with a limp to the counter.

"Shouldn't sit so much. Bad for my hip. How can I help?"

I tell her we want to speak to the sheriff. She tells me they don't have a sheriff at the moment, not until the next election. Sheriff Bergen is the front-runner for the job, but in the meantime, he is the interim, filling in for Sheriff Anderson, who retired early due to illness.

"May I ask what this is about?"

"It's about a rape."

She looks at Ava. Her faces morphs into motherly concern. "Just a minute, dear. Let me call him." She limps back to her desk, picks up the phone, says a few words to someone, hits a buzzer, and motions us through the door to her desk.

"He'll be along in a minute. You just wait right here with me at my desk." She turns to me. "May I have your name?" I give her my name and my business card. She turns to Ava. "My name is Marge, honey. What's your name?"

"Carmela. Carmela Sabrina Ortega."

The walls in Interim Chief Bergen's office are blank. There are unpacked cartons stacked in a corner. Judging from the thin coat of dust, they've been here a while. Bergen walks behind a large wooden desk, points to two facing chairs, and invites us to sit. He's a big man with gray hair and bushy eyebrows. I'm starting to wonder if the Moss Point Sheriff's Department is a retirement home for elderly cops. He looks at my business card.

"Dr. Meyerhoff, how can I help?"

"I want to report a rape," Ava says.

He picks up a pen, looks at his watch, and starts writing.

"Is she the victim?" He's still talking to me as if Ava isn't sitting right in front of him.

"My mother is the victim," she says.

He looks at her for the first time. "What is your mother's name?"

"Iliana Ester Ortega."

Ava's been practicing, rolling her r's like a native Spanish speaker.

"And when did this happen?"

"October 18, 1998."

"Say again." He puts down his pen. "That's a long time ago. Why is she reporting it now?"

"She's not reporting it, I am. I just found out about it."

"I see," he says, although I doubt he does. "Are you or your mother aware that there's a statute of limitations on sexual abuse? If the abuse took place before your mother was eighteen, she has to report it before she turns forty."

"My mother was thirteen when it happened."

Bergen taps on a desk calculator like he's totaling up a cart of groceries. "That makes her thirty-one or thirty-two now. Correct?" He continues without waiting for an answer. "So what that means is, according to the law, she still has time to make a report." It's like he's talking to himself. "Why isn't your mother making this report?"

"Because my mother's afraid. She doesn't want to relive the rape and she's concerned about running into her rapist."

"Nevertheless, we'll need her statement. Without a victim, I can't do anything." He sighs like he finds it personally painful that frightened victims won't step up to confront their abusers.

"I can give you a statement," Ava says.

"It's your mother who needs to make a statement. She's the victim."

"I was taken from my mother without her permission and put up for adoption. That makes me a victim too."

He stops to consider this. I take it to mean that children born of rape don't often complain. "In your eyes, perhaps. Although, I have to say, some people might consider you lucky to have been born and not aborted. Were you adopted or put in foster care?"

"Adopted."

He looks down at his notepad. I look around the room for his pro-life posters.

"The bottom line is I cannot do anything without a statement from your mother. It's not my decision. It's the law."

"What if he's raped other little girls?"

"Then I would surely like to know his name." Bergen stares at Ava as though she might look so much like her rapist father he could go out and make an arrest. He shifts in his chair, glances at his watch again. It's lunchtime. I can hear his stomach growl. "How long have you known your birth mother?"

"I just met her."

"And you believed her?"

"Of course I believed her. She's my mother."

"Did your birth mother or anyone in her family ever make a police report about this incident?"

Incident? An incident is when there's a fender bender. Or somebody TPs their neighbor's tree. Child rape is not an incident.

"Yes. When she was thirteen. The police didn't believe her. Thought her boyfriend got her pregnant and she was trying to get money by blaming someone else."

Bergen leans across the desk. "Just because your birth mother said she was raped doesn't mean it really happened. When young girls get into trouble, sometimes they're too ashamed to admit they had consensual sex, so they make up a story that they were raped. We get these kinds of reports all the time." He pauses, like something has just occurred to him. "Do you think you know your mother's rapist?"

Ava looks at me. She looks scared.

"No. Maybe. It depends."

"Depends on what?"

"On DNA."

Bergen groans. "Here we go with the DNA. DNA is not all it's cracked up to be. Not like on television. We use the state lab. It takes us at least six weeks to get results on a current case. Probably six months on a cold case. Whatever you do, you or your mother, do not publicly accuse this guy because, whoever he is, he's going to have you in his crosshairs for six months or more while you wait on the lab results."

I put my hand on Ava's arm. She yanks it away. Bergen notices this.

"Just in case you have an idea about this guy's identity and for some crazy reason you aren't telling me, you need to know two things." He starts counting on his fingers. "Number one, making a false police report about a rape is a serious misdemeanor. Number two, false accusations of rape can result in you and your mother being sued for defamation of character. So, before you go around accusing anyone based only on what your mother wants you to believe, you need real evidence."

"Can you at least look for the police report?" Ava's not backing down.

Bergen gives a martyred sigh, like he has the world on his shoulders, and now this crazy girl is adding to his misery.

"What was that date again?"

"The date she was raped, the date I was born, or the date she made the report?"

He looks pained. "All three if you have them. And your name again."

"My real name or the name I was given when I was adopted?"

"Both." He picks up his pen. Holds it like he is considering which of us to stab first, Ava, me, or himself.

"Carmela Sabrina Ortega. Or Ava Sower."

His eyebrows go up. "Sharon and Dan's girl?"

"You know my parents?"

"I know everybody in town, it's my business." He picks up his phone. "Lemme call Marge and ask her to check the files from 1998 to see if anyone took a report from Iliana Ester Ortega claiming rape or child abuse." He pronounces it "Orteger." I can hear Marge tell him that the old reports have been moved to a warehouse, but she'll be happy to go over there and look.

"You're wrong about no evidence, you know," Ava says as soon as he hangs up. "I'm the evidence. Take my DNA; when you find the rapist, it will match his DNA."

"How am I going to find this alleged rapist? You've given me nothing to go on."

"What about talking to the officers who were working then, ask if they remember my mother?"

"Ms. Sower, please. Most of the deputies working back then have retired to Florida or moved on to bigger departments where the pay is good and they aren't bored to death. I'm interim sheriff. I'm only here because no one else wants to work in a two-horse town like Moss Point. They want motorcycles, tanks, command vehicles, and real crime. It's just old folks like me and Marge and a couple of young deputies who'll jump ship with the first offer they get."

"No crime in Moss Point? My mother was raped at thirteen and forced to give me to a child trafficking social worker who sold me to the highest bidder. If that isn't a crime, what is?"

"Evidence, I need evidence. And names. I don't have the time, the patience, or the staff to go off on a wild goose chase." He looks at his watch. "We have to leave it here. When or if we find a report, I'll let you know." He gets up, resting his hands on his desk as though he's so stiff he can't stand straight. "If you were my daughter, young lady, here's what I'd tell you. Thank your lucky stars you had a good home and let it go. Grow up. Accept that even good people, like your mother is, I'm sure, make mistakes and bad choices."

Ava's tiny hands ball into fists.

"And if you were my father, here's what I'd tell *you*. Rape is not a mistake. My mother never had a choice. Neither did I."

By the time we get back in the car, Ava's trembling with anger. I give her a minute to settle down.

"Things have changed for the better? Bull crap. He treated me like dirt."

"Why didn't you tell him what Iliana told you, about her rapist saying he was a cop?"

"Because he's an asshat. If he knows my father, he knows Lonny. I don't want to get Lonny in trouble. I feel stupid even thinking he could have raped my mother." She goes into a pout, her arms crossed over her chest. I start the car. "I'm tired of saying Lonny didn't do this when I can prove it with a DNA test. Drive by Cody's house. I'll take something of Lonny's. He won't know. It will only take a minute."

"Why are you so certain Lonny is not your birth father?"

"Wouldn't I have known? Wouldn't I have felt it? He and Marlene and Cody are like my second family."

"Then ask him to give a sample, don't sneak around. He should be willing to do that."

"I'd rather die than have him know I thought for even one second that he could be responsible."

"If you're that certain he couldn't be the rapist, then why bother to get his DNA tested at all?" She doesn't answer. Just stares out the front window, her eyes scanning the street, not looking at me. "Answer me, please. I'm confused. Why bother to get Lonny's DNA tested if you're so certain he didn't assault your birth mother?"

"Because of Eddie. He's been helping me at the café. Teases me all the time because he likes me. I can feel it. I trust him. He wouldn't lie to me." There are shadows under her eyes that weren't there an hour ago.

"What if you get Lonny's DNA tested and he turns out to be your birth father?"

Her face flares with alarm as if I've called her bluff, ripped the cover off her armor-plated facade of super self-confidence.

"I'll kill him and then I'll kill myself," she says like it's a fore-gone conclusion. One I should have known and is not open for discussion. Then she snaps her seat belt into place and folds into a small bundle, like a contortionist, her head on her knees.

I start the car, let it run for a minute, and turn it off. *I'll kill him and then I'll kill myself*. Is this hyperbole? Teenage hysteria? A cry for help? This is the second time Ava has hinted, not threatened, but hinted at suicide and the first time she has ever said a word about killing someone else. I catch hold of my breathing, slow it down. Hysteria is contagious. I order myself to focus. I'm gripping the steering wheel so hard my fingers ache. What if Ava is trying to manipulate me? Get me to do what she wants by threatening to hurt herself? If I asked her how she would kill herself, I'm betting she couldn't answer because she hasn't really thought about it. Ditto with how she plans to kill Lonny Wilson. Ben Gomez had a plan. He didn't tell me or anyone about it, but it was clear that once he chose suicide, he planned it with the same precision he would have applied to a tactical operation. Ava isn't Ben. She's more impulsive, less organized. I'd bet my license as a psychologist she doesn't have a plan. Still, I'm not taking any chances. I start the car again. The sooner we eliminate Lonny Wilson as Ava's birth father, the sooner the specter of her committing suicide is off my radar.

21

There are two trucks and a car parked in the open space at the side of the Wilsons' single-story ranch-style house. Two boats on trailers are stationed next to a big shed. As soon as we pull in, the garage door rolls up and Cody comes out, grinning from ear to ear as if his and Ava's blowout never happened.

"C'mon in. We're just finishing lunch." He walks us through the garage, his hand at Ava's back, past two SUVs and Lonny's gun safe.

Marlene and Lonny are sitting at a long farm table with eight chairs. Lonny is at the head of the table. He has Cody's long pointed nose. His skin is pale and marked with white patches, cancer scars from working in the sun. His silky light brown hair is gathered into a ponytail. He smiles at me with a lopsided grin and stands. He's tall and rail-thin with a soft belly that flops over the top of his belt. He looks nothing like Ava.

"Hey, Ava girl." They hug. "Who'd you bring with you?"

I introduce myself. We shake hands. His is dry and scratchy with calluses. Marlene's is soft with long scarlet-colored acrylic nails. She is simply dressed in jeans and a sweatshirt, her long brown hair streaked with dark red highlights. She offers us lunch, saying it won't take but a minute to whip something up. Ava and I decline everything but coffee.

"We can't stay long," Ava says. "The doctor needs to get back to her office."

"So you're the doctor Dan's been talking about. Glad to meet you."

Given my interactions with Dan, I can't imagine I got a good review. Lonny pulls out a chair, motions for me to sit. Ava takes the chair next to mine. Cody takes the chair next to her. Marlene pours coffee and gets a glass of milk for Lonny because he's off caffeine. Doctor's orders. She's chattering away, like Sharon Sower did at first when we met. People get nervous around me. They think because I'm a psychologist I can read minds.

Ava is holding her coffee cup with two hands, her eyes crawling inch by inch over Lonny's face.

"What?" Lonny says. "I missed a spot when I shaved this morning?"

"Sorry," Ava says. "I was just thinking."

"Thinking is overrated. Causes trouble." He laughs and shifts in his seat. "What brings you two over the hill?"

"Dr. Meyerhoff has never been to Moss Point. I wanted to show her how beautiful it is."

"Welcome to our little piece of paradise." He touches his fingers to his forehead and gives me a salute. Nothing about our unannounced arrival or me being a psychologist seems to have rattled him.

"Dr. Meyerhoff is a friend of Fran's. She works for KPD. She says you used to work for KPD with my dad. I never knew that."

Cody straightens. "No way. You were a cop. Dad? How come you never said? That's hella cool."

Marlene looks uncomfortable.

"No point in talking about it. It didn't last long. I took early retirement. Turns out, it wasn't my thing. I wanted to be near the water. I like boats better than people." I remember what Pence said; Lonny didn't leave on his own terms, he was fired. "So, Ava, what's going on with you and your, what do you call her, birth mother? Your dad's been talking to me, you know. He's pretty upset. He said you met her. What's she like?"

"She's okay."

"Just okay? You're talking to your uncle Lonny here, Ava girl. Dan said she had some crazy ideas that got you all turned around. I've been waiting for you to come over, tell us about her."

Marlene leans in, the coffeepot suspended over my empty cup. "Speaking of your dad, while you're in town, why don't you take a minute to drop by and say hi to your folks? It would mean the world to them. They're worried about you, you know."

"I'm sorry," I say. "Good idea, but I'm running out of time." I look at my watch for emphasis. Marlene set the coffeepot down. Lonny doesn't move.

"You know, Doc," he says, "they didn't have anybody like you when I was at KPD. Probably could have used your services at the time. We just handled stress by going out back of the station and getting hammered. I had to get out of there before I turned into a hopeless drunk."

Marlene flicks her eyes toward Cody. "That's enough, Lonny."

"How's my old friend Eddie Rimbauer? He still around?"

Ava stands up. "I need to use the bathroom before we go." She grabs her backpack and heads down a hallway.

As soon as Ava's out of earshot, Marlene asks me if she's going to be okay. "Sharon and Dan are very worried about her. Does she really believe everything this crazy woman told her about being stolen?"

Cody looks confused. "What are you talking about?"

Lonny snaps at him. "None of your concern, son. Nothing to worry about."

Cody looks as if he's been slapped. Marlene puts her finger to her lips as Ava comes back to the room.

"We better get going. Don't want you to be late, Dr. Meyerhoff." Ava hoists her backpack over her shoulders, gives Cody a high five, hugs Lonny, then Marlene. They walk us to the door.

"Thanks for dropping by. Like boating, Doc? I own the boat-yard in town. If you or your husband—I noticed your wedding ring—like fishing, I'd be happy to take you out for a spin. We got flatfish, rockfish, halibut, salmon, sometimes even shark."

I thank him for the offer. I don't fish and Frank prefers fly-fishing to bait fishing.

"Fly-fishing? One of those, huh?" Lonny elbows me. "Just kidding. Give him a day with me and I'll show him what real fishing is like."

As soon as I start the car, Ava starts talking. "We don't look anything alike, do we? If he was my father, we'd look alike. And I'd feel something when I was around him, wouldn't I?"

"I don't know." I remember what I felt when I was around my father. A brothy mix of love, fear, resentment for his pie-in-the-sky ideology, and envy for his brilliant mind and oratorical skills.

"Lonny used to say that if he had a daughter, he would like her to be like me. He wouldn't say that if I was really his daughter, would he? If I was really his daughter, he would have kept me. He would have made sure I had a good home."

"You did have a good home, with his best friend."

She slaps her hand on the dashboard. "No, no. Not going there."

"Don't forget, Iliana said your biological father may never have known she was pregnant."

Ava digs into her backpack and pulls out an empty can of soda.

"I got this from Cody's room. It's next to the bathroom. The only other bathroom is in Marlene and Lonny's bedroom and their bedroom door was closed. I didn't want to open it. You said the lady from the lab told you a sample from a half sibling was good enough. If Lonny is my birth father, then Cody is my half brother, which he isn't, and this will prove it." She dangles the can with one finger like a flag. "As soon as I get home, I'm sending this in."

22

The lab results come back in two days. Fran reads them to me over the phone. I have just gotten home early from the PD; Frank and I are in the living room looking forward to a relaxed evening.

> *The DNA data are inconclusive. They neither support nor refute a biological relationship with the alleged father. For a conclusive result, we would require either the mother's sample or direct testing of the father. Testing the mother's sample can increase the accuracy of testing and raise the probability of paternity in excess of 99.99 percent.*

There's a scuffle on the other end of the phone. Fran tells me to wait a minute, Ava heard her talking to me and wants her to put me on speakerphone.

"Fran's wrong. The results mean Lonny is not my birth father."

"No, it doesn't. Inconclusive means Lonny can't be ruled out." Fran sounds like she's at the end of her rope.

"Just so you know, Dr. Meyerhoff, I called Iliana and asked her for a DNA sample."

"Hello, Ava," I say. "How are you today?"

"Oh, sorry. Fine, thank you, and you?"

"Fine. Thanks for asking."

"I called Iliana and told her."

"Told her what?"

"That I was trying to find my birth father because he needs to be held accountable for what he did to her and to do that I need a sample of her DNA."

"What did she say?"

"She could understand why I wanted to know who my father was but I'm better off having nothing to do with him because he's a rapist and could be dangerous. She said this wasn't my responsibility. That what he did, he did to her, not me. That she'd do anything for me, except this. Would you talk to her, Dr. Meyerhoff? Please. She listened to you before. She'll listen to you again."

"You want me to call Iliana to pressure her into doing something she doesn't want to do?"

"It's just a DNA sample. It doesn't hurt. It's a cheek swab."

"She's not talking about physical pain, Ava. She's talking about emotional pain. We've been over this before. Your birth mother is traumatized. She's been in therapy for years trying to work through it. You need to think about her needs, not just your own."

"I'm in pain too."

"I know you are."

"I can pay you for your time."

I want to throw the phone across the room. Pay me? Damn good thing we're not face-to-face. A string of enticing possibilities flit across my mind. Me out of control, me slapping Ava's face, turning on my heel, and slamming the door behind me. Me losing my license. Me crying myself to sleep for sinking so low.

"You there, Doctor M?"

"Pay me?" I say when I get my voice back. "I don't want your money, Ava. And if I did, there isn't enough money in the world to pay me for all the time I've spent with you or thinking about you. I'm done."

I hang up. Frank looks at me, expecting an explanation. Before I can say anything, the phone rings. I let it ring a few times before I answer.

"It's me, Ava." I don't say anything. "I'm megasorry for being a bitch. I really do appreciate everything you've done for me. And I know you didn't do it for money. Tell me what to do, please. I'll listen. I promise."

"First off, stop pressuring Iliana. Second, talk to your parents, face-to-face. Tell them what's going on. Find out what they know. Maybe there are things they haven't told you. If you don't, you can forget about asking me for help."

There's a short silence.

"Okay," she says. "I'll do it. I'll ask them to come to Fran's house so you don't have to drive over the hill again. I'll do it as soon as we hang up. I apologize for what I said. I get mean sometimes when I'm feeling sorry for myself. I take it out on other people. It's a shit habit. Thanks for everything you've done for me. I appreciate you, really, cross my heart and hope to die."

23

There's a Bundt cake sitting on Fran's dining table, dripping with lemon icing. I smell coffee coming from the kitchen. Ava is dressed up, meaning pants with no holes and a nice t-shirt with eyelet around the neckline. She's called me several times since yesterday, once to tell me she did what she promised and we are on for tonight. The next time to ask what questions she should ask her parents. The third to ask what she should do if Dan goes ballistic again or her mother faints? I told her preparing ahead was a great idea, but she'd need to figure it out for herself. She's the one who started this, she's the one who has to live with the consequences. If anyone's hurt, it will fall to her to repair the damage.

The atmosphere at Fran's is tense, despite her efforts to make everyone at home. Sharon is sitting at one end of the couch, Dan on the other. Ava is curled up in a swivel chair and Fran is sitting in her recliner. I take a chair from the dining table and turn it toward the living room.

Sharon looks awful. Her skin is flaccid and yellowish, all the fat that rounded out her cheeks has melted away, leaving nothing but saggy skin. She warns us all not to get too close because she has the flu, but she didn't want to miss our get-together.

"The flu? That's what you're calling it now?"

"Your father's upset with me. I was feeling sick, I took some medicine. And then I forgot I took it, so I took some more. It was a mistake."

"The hell it was."

"We are here to talk about Ava, not about me, Dan." Sharon looks at Ava. "Your father is having a bad day. It happens every now and then." Dan has a beer in one hand. Probably not his first. "Before we start, I know we're supposed to talk about how we adopted you, but your father has something he wants to say."

Dan rolls his eyes, puts his beer down, gets to his feet, and faces Ava as if he's going to give a book report.

"I'm sorry I slapped you. It was a reflex. I saw your mother on the ground, I thought you pushed her. She told me you didn't. I'm sorry." He sits down again, relieved to get this nasty piece of business out of the way. A tiny bit of foam has collected in the corner of his mouth. I try not to think of rabid dogs.

"Why would you think that, Dad? Have I ever pushed my mother or you?"

Dan shakes his head. Looks at his hands, not at Ava. "Nope. Never. I guess I had a little too much to drink. Like I said, I'm sorry."

Sharon sits forward, looks at me and Fran. "As you know, the reason we're here is because Ava has questions about her adoption. My memory is not the best, but I've been thinking about it. In fact, that's all I've been thinking about for days." She takes a breath. Clasps her hands. "I don't want you to take this personally, sweetie, but you were a difficult baby, colicky, hard to hold. I didn't know what to do. I read several books about bonding with your baby. None of them helped. I felt terrible. I mean, what kind of a pathetic woman can't make a helpless baby love her?"

Dan laughs. "I kept telling you, Sharon. Crying's normal for a baby, but you kept saying it wasn't. You were such a nervous Nellie. Took Ava to the doctor every time she sneezed."

Sharon ignores him. "I've known from the beginning there was something wrong. Felt it. Sensed it. Wrong with you or wrong with me, Ava, I wasn't sure. That's why I went looking for that social worker. I was hoping she could tell me something that would make everything right, something a doctor could fix. When I didn't find her, I kept assuming that whatever was wrong was my fault."

Dan shakes his head. "I told you, over and over, stop worrying so much. But, no, you kept comparing yourself to Marlene Wilson and every other mother in the world. There was nothing wrong with the way you were raising Ava."

Sharon looks at Ava. "If I had been a better mother, Ava, would you have gone looking for your birth parents?"

There it is, the question at the heart of Sharon's fears.

Ava leans forward. She looks tired, as if these last few weeks have worn her down. "I wish I could make you understand, Mother. This is not about you, it's about me. I want to know who I am, where I came from, why I was put up for adoption."

"You blame me, don't you?"

Fran and I exchange looks. The level of Sharon's insecurity is striking.

"I don't blame you or Dad. I blame the man who raped my birth mother and the social worker who covered it up."

"But you still think we stole you." Dan gets up, throws his empty beer can in the trash, pours a cup of coffee, and comes back to the couch. "What do you want to know, Ava? Just ask."

"Did you know my birth mother was raped when she was thirteen?"

Dan's face is stony. Sharon looks alarmed.

"All I knew then and all I know now is that your birth mother was a teenager who got knocked up. Nothing else." Dan puts his coffee down and crosses his arms across his chest.

"Knocked up is not the same as being raped."

"We didn't know she was raped, Ava. *If* she was raped."

"How did you adopt me? What was the process?"

"What do you mean 'process'? Your mother was desperate to have a child. Desperate and depressed. She was going to leave me."

"I was not going to leave you." Sharon sounds indignant.

"We'd been waiting for years to adopt. So when this social worker from my AA meeting said she knew a baby who needed to be adopted, I said fine, great, where do we sign up? Pardon me for not calling the FBI to do a background investigation on her."

"See what I mean, Ava?" Sharon says. "No matter what your father says, it always turns out to be my fault."

Dan continues as if he hasn't heard her. "There was no process. The whole thing happened in a flash. Caught us off guard. The social worker told us there were a lot of people waiting for babies, so we had to make up our minds fast."

"Did you ever meet my mother? Did you know anything about her or my birth father?"

"Only what the social worker told us. That they were young and healthy."

"Seriously? You didn't ask any other questions? You don't buy a truck or a shovel without reading all the reviews and talking to a dozen people."

"What can I say? That's how it was."

"The social worker didn't tell either one of you my mother was raped?"

"How she got pregnant wasn't our business, sweetie. We were

just glad she decided to give you up." Sharon flicks her eyes to me in a silent bid for my approval.

"How did either of you know for certain that the decision was hers?"

Dan looks irritated. "Because the social worker said everything was legit. All we had to do was sign some papers and pay her fee."

"How much was her fee?"

"Ten thousand dollars."

"You bought me for ten thousand dollars?"

Dan flinches like he's been hit. "We didn't buy you. That was her fee for finding you and doing all the paperwork."

"Did she make a home visit? Check to see if you were suitable parents? Did she or anyone else come to see how I was doing after I was placed?"

Sharon shakes her head. She's starting to tear up.

"Didn't that make you suspicious that my adoption wasn't legit?"

"Let me say this again for the last time." Dan's voice drops. Whatever he's trying to say, he says slowly, through clenched teeth. "Your mother was desperate. So was I. I thought if we didn't get a child, she was going to leave me and find somebody who could give her a baby the regular way."

"The regular way?" Ava asks. "What does that mean?"

"Since we're playing truth or consequences here, I guess I should get this off my chest. I was shooting blanks. I got myself tested."

The room rocks a little. Sharon gasps. "I thought it was me. So did the doctors. Oh my God, Dan. Why didn't you tell me?"

Dan curses under his breath. "Because I'm a freaking idiot. I didn't want you to know. I was ashamed."

"Oh, Dan," Sharon says. "Infertility isn't anyone's fault. It's a medical condition. The doctors told me that over and over. You didn't have to lie. I wouldn't have left you."

"I didn't lie. I just didn't say."

"You should have told me."

"I just did. Didn't make you happy, did it?" Dan looks at his watch. "We better get going. It's getting dark. Anything else you want to know?" Ava is silent. Dan stands. "I don't know if you got what you wanted, Ava. To me it's all water under the bridge. We got you, we loved you. End of story. Have we been great parents? No. We made mistakes, lots of them. I've been a crap father. I get it. But this stuff about rape. I don't know what to believe and there's nothing any of us can do about it now." He shrugs his shoulders. "I don't know what else to say. What about you, Momma, got anything to add?" He extends his hand to Sharon, helps her stand up.

"Are we crazy, Doctor? Can we be fixed?" Sharon's voice is pitched high, like a child's.

I'm not sure if she's joking or dead serious. I go for dead serious.

"I don't think you're crazy, any of you. But you're all in a lot of pain. You've been surviving on secrets. Stepping around and over one another until you've become so tangled, it only took Ava pulling on one dangling thread to unravel it all."

"Then is she going to put us back together again?" Dan is looking at me, not Ava.

"I wish I had a crystal ball to predict the future."

"Me too," he says.

"I can say this much. In my experience, when one person in a family is hurting, everyone hurts. It's hard to get healthy when the whole family is sick. For things to get better, you all need to pitch in."

* * *

Ava helps her mother to the car. Sharon hasn't said a word other than a whispered, "No, thank you," when Fran asked if she wants to stay overnight. The minute we go inside, Ava heads to her room. I stop her. Tell her we need to talk about what just happened. She pauses midway up the stairs, thinks it over, and comes back down.

"That was a complete waste of time," she says. "I don't know anything more now than I did." She flops on the couch, her arms and legs going in all directions, not her usual tied-in-a-knot position. "I feel so bad for my mom. Did you see her face when Dan said he was shooting blanks and never told her?"

Fran sits in her usual chair. "Ava, honey. I didn't know about any of this. Swear to God. I would have told you if I had. All I knew is what Sharon knew. That the doctors told her she was too nervous, too stressed, to conceive."

"We're sickos, right, Doc? All of us."

"I don't want to put a label on it, Ava. People do the best they can with what they have."

"Did you hear what Dan said? They got me to keep their marriage from falling apart. I'm the only thing holding them together. Now they'll probably get a divorce." She turns over on her stomach and scrambles to her feet.

"I'm sorry my parents are a hot mess. I'm sorry I've made things worse. I'm sorry and I'm sorry for being sorry." She stomps to the bottom of the stairs. "Thanks for helping me. Both of you. I appreciate it. But tonight didn't change anything. I'm still going to find out who raped my mother."

24

The front door to my office building is still locked at 9:30, meaning I'm the first to arrive at work. I dig in my purse for the keys, struggle with the door lock, then trip over a pile of mail on the door mat to get to the alarm system before it goes off. Some idiot installed the alarm panel in the break room. Gary, who serves as facilities manager, has never bothered to have it moved closer to the front door. I set the damn thing off by mistake at least once a month. But today, luck is on my side and I make it to the break room in time.

When I go back to the lobby, Lonny Wilson is standing at the open front door, holding the pile of mail in his hand.

He steps into the lobby, pulling the door closed behind him. "Okay to put the mail on this table?" He sets it down underneath the board that shows who's in and who's out of the office. He moves the marker under my name to the "in" column. "That's cool. I could use something like that in my shop." He's wearing jeans, a long-sleeved collared shirt, and a baseball cap embroidered with the words *Wilson's Boatyard*.

I turn on the overhead light. My heart is beating at the speed and volume of a taiko drum competition.

"Sorry, didn't mean to startle you."

"Give me a minute to catch my breath. Have a seat." I point to an antique chair with a needlepointed cover. My mother made it as a welcome gift when I first opened my private office. She's moved on from needlepoint to miniature birdhouses. Frank and I already have three.

I go into the break room and set up the coffeepot. It's the duty of the first-in therapist. I welcome the chance to calm down. As soon as I hear the pot begin to burble, I go back to the lobby. Lonny is tapping his fingers on his knee.

"Dan and Sharon came over last night. They were very upset. Seems like that meeting yesterday didn't go so well. I'm worried about them. I thought maybe you had a few minutes to talk to me. If this isn't a good time, I can come back."

"You could have called me on the phone."

"I don't do so good on the phone. I'm better person-to-person. I just want a few minutes."

"Stay here. I need to go to my office and check my calendar."

I could check my calendar on my phone and not move, but I want to clear my head and I can't do that while he's staring at me. My first appointment is at 10:30, a retired KPD officer and his wife are coming for counseling, trying to learn how to live together now that he's home all the time. He's grieving the loss of fraternity and searching for a sense of purpose. She's suffocating under his constant glare and demands for her attention. I open my office door to go downstairs again. Lonny is sitting in the waiting room, not in the lobby where I asked him to wait.

"Thought I'd save you the trip." He smiles.

I gesture for him to come in. We do a little you-first-no-you-first dance at the door. He steps inside, looks around. I follow, leaving my office door open. There is something about him and his easy, self-assured manners that makes me uncomfortable.

"Nice office. Nicer than the office I went to for my fitness-for-duty eval at KPD. Guess you figured out I flunked, so they canned me. The other day, when you and Ava were at my house, I told my family I retired because I wanted to be near the water. I was lying. It's humiliating getting fired. I never wanted Cody or Marlene to know, so I made it look like it was my decision. It was my own fault I got the blue juice. I did a lot of crap in my drinking days." He gives me a weak smile. "Where should I sit?"

He picks one of the two single swivel chairs. I sit in the other, turning to face him. He takes off his hat, swipes his hand over his forehead.

"Dan and I have been buddies for a long time. Drinking buddies in my KPD days. I don't drink anymore. Dan falls off the wagon from time to time. All this Ava's saying about being stolen from a kid who got raped, stuff like this is going to send him right down that fatal funnel. I don't want to see it happen. I don't know the details about how he and Sharon adopted Ava. They were still in Kenilworth and he was still working for KPD. He's an honorable guy, a straight shooter. He wouldn't have done anything illegal." Lonny's twisting his ball cap between his hands as he talks.

"I've known Ava all her life. I love her like a daughter. She's a good kid, but she's impressionable. Always been a little drama queen, kind of like Sharon. I'm worried. These are my people. I don't want to see them go down the tubes. This woman who says she's Ava's birth mother, what is she, some kind of con artist, out for money? You've met her, right? What did you think?"

"I did meet her. That was not my impression."

"Glad to know." He looks at his watch. "Well, I've taken up enough of your time. I just wanted to tell you that Marlene and I are really concerned. We don't want to see this family, which feels like our family, destroyed. Sharon has always been a little fragile and, like I said, Dan can only take so much stress before he starts drinking heavy again. Marlene and I both feel responsible for them. If there's anything we can do to help, please call us." He stands, extends his hand. We shake. "Thank you for your time, Doctor."

I give him five minutes to leave the building before I go downstairs for a cup of coffee. Gary is in the break room holding a mug of hot water. He asks me if anything's wrong because I seem preoccupied. I tell him I'm not preoccupied. He tells me I turned on the coffeepot but forgot to add the coffee. I tell him about Lonny showing up this morning without calling first. That he seems genuinely concerned about the Sower family. On the other hand, he just scared the crap out of me. I can't put my finger on what it is exactly, but there's something off about him. Gary tells me to forget my finger and pay attention to my gut.

25

Ava calls me later that night full of news. She called Marge, Sheriff Bergen's assistant, who had some kind of "brain fart" and remembered Iliana and her mother coming to the station. Not uncommon, I think, for someone Marge's age to forget what she ate for breakfast but recall in detail things that happened years ago.

"It took her ten minutes to get to the point," Ava says. "She went on and on about how I'm too young to understand, but when I grow up I will. Why do adults always say that to kids? Just wait 'til you grow up, then you'll find out how miserable you can be. I'm surprised we don't all kill ourselves first."

I fumble with the phone. She reassures me she's only joking. I tell her joking about suicide is not funny. She should hurry up and finish her story. It's almost ten o'clock, and Frank and I are already in bed.

"Marge said Iliana was so frightened, she didn't want to talk in front of her mother, who looked scared to death herself. She didn't want to go into the interview room alone with the detective, so he asked Marge to sit in. She was happy to do that because women sometimes try to get out of trouble by accusing the investigating officer of making advances. Can you believe it? I almost croaked. My mother was thirteen. She'd been raped, she was pregnant, and Marge thought she was trying to flirt?" Ava pauses to catch her breath. "I asked if that officer was still around. Marge said he left police work and went into computers. She doesn't know where he lives. I asked if Iliana told the officer who had raped her. She remembers Iliana saying the man who raped her was a cop and threatened to have her and her mother deported if she told anyone what he did to her. Marge said the officer thought Iliana was making things up. That it was her boyfriend who got her pregnant. So did Marge, because—and this is a quote—'it happens all the time with those people.'" Ava's voice raises an octave. "*Those* people. Meaning Mexicans. Meaning me."

"Call her, please, Doctor M."

"Who? Marge or Iliana?"

"Iliana. I need her to send her DNA sample to the lab ASAP. Marge is going to tell that dickhead sheriff that she remembers Iliana. He'll tell Dan and Dan will tell Lonny. I don't want Lonny to know I had Cody's DNA tested."

Frank has rolled over in bed and is giving me the stink eye, tapping on his watch. I take the phone into the bathroom.

"I have to ask again, how are you going to feel if your birth mother donates her DNA and the results prove beyond a doubt that Lonny is your father?"

"It's not going to happen."

"But what if it does? What are you going to do?"

"It won't be Lonny. If it is—and it won't be—I'll figure something out. Will you call Iliana? Please."

"I told you I am not comfortable trying to pressure Iliana into doing something she doesn't want to do."

"I'm not asking you to pressure her."

"Why don't you call her yourself?"

"I did. I told her I didn't know that my friend Cody's father used to be a cop. Even Cody didn't know it. I told her I'm sure he's not her rapist, but I need a paternity test to prove it. She told me this was not my concern and she didn't want to get involved."

"You have your answer. She said no."

"Cody keeps calling me, wanting to get together. What if he's my brother, my half brother? What if he wants to kiss me? I'm going mental, Doctor. Ask Fran if you want. Cross my heart, hope to die. I'm not making this up."

I head back to bed, determined not to call Iliana. Ava has got to learn to take no for an answer. The phone rings before I close the bathroom door behind me. It's Iliana. She apologizes for calling so late. But after Ava's last call, she really needs my advice. I wave at Frank and go back to the bathroom.

"Why is it so important to Ava to bring her birth father to justice? What that man did, he did to me, not to her. I understand she's upset because she's worried that her friend Cody's father is my rapist. That would be terrible. It breaks my heart to think about it. But what she doesn't understand is that no matter who he is, if I submit a sample of my DNA and they match it to someone, there will be a court hearing. I'll have to testify. I don't want to face this man. I've spent years trying to put him out of my mind."

I tell Iliana I'm not a lawyer. All I know is that there are statutes of limitations and all kinds of legal impediments that may prevent her case from ever going to court. I don't mention Sheriff Bergen, who seems fixed on making sure it doesn't get that far.

"Here's what I want to know from you. If I don't cooperate, do you think Ava will go after this man on her own?"

"I do."

"Can you stop her?"

"I doubt it. She is very determined."

"Ava and I have lost so much time. I want her to be proud of me. To feel that, whatever happens, she can rely on me. It's like our roles are reversed. I should be the one to right this wrong, not her."

"Iliana, listen to me. Do what feels comfortable and safe. You were raped, it wasn't your fault. You lost your child under deplorable conditions. You were not in control of any of this. If helping Ava makes you feel back in control of your life, then do it. But whatever you decide, it needs to be your choice. No one else can live your life for you or bear the costs of your decision."

26

Fran calls me the next morning to say that Iliana called Ava. After talking to me, she sent the lab a sample of her DNA and paid extra to get the results back in twenty-four hours. Good thing because time is moving so slowly it feels like the clock is running backward. Fran has been trying to distract Ava by persuading her to register for the local community college. No matter what happens next, Ava needs to consider her future, and a future without an education isn't much of a future. Ava isn't Fran's only concern. Sharon is a hot mess, can't get out of bed, and Dan is hitting the bottle hard. I tell her to call me the minute the test results are in.

That minute arrives at 8:30 the next morning as I'm driving to work. RBG's lab is clearly faster than the state lab Sheriff Bergen uses. There's a tremor in Fran's voice as she reads loud enough to be heard over the traffic.

Based on samples from Cody Wilson, Iliana Ortega, and Ava Sower, the alleged father of Cody Wilson cannot be excluded as the biological father of Ava Sower. Based on our analysis, the probability of paternity is 99.99999999%. Please note: Test results are for informational purposes only. Samples were not collected under a strict chain of custody. Patient names and sample origins cannot be verified.

"Where's Ava?"

"She ran out of the house and got in her car. I've called her cell a dozen times. You don't think she's gone over to Lonny's, do you?"

I tell Fran I'm pretty sure Ava is sitting somewhere crying her eyes out. And to please text me the minute she hears from her. I sit for a minute before getting out of the car. My hands are shaking. I feel lightheaded. Ava's worst fears have come true. Lonny is her biological father. The implications of this for Ava's and Cody's futures are almost too mind-boggling to comprehend. Everything they knew to be true has been turned on its head. I start up the walkway, weak at the knees. My briefcase as heavy as a bag full of bricks. I open the front door. Gary's waiting for me in the lobby.

"There's somebody here to see you. I took her into the staff room and made her a cup of tea. She's pretty upset."

Ava's head is buried in her arms like a child napping at her desk. She looks up when I enter the room; her face is bloated and scorched red from crying.

"I'm so sorry." I sit next to her and reach for her hand. She pulls away.

"How could he? How could he know for eighteen years that I was his daughter and never say anything?" She's talking loudly, so loudly I'm sure everyone can hear her. A building filled with therapists is usually quieter than a library.

The door to the staff room opens. Gary sticks his head in. "Everything okay here?"

I tell him we're on our way upstairs. He tells me he's in his office and he'll leave the door open if I need anything. Ava follows me, dragging herself from step to step. I text Fran. She is so relieved to hear that Ava's okay she doesn't know whether to hug her or yell at her when she gets home.

Ava curls up on my couch, hugging her knees and staring into space like she's in a trance. I let the silence between us stand as the enormity of what Lonny's done sinks in.

"That bastard." She jumps to her feet. "I'm going to show him the results, make him eat them page by page."

I stand, position myself between her and my office door. "You need to think this over."

"What's there to think about?"

"Lonny could be dangerous."

"I hope he is. I hope he tries to hit me so I can hit him back."

"Sit down, please." Ava hesitates. "I'm not asking, I'm telling you. Sit down. You need to listen to me."

"Whatever." She flops to the couch like a rag doll.

"Lonny may not ever have known Iliana was pregnant. Remember? You can't just march into his house waving the DNA results. Imagine for a minute that you're him. Wouldn't you deny everything? He's going to want to look innocent in front of Marlene and Cody. He's been lying to them for years, trying to save face, telling them he quit KPD, when he was fired. You can't corner him. Cornered people can be dangerous." She squints at me, trying to decide whose side I'm on. "Lonny needs to be confronted, absolutely, but not by you. We should go to Sheriff Bergen first."

"That fat creep. He won't do anything. He doesn't believe me."

"He has to. DNA doesn't lie."

"I want to call Lonny out. I want him to look at me and tell me what he did."

"There's no rush. No one knows about the DNA results except you and me and Fran. If you go to Lonny's house now—and I understand why you would want to—you'll tip him off and we don't know what he'll do next. You don't want Lonny to go into hiding, do you? Or kill himself?"

"I don't care if he kills himself. I'd dance on his grave."

"Is that what you want? Cody is going to be devastated by this news. If Lonny kills himself, it will make everything worse for him and Marlene."

"It would be better than having to look at Lonny's ugly face or read about him in the newspapers. Because I'm going to call the newspapers." She pulls her phone out.

"Stop. Please. Releasing these results is a very big deal. Remember what Sheriff Bergen said? He may not be likable, but he's not stupid. You could be sued for defamation. Lonny would have you in his crosshairs. It could be dangerous."

"What are you saying? That I should do nothing?"

"That's not what I'm saying. I'm asking you to consider how to bring Lonny to justice and do the least possible harm to everyone involved. Marlene, Cody, Iliana, and yourself."

Ava flushes with anger. "How am I going to hurt myself? I told you a hundred times I'm not going to kill myself. Why do you bring that up all the time?"

"Because I knew a young person about your age who did kill himself and I felt responsible."

"Were you?"

Her question throws me off guard for a second. "No, not entirely. Do I wish I had done things differently? Of course. But even if I had, I doubt I could have stopped him. Still, knowing I couldn't have stopped him doesn't keep me from torturing myself with the what-ifs. You are about to change some lives forever. This is a lot of responsibility. I want you to feel that what you did, you did thoughtfully, not impulsively, with respect and kindness for everyone involved."

"Lonny doesn't deserve my respect and kindness."

"I'll say it again. This is not for him, it's for you and Cody and Marlene and Iliana."

"I only care about one thing, Dr. Meyerhoff. That Lonny gets what he deserves. How I do it doesn't matter."

"It does matter. You may not think so now, but it does. The ends don't justify the means. You've been betrayed. You're hurt. Hurt people hurt others. Let's find a way to deal with Lonny that doesn't hurt the innocent people around him."

She looks at me like I've just forced her to swallow rat poison.

"How is talking to that bonehead Bergen again going to help? I don't trust him. What if he tells Lonny and Lonny gets on a plane to somewhere?"

"If that happens, we'll deal with it. Lonny's more likely to run off if you confront him than if the sheriff does."

"How do you know that?"

"I don't. I'm not sure of anything. I just think it's the best option you have."

She stands, slowly this time. "Okay, but if Bergen won't help, I'm going to Lonny's no matter what you or anyone says."

She waits for me to agree. One concession deserves another. I nod. Right now, I'd do anything to slow her down. We're in dangerous territory. Far more dangerous than Ava imagines. She needs a minder. As far as I know, I'm it, the only one who's willing, able, and available.

27

It's a beautiful day in Moss Point. The sky is blue and full of bird-song. I open the front door of the sheriff's department. Marge looks up from her tea and without a word buzzes us inside.

"He's in his office. Not in a very good mood. I told him I remembered your birth mother and her interview. I'll let him know you're here."

Bergen is at his desk, head down, reading the newspaper. He looks up when we tap on the open door with a "not you again" look on his face. He glances at his watch. Tells us he has a conference call to make in ten minutes.

"Marge remembered Iliana reporting she'd been raped."

"The fact that Marge remembers your birth mother reporting a rape doesn't mean the rape actually happened." He frowns, his eyebrows making a deep V shape like a bird in flight.

Ava is fingering the DNA report she folded into a tiny square and stuck in her pocket.

"Why won't you believe me?"

He holds out his hand and starts counting off on his fingers. "Because I'm a cop. Far as I'm concerned, based on more years of experience than you've been alive on this earth, if your lips are moving, you're lying." He raises a second finger. "Because girls lie about who got them pregnant." And a third. "Because people are innocent until proven guilty." And a fourth. "And, last but not least, because you have no proof." He spits out the final four words one at a time.

"I have proof. I got my DNA test back. Lonny Wilson *is* my biological father. That means he raped my birth mother. Here's the proof. Arrest him."

She unfolds the report and slaps it on his desk. He smooths out the wrinkles with his enormous hands. Puts on a pair of glasses and starts to read, dragging his index finger down the margin. When he finishes, he takes off his glasses, puts them back in his pocket, and looks at Ava with tired eyes.

"I told you before, you don't have any standing to file charges because legally you are not the victim." Ava starts to speak. He keeps talking. "Let me remind you, this is not my decision. I didn't make these laws."

"Did you read the results of the report? Ninety-nine point nine percent probability Lonny Wilson is my biological father."

"Probability isn't proof." He lets out another one of his martyred sighs. "There are many things wrong here. Numero uno . . ." He holds up his hand again, ready to count on his fingers. I wonder if he's having trouble keeping track of his thoughts.

"I speak English."

"Sorry, no offense meant." He gives a second, louder sigh as though, in addition to everything else we're bothering him with, the burden of being politically correct is weighing him down.

"Number one. You have no chain of custody. The court will only honor a legally mandated test with a validated chain of custody. Number two." He looks to make sure Ava's listening. "Only your birth mother can bring legal charges or sue in civil court. You only have one other option. Get Lonny to confess."

"And how do you suggest Ava does that?" I jump at the strident sound of my own voice. It was my intention to stand by and let Ava do the talking, but this joke of a law enforcement officer is irritating me big-time. "Seriously, Sheriff. That's your response? Send an eighteen-year-old girl to get a grown man, a rapist, to confess to his crime?"

Bergen steeples his hands and sinks back into his chair, looking at me like I'm all that stands between him and a nap.

"I cannot, by law, start an investigation on Lonny Wilson or anyone else unless your birth mother, the so-called alleged victim, steps forward to make a complaint."

Ava and I both start to say something. He puts his hand up, traffic cop style.

"Don't start that 'I'm the victim' business again. You have no standing to file a complaint. If your mother won't testify, there is nothing I can do. For Pete's sake, how many times do I have to say that? Your report is worthless. Not admissible in court." He shoves it back to Ava. "I need a search warrant for the alleged assailant's DNA. I can only get that if the alleged victim agrees to go to her local police department to give a DNA sample to ensure the chain of custody."

"Stop saying alleged victim, alleged assailant." Ava is so frustrated she's on the verge of tears. "We're talking about Iliana Ester Ortega and Lonny Wilson."

"Doctor, help your patient, please."

I remind him Ava is a family friend, not my patient. He cuts me off, leans over his desk, and turns to Ava, his face only inches from hers. "The DA will not file unless your birth mother comes here, in person. Let me give you some advice, young lady, based on personal experience. I caution you against trying to talk your birth mother into coming here. It is never a good idea to pressure a victim to come forward. Victims have already lost control of their lives. It is up to them to make their own decisions about what to do. Pressuring a victim to file a complaint never turns out well for the victim or the person who did the pressuring."

It's the same advice I gave to Ava, but coming from Bergen, it sounds like a threat. His phone rings. He stands, thanks us for coming, and asks us to close his door on our way out. Marge waves at us as we go through the lobby, gives us a questioning thumbs-up, thumbs-down gesture. We keep walking.

"I told you so," Ava says as soon as we are outside. "He doesn't believe me."

"Did you notice he referred to Iliana as the victim, not the alleged victim?"

"Big fricking deal. He's still not going to do anything. I'm going to Lonny's." She starts down the steps.

"No, you're not. I drove, remember? I get to choose where we go and I choose lunch. We need to think about our next steps. I don't think well on an empty stomach."

28

"Where's Sharon?"

Sharon, Mom, Mother—Ava changes what she calls both her parents according to her mood. Mom or Dad means she's feeling affectionate. Dan and Sharon, Mother and Father seem to buy her the distance she needs to make breaking away less painful.

Dan is sitting on the front porch of the house, staring into the cup of coffee he's holding. The house is surrounded by open fields filled with wild grasses. Nuthatches, juncos, chickadees, and blue jays are darting from bush to bush. Three mangy-looking cats circle around Dan's feet. Ava says he never feeds them. He wants them mouse-hungry.

I managed to calm Ava down over lunch. It was her decision to tell Dan and Sharon about Lonny. She didn't want them to hear about it from anyone else because this was going to hurt, big-time, and she's hurt them enough. It's her second concession of the day. I keep my fingers crossed that this means I've been getting through to her and she's listening.

"Where's Mom?" Ava asks for the second time. "She over the flu?"

Dan looks up; there are circles under his eyes and he's unshaven. "Your mother is in the psych ward at Moss Point Community Hospital. I'll tell her you asked about her."

"What?! When? Why?"

"Been there since that night at Fran's. The night I got to humiliate myself in public. We stopped by Marlene and Lonny's house on the way home. She barely said a word. The minute we got in the house, she went for the pills. I found her lying on the floor of our bedroom. She was unconscious. I called 911."

Ava's knees buckle. She grabs hold of the porch railing and hangs there speechless.

"Thank you, Dad," Dan says, "for saving my mother's life. By the way, how is she doing?" The mockery in his voice is unmistakable.

"Why didn't you call me?"

"I didn't think you cared. You have another mother now."

Ava looks up. "That's not fair. I love Sharon. You know that."

"You got a funny way of showing it."

"Why did she take the pills? Was it because of me?"

"You'll have to ask her. This isn't the first time."

"Not the first time? You should have said." Ava's still gripping the porch rail. Her voice is a mix of outrage and panic.

"There are some things a kid shouldn't know."

Ava looks up. "What the fuck? Iliana, now you. Why is everyone trying to protect me? I should have known. I could have helped."

Dan smirks. Then he shakes his head as if to say if he couldn't help Sharon, no one could.

"How is she doing?" I ask.

"Dunno. The hospital staff thought it was better if she didn't talk to me for a while." He drains his cup and puts it down. "So what's on your mind, Ava? To what do I owe the pleasure of your company?"

Ava lets go of the railing and walks up on the porch steps. She pulls the DNA report out of her pocket and hands it to him.

Her mouth is turned down at the corners, her delicate nostrils flaring in and out with every breath.

"Read this. I'm sorry, Dad. I wish it was different."

He starts to read. Gets to the end and reads it again. "Bullshit." His voice startles a flock of quail out from under a bush and sends them over a fence. He throws the report on the ground. "Get that thing away from me."

"It's DNA, Dad. DNA doesn't lie. I hate knowing this as much as you do."

Dan gets to his feet. Starts pacing across the porch, talking to himself more than to us. Ava flattens against the wall of the house to stay out of his way.

"No. No. Not Lonny. I know him. He's like a brother. I would've known. I've been a cop. I got a gut feel for creeps. You think I would have let you be around him if I had known? He's not a rapist. He's not your father. I'm your father. This is not happening." Dan leans against the rail trying to catch his breath. Ava steps to his side, closer but not too close.

"Dad, listen to me, please. I don't think Lonny knew my birth mother was pregnant. Even she didn't accept it until she started showing."

"This is crazy. I'm telling you, Lonny Wilson is not a rapist. Get off my property. Both of you." He kicks his coffee cup against the side of the house. The cup shatters. A dark stain oozes along the wall.

"I need your help, Dad."

"Don't you dare say a word of this to your mother. You'll kill her."

"I didn't know it would turn out this way." She moves a tiny step closer to Dan. "I need Lonny to confess. Can you help me?"

Dan stares at Ava, his eyes wide. "You got a helluva nerve asking me to help you send my oldest friend to prison on this bullshit. Especially since you've been so kind and concerned about your mother and me."

"I'm afraid of him. Dr. Meyerhoff thinks he could be violent."

"She put that in your head?" He glares at me. "I've known Lonny Wilson all my adult life. He's a peaceful guy. Know why he quit being a cop? Because police work was too violent for him."

"He didn't quit, Dan," I say. "He was fired for drinking on the job and roughing up a suspect."

"Bullshit."

"Ask Chief Pence. There was a lawsuit. The city settled out of court to keep it out of the papers."

"Never heard of it."

"Because he didn't tell you. He didn't tell anybody. Not even his family knew."

Dan stares at me, struggling to take in what I've just said. Like a deaf man whose hearing has been suddenly restored.

"My birth mother is scared of facing Lonny." Dan starts pacing. Ava follows him. "If he confesses, she won't have to. He trusts you. I was hoping you could persuade him to do the right thing."

"You're going to kill Lonny if you keep this up. Destroy his entire family. What about Cody? You're going to destroy him too."

"None of this is Cody's fault."

"Kind of a day late and a dollar short to be thinking about that now, isn't it?" Dan stops suddenly to pick up the broken pieces of his coffee mug. Ava tries to help. He pushes her away, and she stumbles and catches herself before she falls.

"Out of here, both of you. I need to think and I need a drink. I can't do either with the two of you staring at me."

Ava doesn't move. I reach for her hand and tug her gently out to the yard.

"There's something about you, Ava, I don't get." Dan is standing at the top of the steps. The sun is behind him, throwing his shadow at us as if there were two Dans. "You're hot to protect this mother you barely know, yet you don't give a damn about the mother who raised you. The one who's having a nervous breakdown and asks every day if you're going to visit her."

Ava turns around. "You should have told me she was in the hospital."

One of the cats rubs against Dan's legs. He shoves it off with his foot. "How about this? Go see your mother. Tell her what you just told me. See what she has to say."

"I thought you said not to tell her, that it was going to kill her."

"I changed my mind."

"If I do, will you talk to Lonny?"

He looks at me. "See how she is? The only reason she'll go see Sharon now is because she wants something from me." He puts his hands up to his head like it's about to explode and turns back to the house. The cat runs under the porch.

Ava gets in the car, buckles her seat belt, and stares out the window, her eyes unfocused. I've seen that thousand-mile stare before. It's the face cops wear when their lives have been shattered by unspeakable violence and unbelievable cruelty.

"Is it my fault Sharon tried to kill herself?"

"No one can make another person harm themselves, Ava. Or drink to excess. It was obvious from our meeting at Fran's that your mother and father have both had a lot of problems for a long time, maybe since before you were adopted."

"And I made everything worse by looking for my birth parents."

"That's too harsh. Looking for your birth parents was a tipping point, the proverbial straw that broke the camel's back.

Your parents are adults. What they do with their lives, both the good and the bad, is up to them. Dan won't get better until he stops drinking. Sharon needs therapy. I hope she's getting what she needs at the hospital."

"Then let's go to see her and find out," Ava says. "The hospital isn't far."

29

The sun is so bright the fields on either side of the road look like they're on fire. For a small town, the Moss Point Community Hospital is impressive. Red brick with tall white columns spaced along the front. We follow the signs to the mental health clinic and wellness center. The visitors' entrance stands at the top of a wide grassy courtyard rimmed with flower-filled planters. If I didn't know where we were, I'd think we were at a library or on a college campus.

The reception lobby is painted a cheerful yellow. A large fish tank hangs on one wall, a huge aviary on another. The furniture is arranged for conversation, face-to-face chairs, face-to-face love seats. Someone in an alcove is playing the piano. Four people are seated at a card table working a jigsaw puzzle. The receptionist calls Sharon to the front.

Sharon looks better than she did at Fran's. There's color in her cheeks and her face has filled out again. She's overjoyed to see Ava, introduces her to everybody in the room, even the sour-faced orderly who is overseeing the lobby for potential runaways and contraband. Sharon is apologetic. If it weren't so close to the end of visiting hours, she would have given us a tour of the facilities, the fitness room, the hair salon, and the library.

Too bad her therapist has gone home early. She and Ava could have joined her for a session because they need family therapy. It's one of the items on her postrelease plan along with couples' therapy, AA, NA, Al-Anon, and Co-Dependents Anonymous.

We sit in a triangle of purple plastic chairs. Sharon on one side, me on the other, Ava in the middle. I'm beginning to understand that being in the middle has been Ava's position for most of her young life.

Sharon turns in her seat to face Ava. I move my chair so I don't miss any of what she's saying.

"I'm so glad you came to see me. I've been thinking about you every day, talking with my therapist about our relationship. I've only been here a short time, but I've learned a lot. I'm a very insecure person. Being unable to have children only fortified my insecurity. Even now, knowing Dan was the problem hasn't helped. I wasn't prepared to be a mother—even though I thought I was. None of this is your fault, Ava. Your father and I have things to work out. Not your fault or your responsibility. I'm sorry I scared you and your father when I took those pills." She reaches for Ava's hands. Her cheeks are flushed. She exhales. "I really needed to say that. I've been rehearsing it, waiting for you to visit."

"So, it wasn't a mistake, Mom? You were trying to kill yourself?"

"No, no. I wouldn't do that to you or Dan. My therapist said I was only trying to stop the pain, the mental pain. I'm very glad to be alive. And very glad to see you." She squeezes Ava's hands. "Too much about me. How are you, sweetie? What have you been up to since I've been here?"

"A lot has happened."

Sharon's face lights up. "Tell me. I want to hear all about it."

"It's about my biological father. I know who he is."

Sharon pulls back. She looks alarmed. I put my hands up, signaling Ava to stop talking.

"This may not be the best time to discuss this with your mother, Ava. Perhaps save it for another day when she's feeling stronger."

"I don't want her to hear it from anyone else but me."

"Hear what?" There's a tremor in Sharon's voice. Her legs are starting to shake. She bites down on her bottom lip. "If it's good news, that's fine. But this isn't the best time to talk about serious things. I'm still a little shaky. My therapist thinks I'm too fragile to take on anything other than my own healing. She'll let me know when she thinks I'm stronger." She takes Ava's hand again. "I wish I were brave like you."

Ava isn't brave, she's scared to death. Scared of the truth. Scared of wrecking the lives of people she loves. Scared that without the truth, she's condemned to a future full of lies.

"Not a problem, Mom. Don't worry. You're doing fine. I'm proud of you." Ava leans over and gives Sharon a kiss. "Keep it up. I'll visit again soon."

We drive back over the hill to Kenilworth. The air is dusky. Behind us, the sky is streaked with pale pink tendrils. Ava avoids talking by pretending to be asleep. I can't blame her. It's been a devastating day. She needs the rest and I appreciate the silence.

I drop Ava off at Fran's. Dan's truck is parked in front, the wheels half on the street, half on the sidewalk. Ava looks scared. I walk her inside. Fran is making coffee in the kitchen. She's in her bathrobe. Dan is slumped in a chair. His face is bruised and he has a black eye. The minute we left him, he started drinking, and while we were visiting Sharon in the hospital, he went to Lonny's house, demanding to know if Lonny was Ava's father.

"The fucker denied it, of course." Dan's slurring his words. I can't tell if he's still drunk or having trouble talking because his bottom lip is the size of a plum. "He couldn't imagine I would believe my quote 'dope-smoking daughter' over him." He looks at Ava with his good eye. "You don't smoke dope, do you?"

"Tried it, didn't like it much. Cody smokes."

"Then he starts lecturing me about the evils of alcohol. I was drunk. I admit it. Like he's one to talk. He was drunk on his ass for years." Fran hands him a cup of coffee. He takes a sip and grimaces. "Too hot. My freaking lip hurts."

"I didn't mean for you to go over there tonight, Dad. I'm sorry he hurt you."

It's not enough that she feels responsible for Sharon's pill-taking, now she's carrying Dan's idiotic behavior on her bony little shoulders.

Fran replaces Dan's coffee with a glass of water.

"The thing that really pissed me off is when he told me to slap the crap out of you for spreading lies. And if I didn't, he would. I told him I'd kill him if he laid a hand on you. That's when we started trading punches. Cody and Marlene heard the whole damn thing. Broke us up." He drinks some water.

"What are you doing here?" I ask.

"I was afraid Lonny would come gunning for me if I stayed home. So I came here looking for Ava. Aren't you proud of me, kid? I did what you asked."

Ava doesn't respond. She's just standing there, looking at the floor. I can't see her face, only her boisterous curls bouncing as she shakes her head. Without a word, she turns and walks up the steps to her bedroom. Fran starts after her. I stop her.

"Let her be. She needs time to think."

"Think about what? The fact that she might as well be an

orphan? That she's got one parent in the nuthouse and another who drinks like a fish and acts like a jerk?"

"Exactly," I say. Dan's fallen asleep in his chair. "Okay for him to sleep it off here?"

Fran nods. Pulls his keys out of her bathrobe pocket. "I won't let him go until he sobers up and promises me he'll stay the hell away from Lonny."

30

The next afternoon, I head to the café for a cup of coffee after my last client, a young officer who is having trouble processing the world of pain that is becoming his daily fare. He joined the force to put bad guys in prison, not to console the grieving parents of a dead child, their agonized screams reverberating in his sleep.

Yesterday was rough. I want to connect with Ava, if only to reassure myself that she isn't planning some kind of stealth assault on Lonny. Dan's battered face has erased any doubts I had about Lonny's propensity for violence. As for his threats to slap the crap out of Ava, I'm taking those seriously. Ava could be in danger. I only hope she understands how much.

Eddie comes to the café door, wiping his hands on his apron.

"If you're looking for Ava, she's not here. Fran just called. That little pisshead Cody is standing in front of her house, yelling and throwing shit, demanding to talk to Ava."

By the time I get to Fran's, clusters of neighbors are standing around watching the action. Cody has upended Fran's garbage and recycling bins, littering her front yard with refuse. Tire tracks from his truck have turned her lawn into a muddy mess. Fran is standing on the front step, one hand on the doorknob, the other holding a broom. Ava has locked herself in her car. Cody is trying to pull open the passenger-side door.

"Bitch, what do you think you're doing?" He keeps pulling on the handle.

Eddie's beat-up truck zips to the end of the block, makes a U-turn, tires screeching, and parks a few houses away, following standard police procedure to not park directly in front of an in-progress crime. He gets out, still wearing his apron, and starts down the street, motioning the neighbors back into their houses. "Move on, nothing to see here."

Cody is making put-your-window-down gestures with his hand. Then he jumps on the hood of Ava's car and sits there, banging his legs against her tires.

Ava rolls her window down a few inches and tells Cody to chill out. Somebody will call the cops, if they haven't already, and he's going to get arrested.

"Why didn't you answer your cell? I want to talk to you. Come out."

"I will if you calm down."

She's working him like a hostage negotiator, don't give anything away, always ask for something in exchange.

Cody jumps off the hood. Stands like a statue in front of her car.

"I'm calm. See." He turns in a circle. "Come out." Ava opens her car door. I yell at her to stay inside. She gets out, positions herself between the door and the car, using the door as a shield. Cody starts to pace back and forth. He's mumbling. I can't tell if he's talking to himself or the neighbors. He stops suddenly, turns, and starts for Ava.

"You're a bat-shit crazy liar, Ava Sower!"

Eddie is on him in a moment. He twists Cody's arm around his back, hard enough to make him yelp, and drags him away.

Now Ava is yelling at Eddie not to hurt Cody. Fran opens her front door and waves us all inside.

Eddie pushes Cody to the couch and sits next to him, using his body to hold him in place. Cody is rubbing his arm, complaining that it's broken. Fran goes to the kitchen to make coffee. She didn't call the cops and doesn't think any of her neighbors would.

Ava and I sit in separate chairs facing Cody. The room is filled with the sound of him trying to catch his breath. His face is streaked with sweat and tears. Eddie drapes his arm over Cody's shoulder. He's talking in a low voice, telling Cody that there's nothing that can't be solved by talking. That he's been lower than whale shit in his life, which is how Cody looks now, but give it day and things will look better.

Cody throws off Eddie's arm. "You're a fat fuck. You don't know what's going on."

Ava just sits, examining Cody's face, looking for evidence that they're related. She's darker than he is. His eyes are blue, hers are brown. He has a long, pointed nose. She doesn't.

"She's a skanky, crackhead bitch. Arrest her." He reaches for Ava, and Eddie knocks him back to the couch.

"Talk to me, buddy; tell me what's going on? Maybe I can help."

"She's lying, telling everyone my father raped her slut mother." He glares at Ava. "I know why you're doing this. You're making this crap up to get at me. Stop it. You don't have to be my girl-friend. You don't even have to be my friend. I'll move away, you won't ever have to see me again."

"None of this is your fault, Cody," Ava says. "None of it."

"Then stop lying." He starts to push his way to his feet. Eddie halts him with a bear hug. Cody keeps wriggling. His face is red and he's hyperventilating.

"Cody," I say, "this is not your fault and it's not Ava's fault. Ava isn't lying. Your father is Ava's biological father. She has a DNA report to prove it. DNA doesn't lie. I know you don't want to hear this, but you are her half brother."

Cody yanks on Eddie's arms. Eddie doesn't budge. "Bullshit. You don't even look like him."

"Lonny threatened to slap the crap out of me. You heard him. He said it in front of you. He's never threatened me before. Never called me names. Why do you think he's doing it now, Cody? Why? Because he's guilty. He did what I said he did. He's cornered and he's scared."

A car pulls up in front. Marlene Wilson gets out, looks at the mess on the lawn, walks to the front door, and lets herself in without knocking. Her eyes sweep the room for Cody. She spots Eddie and orders him to take his hands off her son. Eddie mutters something like "Nice to see you, Marlene, it's been a while," then moves over to give her his seat. She puts her arm around Cody and pulls him in. He collapses against her, burying his face in her shoulder.

"Tell her, Mom. Tell her to stop lying."

"I will, son. But first I want to talk to Ava in private. Go outside with Eddie. I'll just be a few minutes."

"I'm not going anywhere with that pig."

"Now, Cody, please. I'm serious."

Cody pushes his way up. He's totally depleted. Eddie moves faster than he does.

"While you are out there, son, pick up that mess you made. All of it." Her voice is firm, yet soft. Full of sorrow. Eddie opens the door and makes an after-you gesture. Cody swats at his hand and stomps out.

Marlene looks like she hasn't slept in a week. Her eyes are swollen, her face is pale.

ELLEN KIRSCHMAN

"Marlene, I'm so sorry." Ava's eyes gloss with tears. "I didn't tell Dan to go to your house. I was going to tell you about the DNA, but not the way he did. I didn't want to hurt you or Cody. Never."

"As they say, the road to hell is paved with good intentions." She looks at her palms as if trying to tell her own future. "I'm not here to fight with you, Ava. I'm here to talk, to understand whatever the hell is happening. Men don't seem able to do this. They run into something they don't understand and all they want to do is hit someone or something."

"Has Lonny hit you, Marlene?" I ask. She looks surprised at my question.

"I have put up with a lot from him, Doctor, more than I should have, but never that. If he ever hit me, I'd be gone." She turns back to Ava. "First Dan came over, drunk and noisy, accusing Lonny of being your biological father. Next thing I know, they're rolling around on the ground, punching each other. Cody and I heard the ruckus and went outside. Then Cody jumped on the pile. I had to turn the garden hose on all three of them to get them to stop. Your father left, Lonny punched a hole in the living room wall, and Cody was so hysterical I took his keys away to keep him from driving over here last night. Somehow, he found them this morning."

"Where's Lonny now?" I ask.

"He'd have driven over here himself last night, except I reminded him he had a prepaid fishing party booked for today." She looks at Ava. "Tell me what's going on."

Ava rolls out her story in sequence, right up to the DNA report that she offers to share with Marlene.

Marlene looks at me. "Is there any way this DNA report could be wrong?"

"I'm not an expert in DNA analysis, but ninety-nine point nine percent is pretty definitive."

Ava leans in. "The report is based on DNA from Cody, my biological mother, and me. Cody and I have the same father and different mothers. Do you want to see the report?"

"No." Marlene looks at Fran. "You've known us for years. Do you believe this story? Do you think Lonny could have raped a thirteen-year-old girl?"

Fran shrugs, clearly uncomfortable. "I don't know, Marlene. I guess anybody's capable of anything. I've made coffee. I think it's done." She scurries off to the kitchen.

"You've met Ava's biological mother, Doctor. Is she crazy? Is she making up this story about being raped?"

"I have met her. First impressions, of course. I think she's telling the truth. Please remember that I'm not here in a professional capacity. I'm doing this to help Fran, who asked me to help Ava."

"Then help her. She's killing her parents. Her mother is in a psychiatric ward behind all of this."

"I know that. I went with Ava to the hospital," I say.

"Marlene, did you tell my mother about Lonny?" Ava looks frightened. "She wasn't supposed to know. Her therapist said she isn't ready."

"I did not because I don't believe it. Lonny's capable of a lot of things, but not child rape. Never that. Where did this rape take place, Ava? Did this woman ever make a police report?" Ava doesn't respond. "You've known Lonny and me all your life. We're like your second family. Please tell me what you know."

"My birth mother said she was babysitting. The child's father drove her home and raped her in his car. He told her he was a cop and would deport her and her family if she reported it. After she realized she was pregnant, she went to the police. They didn't believe her, thought her boyfriend got her pregnant, and she was trying to blame some white guy so she could get money."

The pupils in Marlene's eyes widen for just a second. It's a stress response signaling a perceived threat.

"A white guy? Why a white guy?"

"Iliana is Mexican. And small, like me."

It's the first time Ava has mentioned her birth mother by name. Something flickers across Marlene's face.

"We had a lot of babysitters. Most of them were Mexican. They all looked like you and they were all named Maria or Iliana or Elena, something ending in an *a*."

"There is a police report, but no one can find it. It's probably in storage. They're still looking."

"It won't be Lonny, Ava. Can't be. He wasn't a cop when we lived in Moss Point."

Cody opens the front door. "Can I go home now? I picked everything up. You can ask the fat Nazi."

"Apologize to Miss Fran."

Cody barely looks at Fran, who is standing at the door to the kitchen. "Sorry, ma'am. It won't happen again." She nods and waves goodbye.

"Straight home. No place else."

"Where am I going to go? Who's going to talk to me? Everyone thinks my father is a rapist."

Ava stands. "The only people who know about this are you, your parents, my father, Fran, and Dr. Meyerhoff. Even Sharon doesn't know."

Marlene stands. "Straight home. I'll be right behind you."

Cody closes the door without looking at Ava or his mother.

Marlene loops the strap to her purse over her shoulder. "I came over here to have a reasonable conversation and straighten everything out. I'm asking you to drop this insanity. Lonny did not rape your birth mother or anyone else. I don't know who did, and I hope you find him. But it wasn't Lonny. As for the

DNA report, there must be some mistake. No way Lonny could have known who you were all these years and not told me or done something about it. He's a good father; if you were his child, he wouldn't have abandoned you."

"He may not have known I was his daughter. I don't think he knew my mother was pregnant."

"Like I said, he's done some bad things, especially before he got sober. But he would never knowingly have had sex with a thirteen-year old girl."

"Marlene, please." Ava looks desperate. "You have to believe me. I never meant for this to happen. I wish it wasn't so more than anything in the world."

"Then drop it, let it go. It's not true. Stop talking about it. Move on."

Ava drops her head. "I can't. I'm sorry."

Marlene stands. "Listen to me, all of you." There's a quaver in her voice that wasn't there a minute ago. She turns to Ava. "I don't know who you are anymore. And I don't know what we've done to deserve this load of crap. I don't fight with my hands like the men. But make no mistake, I'm going to do whatever it takes to protect my family."

Ava stares at the door after Marlene leaves. Fran leans over her, starts massaging her shoulders. I feel for Ava. She's only now truly beginning to understand that her determination to bring Iliana's rapist to justice will be a Pyrrhic victory, won at great cost.

"I love Marlene and Cody. I don't want to hurt them. I hate myself."

"Lonny is the one who hurt them, Ava. Not you," I say.

"But I'm like him. I have half his genes."

"Who you are, Ava, has more to do with how you were raised than the genes you inherited. Lonny didn't raise you, Dan and

Sharon did. They weren't perfect, but they did their best. And, in my professional opinion, I think you turned out just fine."

"I agree," Fran says. "You're fine the way you are. Except for that crazy business about not eating meat." She squeezes Ava's shoulders. Ava squeals and shrugs her away.

"I'm hurting Iliana, aren't I? I'm forcing her to get involved against her will. That's what Lonny did. He forced her."

"Ava, listen to me," I say. "What Lonny did to Iliana and what you are doing are not comparable. You're not forcing her to do anything, you're asking."

"I feel like I'm forcing her. Making her feel bad for refusing."

"She's struggling. I know that. On the other hand, it's possible she might find speaking out against Lonny to be healing. Her testimony could keep other women from being harmed."

"I only wanted to find my birth parents. I never wanted to hurt anyone. If I had known how this would turn out, I wouldn't have started it. I would have waited until everyone died."

"Listen, kiddo," Fran moves around to face Ava. "You can't unring a bell or tell the jury to disregard what they just heard. Actions have consequences, some of them good, some of them bad, some of them unintended. You can't rewrite history. What's done is done."

"I agree with Fran," I say. "Not only can't you change the past, you don't have time to spend on regret and self-condemnation—you have more pressing things to consider."

"Like what?"

"Like being careful. Lonny is trapped. A guilty man who feels trapped can be very dangerous."

31

Lonny Wilson is sitting on the tailgate of his truck in front of my office the next morning holding two cups of coffee. He's dressed as before, jeans, a long-sleeved collared shirt, and a ball cap embroidered with the name of his boatyard.

"Morning, Doctor. Hope you like your coffee black." He jumps down to the sidewalk.

"I don't want any coffee, thank you." He looks disappointed. "How can I help you?"

"I need to talk to you. Just for a few minutes. I'm happy to pay for your time. Can we go up to your office?"

I tell him I prefer to talk right here on the street, in public.

"I'm really not the ogre everyone seems to think I am. I didn't poison your coffee. I could have, but I didn't."

It's a sick joke or a veiled threat. He laughs. I don't.

"Cody's gone completely off the rails over this crazy accusation. I know what he did to Fran's yard. I'm willing to pay for any damages."

I tell him to make that offer directly to Fran, not me. He's sorry he didn't know Marlene was coming to see Ava, because if he had known, he would have stopped her. But he couldn't because he had a fishing trip planned. It's bad for his reputation

181

to cancel a trip when the weather is good. I ask him again what he's doing here and how can I help him.

"I'm still worried that Ava is being conned by this woman who claims she's Ava's mother. No disrespect, but I think maybe you're being conned too. I haven't been a cop for a long time, but I still think like one. Cops see things that civilians don't. Happens all the time. Ava's a kind kid. Likes to help people. That makes her easy prey."

I want to ask if Ava's such a kind kid, why did he threaten to slap the crap out of her? I look around and decide against it. The street is empty, not even a dog walker or a jogger to help if Lonny decides to slap the crap out of me instead.

"We've already talked about this, Mr. Wilson. Ava and I are not being conned. Now what else can I do for you?"

"I would like to see the DNA report, the one that pretends to have ninety-nine point nine percent proof that I'm Ava's birth father. It's all my wife has been talking about since yesterday."

"I don't have it. It's not mine to give. It's Ava's."

"That's why I'm here. I can't talk to Ava. I don't dare get within ten feet of her. If I even touched her by accident, she'd probably call the cops on me."

"Then call her on the phone. She can send you a copy if she wants to." I look at my watch. "I need to go." A car drives by, slows down, then speeds up. I'm sending every thought I can muster to will Gary or one of the other therapists to show up and help me.

"If I did something to Ava when she was a kid to make her hate me, I regret it with all my heart. Ask her, did I ever touch her in a bad way? Tell her nasty jokes? Show her dirty pictures? She'll tell you no because I didn't. I took her camping, fishing. Just me, Cody, and her. If I was going to do something bad to her, I had every opportunity. And if I had, wouldn't she have told her parents? Refused to go camping with me again?" Small trickles of sweat are running down the sides of his face despite the cool morning air.

"No one is accusing you of assaulting Ava, Mr. Wilson. You're being accused of assaulting her biological mother." I look at my watch again. "I have to go now."

"I'm not perfect, Doctor. I did some shit when I was drinking, but I never raped anybody. I haven't had a drink for almost twenty years because I could see I was hurting my family. Isn't that proof of the kind of guy I am? Tell me what I did to make Ava act so crazy. I'll do anything I can to make it up to her."

"Please leave. I don't want to call security." The only security on-site is Gary, who isn't even here. He's twenty years older than Lonny, twenty pounds lighter, and has probably never raised his hand against another human being in his entire life.

"I want to talk to this mother. Could you make that happen?"

"No."

"We had a lot of babysitters when Cody was little. Marlene did the hiring. Here's what I'm thinking." He puts his coffee on the bed of the truck. He needs his hands to plead his case. "Maybe I offended this babysitter. I'm not always the most politically correct guy on the block. When I drank, I liked to joke around. If she's Hispanic, maybe she misunderstood something I said. I'd like to talk to her, apologize. Could you make that happen?"

"That's the second time you've asked. I already said no. You need to leave now, Mr. Wilson."

"I'm a good man, a good father. I don't have so much as a traffic ticket on my record. I shouldn't lose my family and my reputation because somebody I don't know is accusing me of doing something almost eighteen years ago. Can you remember what you did eighteen years ago? Can you?"

"Did you recently tell Dan Sower to slap the crap out of his dope-smoking daughter for telling lies? That if he didn't, you would?"

Lonny's face crumples. "I did. I could slap the crap out of myself for not keeping my mouth shut. And then I hit him. Can you believe it? My best buddy and me, rolling around on the ground, fighting like snot-nosed schoolboys. I've tried to apologize. Dan won't answer his phone."

"I'm going to go inside now, Mr. Wilson. I have appointments."

He reaches for my arm. I yank it away.

"Dan showed up out of nowhere. He was drunk, saying shit about me in my own house, in front of my wife and kid. Accusing me of rape. Calling me names. He was out of control. I was scared. He hasn't been that wasted in a long time. I thought he was having the DTs. I should never have said that about Ava. I didn't mean it. You got to believe me. I'd cut off my own arm before I'd hit Ava."

He sinks against the side of his truck just as Gary pulls into the driveway; his window is open. "Morning, Dot. Is there a problem here?"

"No. I believe Mr. Wilson is leaving."

Lonny looks like a whipped dog. His head is hanging, his chest caved in. He pushes himself off the truck.

"Sorry to bother you, Doc. Thanks for your time." He shuffles to the cab of his truck, starts the engine, and drives away.

"Who was that guy?" Gary asks as we walk up the front steps together.

I tell him the whole story. He remembers Ava and her tears. How she showed up in the lobby in hysterics and he gave her a cup of tea to settle her down.

"What do you think, Dot? Is he guilty or not? And if he is guilty, what is he guilty of?"

"I'm not sure. Whatever it is, he's desperate, like a trapped animal. He's flailing around. Reaching out to me was a move of last resort."

"Watch yourself," Gary says. "Desperate people panic. And panicked people will stop at nothing to protect themselves."

32

It's after five. Frank's going to his photography class, so I'm on my own for the evening. I want to go by Fran's house to check on Ava. I don't plan to tell her about Lonny's unexpected visit. Gary and three other therapists are still in their offices seeing clients. I move the little marker to show that I've left the building. Outside, the air is balmy and fragrant. I could take a walk. Enjoy the evening air. Get some exercise. I look up and down the empty street. My shoulders tighten. I look for Lonny's truck. Then I look for Lonny. I see him behind every tree, crouched in every doorway. I change my mind and drive to Fran's.

Once I'm settled inside Fran's, she updates me. "Ava's in her room crying. She just got off the phone talking to Marisa. She put it on speakerphone. I heard the whole thing. Marisa met Cody last night for pizza and he was a wreck. Marisa thinks he's going nuts. His parents got into a fight. Cody couldn't hear what they said, but he thinks someone threw something because he heard glass breaking. Apparently, Marisa thinks she can predict the future. She's one hundred percent certain that if Cody's father goes to jail, his parents will get a divorce and Cody will have to drop out of school. Meaning his whole entire life is trashed. Marisa begged Ava to stop going after Lonny. Asked her why she couldn't be satisfied with finding her birth mother. Why did she have to wreck Cody's life too? Then she called Ava a selfish bitch and a bunch of names I never heard before. Told Ava if she didn't stop hurting Cody, she was going to tell everyone in Moss Point that Ava is a whore and a liar. But perhaps Ava wants to tell you this herself. I'll tell her you're here."

Ava saunters down the steps in a pair of baggy flannel pants and an oversized t-shirt. She's plaited one half of her frothy hair into tiny, tight braids. The other half billows like a cloud.

"Like it? I'm bored, always looking the same." She sits, cross-legged on the floor, her small hands making busy work of twisting her hair into knots. It's a harmless distraction, far safer than skulking around Lonny's house.

"Fran just told me about Marisa. She said some pretty cruel things to you."

"No biggie."

"I thought she was one of your best friends."

Ava waves my comment away with her hand. "She's in a mood. Cody will say something to make her mad and she'll be back all lovey-dovey, saying how I'm her BFF and Cody is a monkey-faced skunk."

I try making a mental picture of a skunk with the face of a monkey and can't. Fran announces she prefers her dramas on television. She looks at her watch. It's time for a rerun of her favorite program, *Fawlty Towers*, about a nutty English hotel manager who hates the guests at his hotel. She starts to look for the remote and finds it hidden between the sofa cushions. There's a knock at the door. We freeze.

Fran grabs the fireplace poker before she opens the door. There's a brown paper sack on the front mat. She orders Ava into the kitchen for rubber gloves.

"Not taking any chances," she says. "Could be Anthrax. Or a bomb." She picks it up like she's holding a dead rat by the tail and carries it inside. Ava covers the dining table with newspapers. Fran cuts the package open with a kitchen knife.

Inside is a used toothbrush wrapped in a sheet of computer paper. It's blue and white with misshapen bristles. Fran flattens the paper out with her hands. "For DNA" is spelled out in mismatched letters, each one cut from a different magazine page. Fran laughs.

"Whoever sent this has been watching too many old black-and-white movies."

Ava looks disgusted. "It's Cody. Marisa put him up to it. He could have gotten that toothbrush from anywhere, taken it out of anybody's garbage. He's not trying to help me, he's trying to stop me. All he wants is to protect his scumbag father. Well, screw you, Cody Wilson. It's not going to be that easy." She picks up the toothbrush, waves it in the air, and ceremoniously pitches it in the trash. "Night all, I'm going to my room."

I watch her walk up the stairs, her back straight as a pin, her head high, as though she can feel my eyes on her. Her losses are mounting. Lonny, Cody, Marlene, and now Marisa. All of them are desperate to protect life as they know it, all of them backed against a wall, guns raised, ready for a fight.

33

Fran calls me at the crack of dawn. It's dark out and Frank is still asleep. I roll over to muffle my voice.

"Ava's gone to Lonny's. He called her last night after she went to her room. Did you tell him that if he called her, she'd show him the DNA report?"

"I did not. He came to my office asking to see it. I said it wasn't mine to give. That if he called Ava, she could mail it to him. If she wanted to."

"Apparently she wants to because she's on her way to his house. Can you go Lonny's, please? I'm terrified."

"Why should *I* go?"

"You can calm Ava down. You don't think she listens to you, but she does."

Frank grunts, turns over, and falls back to sleep.

"Call Sheriff Bergen, then call Dan." I'm whispering.

"I already did," she says.

The sun is coming up behind me as I head over the hill toward Moss Point. The traffic coming toward me is heavy, a long line of cars snaking toward Silicon Valley, where the jobs are. Unless you fish, farm, or build, Moss Point doesn't offer much in the way of good-paying careers or employment.

Ava's car is parked in front of Lonny's house. I pull in behind it. I can see them, still as mannequins, through a bay window. Lonny is sitting at the head of the dining table. Dan is seated at the opposite end. Marlene is standing in a dark corner, arms crossed over her chest, her mouth pressed into a skinny red line. Cody is sitting on top of a low cabinet, his legs dangling off the edge. Ava is leaning against a wall, clutching the DNA report in her hand, surrounded by a menagerie of happy wallpaper ducks. There's no sign of Sheriff Bergen or any of his deputies. I knock on the door and walk in. No one looks at me or asks why I'm here.

Dan speaks first. There's a small tremor in his voice. His face is still swollen. "Let's get this over with. Show him the report." Ava hands the report to Dan, who pushes it across the table to Lonny. "Just read that part at the bottom, the statement of results part."

Lonny pulls reading glasses from the pocket of his flannel shirt. The glasses make him look old. He studies the report, holding it for so long I begin to wonder if he can read.

"Worthless." He throws the paper on the table using the same word Sheriff Bergen used when Ava handed him the DNA report. "This is not a legal document. No chain of evidence. You could have got that DNA from anyone."

No chain of evidence? Just the sort of thing a former cop would know, especially if he was scared enough to consult a lawyer. Or talk to the local sheriff.

"Ava, baby girl, how can you do this to me? To us? We're like your second family. I never hurt you, never threatened you. Never did anything but look after you. When your father was drinking and passed out on the couch, who took you for ice cream? Me, Uncle Lonny."

Marlene steps forward, snatches the paper off the table.

Lonny tries to stop her, but she's too quick. She walks back to her corner. She's been crying. The skin around her eyes is scaly and red.

"I didn't get the DNA from anyone, Lonny," Ava says. "I got it from Cody and from my bio mom."

"Liar!" Cody shouts. "I didn't give her anything, Dad. I promise. It wasn't me."

Ava swivels toward Cody. "You didn't *give* me your DNA, Cody. I took a soda can out of your room."

"You bitch." He starts to get off the cabinet. Lonny tells him to stay put.

"Not to worry, son. I know my rights. There's only one way Ava can prove I'm her father. She needs a court-ordered DNA test. And the only way to do that is to take me to court. And she can't do that unless her so-called mother files charges against me."

He's staring at Ava the whole time he's talking.

"Stop calling her my so-called mother. She *is* my mother."

"I don't see your so-called mother around. Of course, I wouldn't know her if I stepped on her because this whole thing is a fantasy." He turns to Dan. "What's she after, Dan? Money? Are you broke? Do you need a loan? You only had to ask. You didn't need to concoct a bullshit story like this, get Ava all involved. I would have given you whatever you needed, pal. You know that."

"Talk to *me*, Lonny." Ava moves forward. "I'm standing right here. This has nothing to do with Dan." Lonny turns in his seat, his eyes on Ava, looking at her the way she looked at Cody, searching every inch of her face for a reflection of his own. "You raped my biological mother when she was thirteen. You need to pay for what you've done to her and to me."

Lonny turns to Marlene. "I need to pay? See, it's what I've been saying. This is about money." Marlene inhales through clamped lips.

"I don't want your money. I want justice for Iliana."

"But she'd settle for a little money, wouldn't she?" Lonny starts to get up. Dan stands, his fists clenched. Cody scoots forward.

"Sit down, all of you. Now." It's the first thing I've said since I got here. I hardly recognize my own voice. I sound like a cop. Ava looks at me for the first time.

"What are you doing here?"

"If you've finished, Ava, let's go." I hold my hand out. She turns her back to me.

"I'm so sorry, Marlene. It's breaking my heart to hurt you and Cody." Cody curses under his breath. "You asked me to tell you more when we were at Fran's house. My birth mother's full name is Iliana Ester Ortega. She was babysitting for a white family who was having a party. She told the police the boy she was babysitting was about a year old. He was dressed in a cowboy suit and his name was Cody."

Marlene makes a noise, half grunt, half gasp. She turns her head to keep from flicking her eyes at an arrangement of family photos on the wall. One of them is a picture of baby Cody dressed like a cowboy.

"That doesn't mean shit. Lots of people dress their kids like cowboys." Cody bangs his feet against the cabinet door and keeps kicking until Lonny tells him to stop. He glares at Ava—his face is pure hate—then he jumps down and walks across the room, deliberately bumping into Ava. She doesn't react. He leans against the wall next to Marlene. She doesn't move, doesn't look at him, doesn't try to touch him, just stands there frozen, her eyes unfocused.

"Here's all I'm going to say." Lonny leans forward in his seat.

"And it's more than I should. It's no big secret that I used to drink." He looks at Dan. "*We* used to drink. I don't remember much about those days. I may have done some stupid stuff, but I swear to God I never raped anyone, never hurt anyone except my family." He looks at Marlene. She's still gripping the lab report so tightly her knuckles are white. Cody's head is bent. I can't see his face.

"I hurt my family. I'll never forgive myself for that. But I made amends a long time ago, something Dan never got around to doing." He glares at Ava like Dan's drinking is her fault. "I've been sober for years." He fishes in his pocket. "This is my twenty-year token, haven't had a drop, not since Cody was a baby."

"My mother said you smelled like beer when you raped her."

Lonny wheels around to face Dan. "What the hell's the matter with you, Dan?" His face is turning red. "Get some control here."

Marlene curses. She walks forward, stopping an arm's length from Lonny, holding the lab report in her raised hand like a flag of surrender.

"I remember that night. We had a party. I hired this little Mexican girl to babysit Cody. She was very quiet. Did a lot of babysitting for my friends. They all loved her. When I phoned her to come back again, she never answered my calls. My friends said she had disappeared without a word, no forwarding address, no phone number. Why did she disappear, Lonny? Was it because of you? Because of what you did to her?"

"We had a lot of parties in those days, Marlene. Remember? And a lot of babysitters. So she disappeared, so what? That's how Mexicans are. They come and go." Lonny's jaw is jutting out, like a dog with a bad underbite.

"That night. You had scratches on your face when you got home. I asked about them. You told me you drove the babysitter to her house, got out of the car to walk her to her door, and tripped. I remember thinking I should have driven her home because you were drunk. But Cody was crying and I was the only one who could settle him down." Lonny's eyes narrow to slits. "I had almost gotten used to you coming home smelling of beer with lipstick on your face. But this was different. Or maybe I just had had enough." Marlene keeps moving toward Lonny. "That's the night I told you if you didn't sober up and go to AA, I was leaving."

"Whose side are you on? I did what you asked, didn't I? Been sober ever since."

"I should have left you then, except Cody was so small I didn't think I could manage on my own." She flips the DNA report at Lonny. He bats it away. "DNA doesn't lie, Lonny. What a joke. All those years wishing I had a daughter and there she was, right under my nose."

Ava clamps her hand over her mouth as Marlene walks out of the room. A minute later, I hear a door slam in the back of the house.

"Fuck you. See what you've done." Cody goes for Ava. Dan pushes him back.

Lonny stands. "Out, get the fuck out of my house, all of you. I'll see you in court. I'm going to the newspaper with this shit. You won't be able to show your faces around here for a hundred years. Then I'm going to sue you for everything you got." Dan takes Ava by the arm and moves her toward the door. "And take the witch doctor with you. When I'm done with her, she won't have a reputation, a license, or any clients."

Dan looks so tired, I wonder if it's safe for him to drive. He tells me he's fine and we should step on it before Lonny comes after us with a gun. I look over my shoulder. Cody, not Lonny, is standing in the doorway looking at us. I can see Lonny through the window, sitting at the table, his head in his hands. Marlene is nowhere in sight. Dan mutters something to himself.

"I told you Lonny wasn't going to fall on his knees and confess when he read the report."

"He was never mean like this. Never."

"Cops are very good at masking their real selves," I say. "It's part of the job. Some of them get so good at it, they don't know who they are anymore."

"I let you go camping with that pervert. Did he ever try anything with you? If he did, I'm going to kill him."

"Never," Ava says.

"Don't lie to me."

"He never touched me. Swear to God and cross my heart."

Dan takes her by the shoulders. "You see Lonny or Cody, they come around you, call you on the phone, bother you in any way, I don't care how they do it, you call me, anytime, day or night. You hear me?"

"Not to worry, Dad," Ava says. "Nothing bad is going to happen. I can take care of myself."

I follow Ava home. Fran is waiting for us, her worried face looking through the living room window. I pull in behind Ava. She gets out of her car and slides into the front seat of mine.

"She tried to fight him off, didn't she? Marlene said Lonny had scratches on his face the night of the rape. What else could that mean except that Iliana tried to fight him off?"

"According to him, he fell down."

"She scratched Lonny's face. If she fought him once, she could do it again. I am going to text her."

I want to stop her and realize it would be easier to stop a charging elephant.

She taps a message on her phone and sends it. Iliana replies immediately, as if she was waiting for it. Ava reads the message to herself, then reads it to me.

I wish you would move on with your life. I see now that you can't. I am terrified for your safety. Tell me what you need me to do.

Ava texts Iliana that she needs to talk to the sheriff face-to-face because he won't file charges until she does. Fran is watching us from her front door, still in her bathrobe, motioning us to come in. I get out of my car. I want to go inside for a minute, tell Fran what happened, and then go back to bed for an hour before I go to work. Ava trundles behind me, staring at her phone, waiting for Iliana's reply. I put one foot inside the house when she lets out a whoop and jumps in the air like a cheerleader.

"She said yes. She'll talk to anybody and everybody if it helps me move on."

34

Ava tells Fran about Lonny's threats. She asks me if I think he's dangerous. I tell her I do. Later that day, she tells Eddie.

The next day, Eddie starts carrying a weapon to work. Fran threatens to lock him out of the café if he keeps it up. He produces his concealed weapon permit and recites, verbatim, from the Penal Code. "Upon honorable retirement, any full-time sworn officer who was authorized to, and did, carry a concealed firearm during the course and scope of his/her employment shall be issued an identification card with a Carrying Concealed Weapon endorsement, 'CCW Approved.'" It's hard to describe Eddie's retirement as honorable. It's more accurate to say Pence put him out to pasture. If he hadn't had a bulldog attorney, Eddie never would have won his pension or his honorable exit status.

Pepper, happy to be doing "real" police work, joins Eddie's volunteer security squad, eating lunch at the café, and stopping by for coffee in the afternoon. A week goes by with no contact from Lonny and nothing in the newspaper. Eddie thinks Lonny was bluffing, all hat, no cattle.

"Can't blame Lonny for being pissed off, can you, Doc? Happened to a bunch of my guy friends. They're sitting there, fat, dumb, and happy, the doorbell rings and there's this kid on the doorstep with their hand out, asking for Daddy."

"Ava doesn't want money. She wants justice."

"In some people's minds, they are one and the same."

Fran isn't happy or reassured. Even with Pepper and Eddie on the alert, she can't stop thinking about Lonny. She doesn't want Ava to go anywhere but the café or home. Not even to the local community college to register for classes because Lonny's cornered and he's already threatened Ava once. Ava says she can take care of herself. And if someone found her body lying in a ditch, everyone would know who did it. Fran didn't think that was the least bit funny and it certainly wouldn't be any consolation to Ava's parents. At my suggestion, Fran has asked Chief Pence to come over this evening so she can share her concerns and ask his advice about making her house safe from attack. Pence is happy to help because no one ever says no to a police officer's widow, including me.

Shortly after Fran's request, there's a note from Pence on my office door at headquarters asking me to come to his office ASAP. He's in his usual position, sitting behind his desk, staring out the window. As soon as I walk into his office, he looks at his watch.

"What's going on with Fran? Who's threatening her and is this why you have been missing so much work lately?"

I fill him in.

"Why are you involved? This is a police matter, not a psychological matter."

"That's not how it started."

"I wish you had come clean with me to begin with. Lonny was a nice guy, just couldn't handle his booze. Now you're telling me he raped a thirteen-year-old girl? When did this happen?"

"Eighteen years ago."

"Where?"

"In Moss Point."

He looks relieved. "Not my jurisdiction. The case belongs to the Moss Point Sheriff's Department."

"We've been there. Sheriff Bergen won't touch it. Not unless Ava's birth mother shows up in person to file a complaint."

Pence tells me that's standard procedure. I tell him Bergen is compromised; he knows Lonny Wilson, not to mention the fact that he's only interim sheriff. He'll be running for election, meaning he doesn't dare charge a local citizen and business owner with rape unless he's dotted all his *i*'s and crossed all his *t*'s.

Pence boots up his computer, scrolls around for a few minutes. "Just so you know, Lonny Wilson doesn't have a criminal history, not so much as a parking ticket in twenty years."

"More than sixty percent of all rapes go unreported. Lonny's clean record doesn't mean he didn't rape again."

Pence swivels around in his chair, looks out the window. I know this man well. He's evaluating whether or not I've just gifted him with an opportunity to boost his image. Something along the lines of KPD chief drops everything to reach out to KPD's only police widow whose husband made the ultimate sacrifice for his community.

"If I go to Fran's," he asks, "will there be press?"

I get to Fran's around 5:00 p.m. Fran is serving wine and cheese. Pence has changed into his class-A uniform. Ava does not look happy.

Fran is explaining that Lonny Wilson might be dangerous. She's worried that he could break into the house or try to kidnap Ava. She hopes Pence can park a police car in front of her house at night. He tells her that even if she had definite proof that she and Ava are in danger, he hasn't got the staff or even a decoy cruiser to spare. He sounds heartbroken refusing her request. Then he suggests she put in an alarm system, a surveillance camera, and motion-activated lights. She tells him she hasn't got the money, refills his glass, and offers him more cheese. He makes a joke about watching his waistline or no one else will. When he turns his back, Ava sticks her finger in her mouth and pretends to gag.

"Will you at least talk to Lonny? Give him a stern warning that if he does anything to hurt Ava or me, there will be hell to pay."

"No can do, Fran. Not without an open case. I'm not like the Secret Service. I can't offer protection or a security detail. I wish I could because I'm worried about you and Ava. I haven't talked to Lonny Wilson in years. He has no record of criminal activity, domestic abuse, anything that might alert me to his propensity for violence. Do the simple thing, please, put in an alarm, lights, and a camera."

Fran says she'll look at her bank account to see what she can come up with in terms of alarm systems. She's never had one for the café because there's not been a lot of crime in Kenilworth. Pence grins and puts his hands over his heart in appreciation, as though he is single-handedly responsible for keeping the peace. He looks at his watch. He's been here for an hour and the press is obviously not coming. He shakes Fran's hand with both of his, looks into her eyes, and tells her to stay safe, he will have her in his prayers. Then he turns to Ava. "As for you, young lady, be aware of your surroundings. Maybe carry a police whistle or order some self-defense equipment online. It's amazing what women can buy these days. Just be sure you don't pepper spray yourself in the face." He laughs. Ava doesn't.

As soon as he leaves, Ava goes upstairs and comes back

holding a tote bag. For less than thirty dollars, plus ten dollars for express delivery, she has already bought herself a personal alarm, a red-and-white Wonder Woman keychain with a pointed edge capable of puncturing a watermelon, and a canister of pepper spray that looks like lipstick. She leaves the bag by the door to remind herself to take it with her.

Fran invites me to stay for dinner. She's cooking a meatless meatloaf especially for Ava. It's made with mushrooms that are more expensive than steak, which would taste a damn sight better. I tell her Frank is making pasta and I need to go home. We're interrupted by a text from Iliana asking Ava to make a hotel reservation for her because she will need to stay overnight when she makes her trip to talk to Sheriff Bergen. The trains from Silicon Valley to San Francisco don't run frequently at night and she doesn't like traveling in the dark.

"Absolutely not," Fran says. "Iliana will stay with us. There's a foldout bed in my sewing room. Ava can sleep in there and give Iliana her room. We'll fix it up after dinner."

"Before you do that, Ava," I say, "we need to talk about when you are going to introduce Iliana to Sharon and Dan."

35

Lonny's terrorist campaign starts with an anonymous nasty online review of the café. Eddie isn't as much insulted by the nasty things said about his food as he is by the writer's insinuation that Fran is falsely claiming widow's benefits. Fran says she has been accused of worse things in her life, but she won't say what. She tells Eddie that if Lonny or Cody shows up at the café—we all know one of them wrote the review—he should put worms in their salad at no extra charge. Someone professing to be a client posts a comment on an online directory of local health providers accusing me of incompetence and making sexual overtures. Cody tops it all with a video rant calling Ava a "skanky ho" who gives blow jobs for free. Then he writes her phone number on a piece of posterboard and holds it up to the screen. Her phone starts ringing and doesn't stop.

The barrage of intimidation is relentless and so gross Ava, Fran, and I stop sharing it with one another. Fran calls Chief Pence, who is wine-tasting for the weekend with his wife. Then she calls Pepper, who advises us to do what we've already done, block the trolls, unfriend them, report them to the online service provider, change our usernames and passwords, and quit using the sites forever. Ava rebels at this last suggestion. No way can she live without TikTok and Instagram.

Pepper asks if we want her to drive over to Moss Point and tell Lonny and Cody to cease and desist. She's aching for a fight, I can tell. I advise her not to do this. She backs down when I suggest she'll get days off from Pence for going rogue and I'll need to reconsider her readiness to return to the street.

I figure the best way to stop this barrage of harassment is classic reinforcement theory. Ignore the provocation and it will extinguish itself. I turn off my computer and phone and inform the dispatch center that if there's an emergency over the next twenty-four hours to call Frank's phone. This, of course, requires me to explain what's going on to Frank. I reassure him that Lonny is loud, but not dangerous. Neither is Cody. He wants to know how I know this.

"The best predictor of future behavior is past behavior."

"The man has a terrible past. He raped a child. He was a drunk."

"He's been sober for twenty years and has no criminal history."

"Don't give me that 'people can change' baloney." He starts to say something about last year's fiasco when Pepper was kidnapped. I stop him. We've talked it to death with no satisfactory conclusion other than the fact that I was wrong because I was too trusting. As a result, I put Pepper, Frank, and my mother in danger. I've apologized a hundred times. I don't know what else to say.

"I guess in your business you have to be optimistic," he says. "In the remodeling business, if there's trouble in the beginning, it will only get worse when the client's house is torn up and they have to stay in a motel."

"Your point is? Besides 'I told you so.'"

"I did, didn't I? I told you helping Fran and Ava would turn out to be trouble. Only I didn't know how much trouble."

"That makes us even. Neither did I."

36

Today is the last day for Ava to register for college. It's drizzly and muggy. The kind of day when your clothes stick to your skin. Pepper and I are at the café. I'm having coffee, she's checking the doors and windows, making sure they're securely locked. The harassment campaign has continued. A few days ago, Gary found a particularly disgusting photoshopped portrait of me in the office mail. Eddie is in the kitchen preparing vegetable soup for tomorrow's lunch. Fran and I are in a back booth listening to Ava vent about her time on campus.

"I was so scared. I kept seeing Cody or Lonny behind every door and under every bush. Then I ran into Marisa. She started lecturing me again. I'm crazy. I need therapy. Just because my life is a wreck doesn't give me the right to destroy Cody's life. He's going to kill himself and when he does, it'll be my fault. I told her about the video he made with my phone number. She doesn't care about me. She's only worried about Cody. I think maybe she's the one who sent the toothbrush."

"Kids," Pepper says as she slides in next to me. "Like a pack of wild animals." She never misses an opportunity to put in a plug for her return to street duty.

"Wild animals are the ones who kidnapped you last year," I say. "All of them in their thirties."

Ava keeps talking. "Marisa just repeated what she said to me on the phone. She can't be Cody's friend and mine at the same time. It isn't fair of me to make her choose, like when her parents divorced and she had to say who she wanted to live with. I should be happy knowing who my parents are and leave the rest alone. I can't believe it. She actually thinks I could hang out with Cody and his family knowing what I know. Or that Cody could hang out with me." She looks at us for confirmation that Marisa has gone off the rails. "I told her Lonny is to blame for Cody's misery, not me. I hate what's happened. I hate that I'm hurting Cody. I hate that Marisa hates me now. Somedays I even hate myself."

Fran strokes Ava's arm. "Tell them what happened next."

"Marisa said she never wanted to see me again and stomped off. I registered for classes then headed to the parking lot when I see Cody following me. He starts yelling that I'm a bitch. I get in my car and lock the doors. He keeps yelling, banging on the car window, ordering me to let him in. The campus cops drive by and ask if I'm okay, did I need any help? I said we were just playing around. As soon as they leave, Cody starts yelling again, making such a scene that people are looking at us. I tried to drive away. Cody started running after me, throwing rocks, and shouting that I'm a batshit crazy bitch and a skanky crackhead. He and his father are going to sue me and send me to jail. Next thing I see, the campus cops are pulling up next to him, getting out of their cruiser, their hands on their holsters. I just kept driving. I didn't know what else to do. Marisa texted me later. The cops put Cody in their patrol car right in front of all those people and wouldn't release him until he saw a psychiatrist."

Ava leans on the table, arms crossed. Except for her tears, she looks as if she's napping.

* * *

"Poor kid," Pepper says on our way out of the café. "Bit off more than she can chew. Someone's going to get hurt."

We start to walk across the street. A car horn blares, followed by screeching tires. Pepper shoves me aside as Cody's truck stops, his front wheels against the curb. He jumps out of the cab onto the sidewalk.

"Where is she?"

"Hold on, buddy." Pepper steps forward, her hand on her Taser. She's easily six inches taller than Cody. "I understand you've already had one run-in with the cops today. Don't make it two."

"They made me see a head shrinker. He had hairy hands and Coke bottle glasses. The whole world thinks I'm a freak."

"I doubt that." Pepper moves closer. "Settle down now. You're not in any trouble. You drive like a bat out of hell, but so far, nothing to make me put you in cuffs."

He wheels away from Pepper and glares at me. "Stop putting ideas in Ava's head. You're making her crazy." Pepper puts her hand up likes she's directing traffic and asks Cody to move back. "Where's my fucking father?"

The door to the café opens. Fran, Ava, and Eddie are standing there wide-eyed. Eddie asks if Pepper needs backup. She tells him to stay inside and lock the door. "Don't let anyone in or out."

"What do you mean, where's your father?" She sniffs the air. "Have you been drinking? How about we do a little Breathalyzer?"

"I tried to take it away from him. So did my mother. The bottle broke. I'm not drunk."

"Take what away from who, son?"

"Get away from me. I'm not your fucking son."

"Provocative little shit, isn't he?" Pepper turns to me. "What do you think, Dot? Think it's worth jeopardizing my career to tune this kid up a little?" She winks at me and spins Cody around, pushing him up against a wall. She starts to pat him down. "Got any weapons on you, kid? Any needles?" She lets him go. "Clean as a whistle."

"Why are you asking about your father, Cody? Where do you think he is?" I ask.

"I don't know. If I knew, I wouldn't have asked." He's on the verge of tears.

"Tell me what happened."

"He and my mom got into it again. She kept at him, did he rape that girl or didn't he? He was drinking, he gets bad when he drinks. He kept telling her to shut up and when she didn't, he hit her. That's when he took off."

I remember Marlene's bottom line. If Lonny ever hit her, she'd leave him.

"I tried to stop him. Told him I'd drink with him. My mom didn't know he's been drinking because he hides it in the boatshed. He's been sneaking booze ever since Ava started hounding him."

Poor Cody. Covering for his father. Buried under a secret he couldn't share, not with his mother, not with Ava, not with anyone.

"He's got a gun. I'm afraid he's going to kill himself."

"Where's your mother?" Pepper asks.

"The fuck if I know," he says.

The door to the café opens. Again, Eddie asks if Pepper needs his help. She thinks for a minute, then grabs Cody's arm and shoves him toward the door. "As a matter of fact, I do. Take this little piece of crap off my hands so I don't have to arrest him for reckless driving. Give him some chamomile tea and sit on him until he calms down. Don't give him his truck keys back until you think he's safe to drive."

CALL ME CARMELA

"I'm not going in there." Cody tries to squirm out of Pepper's grip.

"You're going where I tell you to go. Or would you rather go to jail for reckless driving and failure to comply with my orders?"

"I refuse to be in the same room with that bitch."

Eddie says that Fran and Ava have left through the back door. "Just you and me, buddy, and we're going to have a tea party."

Pepper shuttles Cody to the café door and hands him off to Eddie.

"I'm really done with teenagers, Doc. I'd take a righteous bad guy with a gun any day of the week over a squirrelly teenager with a half-developed brain. Now if you'll excuse me, I'm going to call the Moss Point Sheriff's Department and tell them to find Lonny Wilson and his wife before we have two dead bodies on our hands."

37

Frank and I have an early dinner, warmed-over pizza with an egg on top, before I head to Fran's to check on Ava. She's had a rough day. So has Cody. Fran opens the door. Ava's sitting at the dining table, talking to Sheriff Bergen on speakerphone. Her books and backpack are discarded on the couch. I pull up a chair to listen.

"Are you going to arrest Lonny?"

"Nope, no can do."

"He's been threatening me, Sheriff. Spreading lies on the internet."

"Really? He says that's what you've been doing to him. Telling everyone he's a rapist and he's your father."

"He *is* my father. Remember the DNA report? Ninety-nine point nine percent probability?"

I move the phone away from Ava. "Dr. Meyerhoff here. According to his son, Cody, Lonny Wilson is missing. He's drunk, he's armed, and he hit his wife. Do your damn job."

There's a moment of silence. "I'm going to chalk that last statement up to emotional distress. It is not a good idea to threaten me, Doctor, especially as you're asking me to help you and your young friend."

Ava moves the phone back. "Help? You haven't given us any help. The only person you're helping is Lonny Wilson." Bergen starts to say something. Ava keeps talking. "For your information, my birth mother *is* going to cooperate and bring legal charges in person. With or without your help, we are going to get what we deserve." She ends the call. Throws the phone on the couch. It bounces off, slides across the floor, and comes to a full stop against a chair leg, like it's dead. We stare at it with the innate revulsion humans feel for corpses.

"Well," Fran breaks our silence, "that was a bust. Glass of wine anyone?"

I ask for coffee, Ava asks for a soda. "Lonny's an alcoholic, I could be one, too, if I start drinking." Ava looks at me. "Couldn't I?"

The pile of unanswered questions in Ava's life gets higher and more frightening every day. I remind her that genetics is not my field of expertise. "As far as I know, Ava, having an alcoholic parent does not guarantee you'll abuse alcohol any more than knowing your father was a rapist puts you at risk to be a violent criminal. Too many other factors come into play."

I'm interrupted by a blaring car horn and a crash so forceful it shakes the house. We run to the window. Lonny Wilson's truck is crushed against the front steps, smoke coming out from under the hood. He tumbles out the driver's door shouting, falls to his knees, then scrambles back to his feet.

"I'm a good father, goddamn it. A good husband. I've done everything for my family, made a thousand sacrifices they don't know about." He stumbles up the steps. "Now they hate me. All because the little bitch who lives here is a moneygrubbing liar."

He rattles the door. Ava looks terrified. Fran yells that the police are on the way. If he knows what's good for him, he should get off her porch. She is holding the fire poker in her hand. She orders Ava upstairs and tells her to hide first, then call the police.

The glass window on the door shatters. Pieces of falling glass drift to the floor in slow motion, glinting like a kaleidoscope. Lonny's bloody hand pushes through the broken shards, flailing around, feeling for the doorknob.

"Go. Now." Fran is shouting at Ava. Pointing at the stairs with the poker. Ava runs, taking two steps at a time.

Lonny is growling and spitting through the broken window. Fran is screaming at him to get away and leave us alone. He keeps trying to open the door. Fran holds the poker like a baseball bat, sweat pouring off her face, tangles of gray hair sticking to her cheeks. She's breathing hard, heart attack hard, banging away at Lonnie's hands. He puts his shoulder to the door, sending splinters of glass in all directions. Fran keeps swinging. Lonny dodges to the right, yanks the poker out of her hands. She stumbles forward, toward the shattered window.

Ava's tote bag is still where she left it, next to the front door. I reach inside, grab the never-used lipstick-sized pepper spray canister, push Fran aside, and aim the spray directly at Lonny's snarling face. He grabs at his eyes, falls back on the porch, ripping his hand on a jagged point of glass. I keep spraying through the broken window until the cannister is empty. Lonny rolls around, his bloody hands scrubbing at his eyes. Police sirens compete with his howling. The air is filled with screeching tires and barking dogs. Lonny gets to his feet and takes off behind the house like a blind man on fire, bumping into trees and tripping over curbs.

38

Fran and I are in the living room shivering like it's the middle of winter. We're talking to Chief Pence and the two officers he has just scolded like naughty children for letting Lonny escape. He asks Fran if she needs to go to the hospital to get checked out. She tells him the only thing she needs is a stiff drink and a good night's sleep.

Pence looks worried. "I'm thinking maybe you two and Ava better check into a hotel until we find Lonny. According to Cody, Lonny has a gun. No ex-cop ever has just one gun."

"Where's Cody now?" I ask.

"With his mother. She called him a little while ago from her sister's house."

There's a commotion on the porch. Pence reaches for his weapon. Except for yearly qualifications at the range, I doubt he has ever fired his gun in the line of duty. Dan is standing wide-eyed at Fran's broken front door. He shakes off the cop who is trying to keep him outside. "Where's Lonny?"

"Gone," Fran says.

"Where's Ava?"

"Upstairs, in her bedroom." Dan's knees buckle and he grabs for the doorframe. "Bergen called me. Told me Lonny was on a rampage. I got here as soon I could."

Pence announces he's organizing a search party for Lonny and needs every available officer he can get. Meaning he can't post a cop in front of Fran's house.

"Not to worry, Chief," Fran says. "After watching that fiasco with Lonny, I'm convinced your Keystone cops couldn't catch a crook if he sat in their laps. I'm going upstairs to check on Ava." She comes back a minute later and pronounces Ava shaken but well enough to be scrolling away on her damn phone.

"Now that you're here, Dan. I'm going to bed. If anyone thinks it's too early, they can go to hell. Can you stick around in case we get a return visit?" Dan nods. "And while you're here, get some plywood out of the garage and fix my damn front door." She turns to me. "You okay, Dot? You were ferocious."

I lie and tell her I'm fine. It's almost 9:00 p.m. Still time to salvage part of an evening with Frank. I pick up my purse and put it down again. I can't leave Fran with this mess, plus I shouldn't drive until I stop shaking. First I need to switch gears, reset my body. Best way to do that is to get a little exercise. Except it's too late to go to the gym and I'm not walking anywhere by myself until Lonny is in custody. I grab a broom and start sweeping up the jagged pieces of glass, dumping them in the recycling bin. It's a win-win decision. I'm helping Fran at the same time I'm spilling off the adrenaline that's coursing through my body like a river gone wild.

Frank grabs me the minute I walk in the door. Eddie called him. He'd been listening to the scanner. Frank checks me over for injuries. I tell him what happened and ask him not to lecture me about getting myself in danger.

"What a shit show. You tried to do a favor for a friend and it turns into a freaking nightmare. I need you to be careful," he says. "Funerals cost money and we don't have burial insurance."

"Lonny's relapsing. It happens. He'll sober up, come to his senses, talk to his sponsor. The man's been sober for decades. He must have learned something from twenty years of twelve-step meetings."

"The guy's a mean drunk. He'll sober up and go after you again."

"I asked you not to lecture me."

"And I asked you not to get yourself killed."

"That must mean I'm doing something right because I'm not dead yet."

"You think this is funny, Dot? I'm scared. All the time you're running around trying to fix the unfixable, I'm home worrying like a crazy man. I want us to die when we're old, not because some lunatic client of yours shot us to death."

"Lonny Wilson is not my client."

"The way it looks to me, the whole effing world is your client. Do what you like, you will anyway." He turns toward the kitchen. "I'm going to make something, not because I'm hungry but because I need to calm down and the best way for me to do that is to cook something."

Frank worries about me because he loves me. It's a strain to love someone who loves a risky job. I hear it from police spouses all the time at work. It's hardly fair, though, to call my job risky; most of the time, I'm sitting at a desk or talking. I don't chase bad guys through dark alleys or serve warrants on people who are determined not to go back to prison. Frank wants me to be careful. I'm happy to be careful, it's the right thing. But how can I be careful when the person who is threatening me doesn't feel obliged to announce the time and place he plans to show up and kill me?

* * *

Lonny's attack was vicious. He was vicious. I see his snarling face every time I turn over in bed. Hear his animal-like howls of pain. See myself aiming the pepper spray at his eyes, as intent on hurting him as he was on hurting me. Only once in my entire life did I try to hurt another human being. I had a reason, not an excuse, but a reason. Mark and I were in the middle of our divorce. Out of our minds with anger and grief. He grabbed me first and I swung at him with a wine bottle. The shame of it turns my stomach to this day. Mark never intended to hurt me, nor did I intend to hurt him. Lonny Wilson is different. If he had gotten his hands on Ava or me tonight, no telling what he would have done. Frank rolls over in bed.

"Trouble sleeping?"

"I keep replaying what happened with Lonny. I can't turn it off." It's 2:30 a.m. "I think I'll go downstairs to the couch so you can get some sleep." I roll to the edge of the bed.

"Stay here," Frank says. "Not a problem. I can sleep any old time."

"I'm okay."

"You're not okay. You were attacked by a madman. No way you are okay."

"I'll be back. I just need to think."

I put my robe on, go downstairs to sit in the dark. The very dark dark. With the unidentifiable creaking noises. I'm afraid to turn on a light. What if Lonny is outside? Or Cody? Lonny is evil. Cody is coming apart at the seams. I'm trained to deal with people in crisis. I'm not trained to deal with evil. Evil people hurt others for their own satisfaction. Lonny has been living like a normal person, a regular citizen. Lying. Pretending, maybe even to himself. No feelings for the girl he harmed, no shame, no guilt, not even a detailed memory. He just brushed it off, blamed it on alcohol, and lived his life like it never happened.

No looking over his shoulder, no worries about being caught. No inner sense of morality, no remorse, no burning desire to change. Only Marlene's threats to leave him drove him to stop drinking.

There's a noise on the steps, the living room light turns on. Frank, looking like a monk in his long hooded bathrobe and bare feet, comes into the living room.

"Why are you sitting in the dark?"

"Because I'm afraid to turn on the lights."

He frowns. "Because Lonny may be hiding outside?" He squeezes in next to me. Puts his arm around my shoulder. "Because you're scared?"

"I've misjudged the situation, Frank. I've misjudged everybody involved."

"Like you think you misjudged Ben Gomez?"

"Like I misjudged Ben Gomez."

He leans back. "Well then, taking a line from your playbook, tell me more."

39

I head to Fran's early the next morning. Still groggy from lack of sleep, but calmer for having dragged poor Frank through every detail of my failure to see what was in front of me. First with Ben. Then with Lonny. Fran opens the front door, still in her bathrobe, pronounces Dan's repairs "Good enough for government work," then goes into the kitchen to make coffee and waffles. Dan, his face creased from sleeping on the couch, asks her for an extra toothbrush. Ava straggles down the stairs in baggy pants and a sweatshirt. She sees Dan and rushes him, her arms open, for a hug. He reciprocates in kind.

There's a knock on the door. We freeze. Dan pulls away from Ava, tells us to stay put, grabs the cast-iron skillet Fran left next to the front door.

"It's me. Chief Pence."

We exhale, all at the same time.

"Good work on the door." He nods to Dan. The bags under his eyes are puffy from lack of sleep.

Fran comes out of the kitchen, wiping her hands on her apron. "Just so you know, Chief, that was custom-designed stained glass made for me by a woman up in Bellingham, Washington. Going to cost a fortune to replace it."

"You're lucky that's the worst of it," Pence says. Fran offers him a cup of coffee and waffles. He refuses. He's been drinking coffee all night and thinks he's given himself an ulcer. He doesn't refuse the waffles.

As they sit at the table, Dan asks the chief about Lonny. Pence shakes his head. Says his officers have been looking everywhere. He's holding them over for double shifts and canceling vacations until they find him. He's concerned that the City Council will go ballistic over the bump in overtime and looks at me like it's my fault.

"What about Sheriff Bergen?" Ava asks. "Is he looking for Lonny?"

"You bet. He's got everyone looking. Moss Point County is big. Lots of farmland and hills. Plenty of places to hide. And he has less staff than I do. I'm going to send him a couple of my guys."

"I don't trust him." Ava looks scared. "I think he's Lonny's friend. And he doesn't like me."

"Not to worry, young lady. I got my eye on everything. I set up a mutual aid incident command system. Bergen reports to me." Pence finishes his second waffle, pushes back from the table, and stands. He's going to make a speech. I know the signs, the little nervous tics he makes before he talks, like a pitcher on the mound. He tugs on his shirtsleeves and smooths invisible flaws from his shellacked silver hair.

"You, Miss Ava, are not to go out. Not to work, not to school, not to see your friends. You are to stay here with your father. Understood?" She nods, willing to do whatever it takes to stay safe. She had enough terror yesterday. Pence turns to Dan. "If Lonny shows up, call 911, but do what you have to. Got a weapon, something more effective than a frying pan?"

"Hunting rifle in my truck."

"Then get it. It's not going to help you in your truck if Lonny breaks in here again. Make sure it's loaded. Don't shoot unless you have to. California is a stand-your-ground state. Only use force if you reasonably believe you or these ladies are in imminent danger of physical harm. In other words, if all he has are his fists, don't shoot him. Hit him with the pan. Am I clear?"

He turns to Fran. "I'll drive you to the café, wait while you hang a 'Closed Until Further Notice' sign on the door then drive you back here." Fran protests, says she needs to make money so she can repair her damn door. Pence shuts her down, tells her funerals cost more than doors. She argues, they compromise. Fran will stay home. Eddie can keep the café open.

"As for you, Dr. Meyerhoff—I am authorizing you to cancel all your appointments at the PD until we get this guy in custody. Unless I'm mistaken, he blames you for putting ideas into Ava's head. Ava may not be the only one around here with a target on her back."

"I'd think headquarters would be the safest place in town."

"It is, but your private office and the streets between HQ and your private office aren't. I'm ordering you to stay here for the day. Keep your eye on these folks." He cocks his head in Ava's direction, as if I didn't know who he was talking about. "Go home before dark, lock your car doors, stick to main streets, and tell your husband to keep his eyes open. Any questions?"

Frank is already concerned about my safety. I'm not going to add to his worries by volunteering him for Eddie's vigilante squad. Catastrophic thinking works for cops on the street. Imagining everything that could go wrong before it does is the way to stay safe. On the other hand, being constantly on high alert, surveying everyone and everything around you for potential threats, makes staying present with your family, when you're at home, damn near impossible. I refuse to do that to my relationship with Frank.

The morning drags into afternoon. Ava jumps at each passing car and almost comes out of her chair when the newspaper carrier throws the paper against the door. We play Scrabble, Monopoly, and cards, using dry beans for money. Fran makes veggie chili and cornbread for lunch. We watch television. Eat popcorn. Dan goes for his rifle every time the wind makes a branch scrape the side of the house. At five o'clock, I announce I'm going home.

I follow Pence's advice and take the main road back to our house. Big mistake. It's commute time. I've been sitting in traffic for five minutes, an easy target for Lonny or anyone else standing on the side of the road. There's a roar to my right. A biker, the shield on his helmet pulled down over his face, barrels up the shoulder and stops, sending a tornado of dirt into the air. Pepper flips up the visor on her helmet and gives me a thumbs-up. I lower the window. My hands are trembling.

"You okay, Doc?"

I nod. The idiot behind me honks at me to move ahead.

"Pence ordered me to tail you home because he thinks you can't be trusted to take care of yourself. Somebody saw Lonny over on the coast, skulking around his boatyard, and called the sheriff. He was gone by the time the deputies got there. Fifteen minutes later, Marlene called the sheriff to report that Cody's missing now. She thinks he's with Lonny."

The traffic loosens. The driver behind me leans on his horn to demonstrate his displeasure with my slow-footed reaction. Pepper says she'll follow me home. I'm relieved to hear this. If Lonny doesn't shoot me, the guy behind me might.

* * *

"Nothing to worry about?" Frank says. "Why did Pepper follow you home? Why did Eddie call here saying 'The coast is still clear.' What the hell is going on?"

"Someone saw Lonny over at his boatyard. Cody's missing too. Marlene thinks he's with his father. I'm worried about him. He's coming unglued."

"What are you supposed to do about it?"

"Nothing, that's what I'm trying to tell you. The sheriff or Pence will find Lonny and Cody in a few hours. Everybody in the world is out looking for them. There's nothing to worry about. Now can we talk about dinner? I'm hungry."

If there's nothing to worry about, how come I can't sleep, while Frank is dead to the world? I'm not checking all the locks on the doors and windows or patrolling the perimeter of the house like a traumatized cop, but I'm close. Every noise sends shivers up my spine. Frank built this house. I'm going to complain to him how noisy it is at night, dozens of creaks and groans, all of them sounding exactly like someone is breaking in.

Pepper texts me around midnight. There's been another sighting of Lonny and Cody about three blocks from their house in Moss Point. The reporting party, who wouldn't give a name, said she noticed them because they were yelling at each other and fighting, rolling on the ground. Weirder still, they both appeared to be crying.

40

Ava and I are at the train station waiting for Iliana. The sky is a dusky mix of blue and pink. Ava insisted we call Iliana, tell her that both Lonny and Cody have disappeared and give her the chance to back out, postpone the sheriff's interview until Lonny is in custody and Cody is at home. To her credit, Iliana insisted on coming. If not now, she feared never again having the courage of her convictions.

I offered to pick Iliana up at her house because she doesn't drive, but she preferred to take the commuter train. She hasn't been far from home for so long, she's looking forward to seeing how things have changed between San Francisco and Kenilworth. Commuters spill out of the train, heading in all directions, like a dropped bag of marbles. Iliana is the last to descend. We watch her hold on to the railing and ease herself over the steep drop to the ground, her delicate figure dwarfed by a black backpack. She scans the platform. I suspect she's not only looking for us, she's looking for Lonny. We wave. She walks toward us. She and Ava hug politely, shyly, like they're meeting for the first time.

Ava offers Iliana the passenger seat of my car, but Iliana prefers to sit alone in the back. The conversation on the way to Fran's is limited. Ava asks about Marisol. Iliana says she is well, but not strong enough to travel even short distances. Ava thanks Iliana for coming, tells her it means a lot. I say something innocuous about the weather, point out a few landmarks, and then we are at Fran's house.

"This is it," Ava says. "This is where I live now." Iliana looks out the window.

"What happened to your front door?" She looks so frightened, I'm afraid she's going to change her mind about being here and insist we take her back to the train station.

Dan opens the door. Starts down the porch steps.

Iliana presses against the seat. "Is that Lonny?"

"That's Dan Sower," Ava says. "Technically he's my adoptive father, but he's really my *real* dad. He's here to help."

Her real dad. Wouldn't Dan be happy to hear her say that? I'm happy to hear it. Happy that Ava is finally acknowledging that her less-than-perfect father, clumsy and troubled as he is, is on her side.

"And the door? What happened to the door?"

"Broken front window, it was an accident," I say. "Ava's father Dan covered it in plywood until Fran can get a replacement." I see no point in adding to Iliana's anxiety by describing how the window got broken. It's been forty-eight hours since Lonny tried to break in, twenty-four since anyone has seen him. For all I know, he and Cody have taken off for parts unknown, never to return.

Fran appears on the porch, wearing an apron over her best sweatshirt. "Welcome to my house," she says, loud enough for Iliana to hear. "Come in, I can't wait to meet you."

Iliana relaxes. Fran's motherly exuberance is irresistible, like a magnet, drawing people in. I know this from personal experience. She ushers us into the living room for wine, cheese, and crackers and an antipasto big enough to feed an army. Iliana hardly takes a bite. Fran offers us wine. Dan asks for a soda. He's studying Iliana's face, comparing it to Ava's. The resemblance is striking.

Our conversation at dinner is awkward. Dan is his usual almost silent self. We all compliment Fran on her cooking. Iliana apologizes for picking at her food. Normally she's not a big eater, but her nervousness about being in a new place and having to face the sheriff tomorrow have left her with an even smaller-than-usual appetite. After dinner, Dan offers to drive us around town so Iliana can see the sights. Kenilworth isn't known for its sights, unless you like massive glass structures honeycombed with high-tech start-ups or overbuilt mansions that belong in the South of France. Iliana declines, saying she is tired, and bids us good night. She needs to go to bed early to prepare for tomorrow's meeting. It's a diplomatic feint. The truth is written all over her face and in her trembling fingers. She's afraid to go out after dark. As soon as she goes to her room, Ava follows. She wants to connect with some friends on Instagram, if she still has any friends left.

"What am I going to do about Sharon?" Dan, Fran, and I are still sitting around the dining table. "She's coming back from the hospital for a few days. Kind of a test drive. I'm worried about what she'll do if Lonny comes looking for me."

"You haven't told her about Lonny yet?" Fran looks incredulous. Dan and Sharon have lots of secrets between them and a built-in aversion to difficult conversations.

"She doesn't want to hear any bad news. Said her therapist told her to concentrate on getting better, that the rest of us could take care of ourselves. I was hoping that Ava or maybe you, Fran, would tell her about Lonny."

Sharon's therapist is dead wrong. The Sower family can't take care of themselves. Ava is scared and confused. She needs support. What she has are two fathers, one a violent drunk and the other too recently and tentatively sober to be counted on. Two mothers, both so psychologically damaged they may be beyond repair. And a raging, suicidal half brother who needs help more than anyone.

Dan and Fran are looking at me.

"It's on you, Dan," I say. "This is not Ava's job, it's yours. You're Sharon's husband and you're the adult. Don't put Ava in the middle. And don't wait. As soon she comes home on leave, tell her."

"I don't know what to say. If I tell her, it will send her back to the hospital." He stands. "Not going to do it. I'm staying here. Lonny could come back. I need to protect Ava."

"Go home, Dan," Fran says. "The doctor is right. This is on you, not Ava. If Lonny does show up, I'll call 911. In fact, I can do better than that," she says, getting up from her seat. "I'm calling my volunteer vigilante to stand watch. Eddie would do anything to play at being a cop again."

41

Dan is waiting for me on the sidewalk in front of Fran's house the next morning. He's wearing a collared shirt and there are dark circles under his eyes.

"The girls are getting ready. Got a minute?" He shuffles his feet. "I talked to Sharon last night. Told her about Lonny being Ava's father."

"How did that go?"

"Like I thought it would. She went ballistic. Started crying. Yelling. Took a few swings at me. Called me a lying SOB. Accused me of buying Ava off that social worker to protect Lonny, so Marlene wouldn't know what he did. She went on like that for twenty minutes."

He drops into silence. His bleary eyes focus on the ground.

"And then what happened?" Getting him to talk is like pulling teeth.

"She called her therapist, talked to her for an hour. That calmed her down a little. More than a little. After she got off the phone, she thanked me for telling her about Lonny, said it must have been hard for me since Lonny's my friend. I'm betting her therapist told her to say that. Gotta give her credit for trying to be nice. Then she went to bed. I slept on the couch. If you can call what I did sleep."

Fran opens the front door. Dan startles at the sound. Whips around to face the house. Ava, Iliana, and Eddie walk out.

Iliana is dressed in a business suit with a silk blouse and a flowered scarf at her neck. Ava's wearing chinos and a sweater set. Eddie's his usual rumpled self.

"Not a sign of Lonny or his kid last night," he says. "Everyone slept like a log, except for me." He opens my car door for Iliana and Ava to get in the back. Does a little bow. "Ladies first. Good luck over the hill."

Dan takes the passenger seat. Fran waves at us from her door.

Five minutes into the drive, Ava takes out her phone and her earbuds. She leans over the front seat. "Iliana and I are going to listen to some music, okay? Iliana loves music. It calms her down. Me too. We talked it over last night before we went to bed. Didn't want you to think we were being rude." She puts one earbud in Iliana's ear and the other in her own. I can see them in my rearview mirror. Ava is looking out the window to her left, Iliana is looking to her right. They're holding hands. Once again, Ava is the one in charge.

The drive to Moss Point is glorious. The sky is cornflower blue. The reflection of the sun on the diamond-bright surface of the Pacific as we head downhill to Moss Point is almost blinding. I pull into the parking lot next to the sheriff's station. Ava takes the earbuds back, puts them in a case, and puts the case in her backpack.

"I would like to say something before we go inside." Iliana looks at her watch. "I think we have time." She sits forward in her seat. "Thank you for driving, Dr. Meyerhoff. It was a beautiful drive." She purses her mouth in thought. "Taking short trips, seeing the countryside, is only one of the things I have let this man take from me. I'm ashamed of how much power I have given him over my life. I am going to do my best today to make sure he gets what he deserves." She pauses again. "I want to say that differently. I am going to do my best today to get what I deserve." Ava and I applaud. Dan doesn't say a word.

Marge greets us at the door. Her eyes are all over Iliana, like she's a rare bird that has flown off course and landed in Moss Point by mistake. Iliana looks around, trying to remember this place and maybe this woman. She takes my hand. Her palm is sweaty.

Marge pulls extra chairs into the lobby so the four of us can sit. She offers cookies and tea as if we're here for a party. Ten minutes go by without a word. Dan is drumming his fingers on a stack of old magazines. Iliana's eyes are closed. I can't tell if she's praying or rehearsing what to say. Ava is staring at her feet. I'm staring at the door, willing Bergen to open it. Marge tells us she'll buzz him again, he knows we're here but he's on the phone, talking to the DA. There's a noise in the hall and the interior door to the lobby opens.

Bergen's wearing an ill-fitting uniform with gaps between the buttons. His pants are too short, hiked up by his thick thighs.

He looks at us, his eyes landing on Iliana. He walks to where she's sitting and extends his hand. "Ms. Ortega, I presume. I'm Sheriff Bergen. Glad to meet you." They shake, his massive hand covers hers up to the wrist. She stands, holding her purse to her chest like a shield. "Not to worry, ma'am, I don't bite." He smiles and opens the door to the hallway. Ava and I stand, ready to follow. Bergen does that traffic stop thing with his hand, telling us to wait in the lobby. He appreciates our interest, but the only person he needs to talk to is Ava's birth mother.

Iliana looks panicked. Her face goes white.

"Unless of course," he says, bending to look her in the face, "you would be more comfortable having my assistant, Miss Marge, in the room with us."

ELLEN KIRSCHMAN

Iliana looks over at Marge, who is smiling in anticipation of partaking in Moss Point's crime of the century.

"I'd like my daughter to come in with me, please." Her voice quavers.

Bergen shakes her head. "Sorry, official people only." He holds the door open, his hand inches from Iliana's back. Iliana looks over her shoulder, as if she might never see us again. Takes a big breath and walks down the hall toward Bergen's office.

As soon as the door shuts, Marge comes out from behind her glassed-in desk.

"That's her," she says. "There's days I can't remember my own phone number, but I remember her. She's older, of course, but hardly changed. Wish I aged that well."

The front door to the lobby opens. A tall man holding a brief-case enters and looks at us. He's wearing a shirt so white it's blinding. The creases on his suit are sharp enough to cut paper. He nods at Marge. She scurries back to her desk and buzzes him through. Then she tiptoes back to the lobby, her voice barely more than a whisper.

"That's the county district attorney. He's the one who files charges. Must mean the sheriff thinks he has enough evidence to go to court." She's positively radiant with her conspiratorial messaging.

If Iliana is uncomfortable around even one man, as she said when I first met her and she wouldn't let Frank into her house, how is she going to react around two men? Both of them strangers and authority figures. Bergen is intimidating, despite his efforts to play the friendly, small-town sheriff. I don't know the DA, but he reeks of self-importance. Easy to imagine him steamrolling over Iliana, pummeling her with warp-speed questions, shattering the little bit of self-confidence she has. What if she panics? Or freezes? What if she's too scared, too over-whelmed to talk?

I knock on Marge's window. "Let me through, please." Dan and Ava are looking at me.

"Sorry, no can do. If you need a bathroom, you can use mine."

"Ms. Ortega should not be in there by herself with two men." Marge looks puzzled. Evidence that there are holes in both her long- and short-term memory. "She's a rape victim, remember?"

Marge thinks this over, sweeps her hand over her desk, pushing some papers onto the floor. She bends over to retrieve them and hits the door buzzer with her shoulder. "Oopsy," she says. "Clumsy me."

As soon as the door pops open, Ava is out of her seat, ready to follow me. I ask her to stay with Dan. No mother wants to describe being raped in front of her daughter. Dan puts his hand on her shoulder, says something I can't hear, and they both sit down.

The door to Bergen's office is open. Iliana is sitting in a leather chair so big it makes her look like a child. There's a box of tissues on the small side table next to her. The DA is seated at a small desk about five feet away. His head is down and he's making notes on his laptop. Bergen is behind his desk, facing Iliana. He gets to his feet the minute he sees me and orders me out of the room.

"Iliana Ortega is a rape victim. She should not be alone in a room with two men."

"She can have Marge present if she wants. You heard me tell her she could." His face is turning watermelon red. "What do you think we're doing in here, Doctor? Waterboarding Ms. Ortega? Hanging her from her thumbs? We're not blind and we're not monsters. It's obvious she is under a great deal of stress."

Iliana moves forward in her chair. "I would like Dr. Meyerhoff to stay. I believe it's my prerogative as a victim to feel safe and comfortable during police procedures."

I'm impressed. Iliana has been researching victims' rights. Taking steps on her own behalf.

"Are you feeling unsafe with us, Ms. Ortega?" It's the first time the DA has spoken since I came into the room. He has a soft funereal voice, not the voice nor the manner I imagined when I first saw him. "Have the sheriff or I done something or said something to make you feel uncomfortable?"

Iliana hesitates. "No. Neither you nor Sheriff Bergen have done or said anything to make me feel unsafe. Unfortunately, given my history, that doesn't mean I'm not still afraid."

The DA and Bergen exchange some secret law enforcement eye-to-eye message. "Not a problem, Ms. Ortega," the DA says. "The doctor can stay. I don't want burden you. I appreciate the effort you have taken to be here in the first place."

"As do I," Bergen says before turning to me. "Take a seat, Doctor." He points to a side chair shoved into a corner. "But remain silent. Say one word and I'll throw you out of here so fast you won't know what's happened."

"Thank you again, Ms. Ortega," Bergen says, walking us into the lobby. We've been in his office for a grueling hour and a half listening to the unspeakable details of Iliana's experience. Not only the rape, but the following years of shame and terror that shaped her existence. Despite everything, she had the persistence and intelligence to build a decent life for her mother and herself. The magnitude of her derailed potential hits me hard. What might she have done with those skills? Who might she have been had she never crossed paths with Lonny Wilson? Ava's right. Lonny Wilson needs to pay for what he's done.

42

Iliana is again sitting in the back seat next to Ava. Dan offers to buy everyone lunch at a coast-side restaurant with a view of the ocean. Iliana thanks him for the offer, but asks instead to go to Fran's café. She wants to see where Ava and Fran spend so much of their time.

Three Kenilworth patrol cars, light bars flashing, are haphazardly parked in front of the café, car doors ajar and sirens blaring. A fire truck is parked at the corner. Eddie is sitting on the curb. A paramedic is bandaging his head. There's a blood pressure cuff on his arm. Iliana slinks down in her seat. Dan tells Ava to stay in the car with her mother.

"Here comes the cavalry. A day late and a dollar short as usual." Eddie gives us a weak wave. The medic asks if any of us have enough influence to make Eddie go to the hospital to get checked out for a possible concussion.

"Look, buddy," Eddie turns to the medic, "I know you're just doing your job, but the guy only hit me in the head. It's full of rocks, hard as hell. No harm done." He turns to the cops. "Turn those freaking things off. We're code four here, if you haven't noticed. Do something helpful like finding the asshat who clobbered me."

The medic warns him that if he feels dizzy or nauseous or has a bad headache, he should go the emergency room immediately. Then, before heading back to his ambulance, he makes Eddie sign a waiver acknowledging that he's refusing medical attention.

"When did they start hiring twelve-year-old kids in the fire department?" Eddie struggles to stand and staggers. Dan grabs his arm and steadies him.

We go into the café. Except for a few overturned chairs, the place looks normal. Eddie sits on the first stool he sees. "Just my luck. There's usually two or three coppers eating in here. Not today."

"What happened?" I ask. "Was it Lonny?"

"No, it was Santa Claus and his six elves. Who do you think?" He slumps against the counter, unable to keep acting like he's okay. "He was looking for Ava, yelling, waving a gun, scaring the crap out of everybody in the joint. I told him she wasn't here, he should hit the road before I called the cops. He threw a punch at me, knocked me into the counter. That's how I cut my head. Then he was gone. Five minutes, the whole thing was over. I called 911, comped everybody's lunch, gave a statement to the cops and the medics, then you showed up."

"No one else was hurt, only Eddie, thank God." Fran comes out from the kitchen.

"You might get a few bills for dry cleaning. About half the customers pissed their pants. And I'm going to file a worker's comp case that requires a year of paid R and R in Hawaii." Eddie winks at me, then winces. One side of his head is starting to swell.

"I'll close up." Fran is not amused. "Dan, take Eddie to my house in his truck. Don't let him drive." Eddie starts to protest. Fran shuts him down. "You heard the medic, I don't want you alone when you pass out because you're too stubborn and too stupid to take care of yourself."

Ava and Iliana appear in the doorway, holding hands.

"Eddie, what happened to your head?" Ava lets go of Iliana, rushes Eddie, and hugs him hard enough to make him grimace. Pence shows up next, then Pepper comes roaring on her Harley. It's her day off, which makes me wonder why she was listening to her scanner instead of studying or having fun with friends. Eddie repeats his story, adding some dramatic embellishments about how he chased Lonny away and prevented a mass shooting. Pence orders us back to Fran's house and commands us to stay inside. Pepper volunteers to come along and provide security. Pence reassures us he has an all-points bulletin out for Lonny and Cody.

"Not Cody, just Lonny," Eddie says. "I followed him out the door, there was no one else in his truck. Only him."

"Was he drunk?" Pence asks.

"Whaddya think, Chief?" Eddie answers. "Is the pope Catholic? Does a bear crap in the woods?"

43

We gather in Fran's living room. Everyone except Eddie, who is taking a nap in Fran's bedroom, and Pepper, who has stationed herself as a lookout on the front porch. It's not cold, but Iliana's bundled up in one of Fran's souvenir blankets from San Francisco, the Golden Gate bridge on one side, Coit Tower on the other. Ava is sitting next to her on the couch.

Fran starts to ask what everyone would like for lunch and Iliana stops her.

"I have something to ask. I want to be sure I understand." She shrugs off the blanket. "The man who raped me, this Lonny Wilson, is the same man who hurt Mr. Eddie?" We all nod. Ava starts to reassure her that we are safe, Lonny can't hurt us. Iliana raises her hand. "Let me finish, please." Ava sits back. "Lonny Wilson is your friend Cody's father? The man you were hoping to prove was *not* your father, therefore *not* my rapist. The man you have known all your life? Whose wife and son are like your second family?" Ava nods. Iliana puts her hands over her heart. "All this time, until you heard my story, you had no idea he was your biological father?" Ava nods again.

The room is totally silent except for Iliana's soft voice. Fran, Ava, Dan, and I are sitting like stones, stones with beating hearts.

Iliana turns to Ava, takes both Ava's hands in hers. Like a matching pair.

"I ache for you, Ava. You have lost so much. Because of me. Because I am weak." Ava starts to say something. Iliana stops her. "I should have been taking care of you, not the other way around. I thought I was doing the right thing by keeping you from finding me. I felt it in my bones that meeting me would turn out badly for you. And it has. It's worse than I ever imagined. I am so sorry. I owe you an apology." She looks around the room. "I owe you all an apology. My decisions have hurt everyone."

Ava squeezes both of Iliana's hands. "Don't apologize. Don't ever apologize. You did what you thought was right at the time. I don't care about Lonny. He's dirt. You're all that matters to me. You and knowing that you didn't keep me because you loved me, not because I wasn't worth loving."

Fran manages to throw together a salad for lunch. We're setting the table when Pepper comes through the front door holding her phone. "Got him," she says, pumping her fist in the air. "CHP pulled Lonny over on his way to Moss Point, doing a buck twenty. For you civilians, that's a hundred and twenty miles an hour. Drunk as a skunk. It's a miracle he didn't kill himself or someone else."

Killing himself is exactly what I think he was trying to do. I decide to keep this to myself.

"Tried to run the chippie down. Lucky he didn't get shot. Instead, he's enjoying KPD hospitality, sobering up in our jail."

"Where's Cody?" Ava asks.

"Beats me. All I know is when they stopped Lonny, no one else was in the truck with him."

"Chippies got him?" Eddie is coming down the stairs, one step at a time, his hand on the railing.

Ava starts to get up. "I'm going to the jail. I'll make Lonny tell me where Cody is."

"Mija," Iliana takes hold of Ava's hand. "You just told me you don't care about this Lonny. Leave him be. He's dangerous. He'll get what he deserves."

Eddie hobbles off the bottom step into the living room. He's moving gingerly. "Your mother's right. Talking to a drunk is like trying to herd cats. All you can do is move their food. With the amount of booze Lonny has in his system, it will take him at least forty-eight hours to sober up and talk sense."

After lunch, I head to my private office. Gary is standing in the lobby saying goodbye to a client. He smiles when he sees me. "Dr. Meyerhoff, I was beginning to think you didn't work here anymore."

I fill him in on where I've been and what I've been doing. He whistles.

"Better find that kid, sounds like he's decompensating. Wouldn't be surprised if he tries to emulate his father and get some cop to kill him so he doesn't have to do it himself."

I thank him for his optimism and head upstairs. It's up to the cops to find Cody, not me or Ava. Things on my desk have stacked up. My inbox is full, every email needs a response, and I have a dozen reports to write. There goes the weekend. Frank will not be happy. I pick up the first report, start to reread my notes when my phone buzzes with a text from Fran.

Call me asap.

She picks up on the first ring. "Marlene Wilson called right after you left. She was in hysterics. Cody went to the jail to see his father. The officers wouldn't let him in. He threw some kind of fit and almost got himself arrested. Then he took off.

Marlene doesn't know where he is. He has a gun. She thinks he wants to kill Ava and then himself."

Ben Gomez's face rises in front of me. I shut my eyes to block his image. When I open them, he's still there. It's not Ava I should worry about committing suicide, it's Cody. He's out of control, emotionally dysregulated, and armed.

"Dot? Are you still there?"

"Where's Ava now?"

"In her room with Iliana. I tried to get the two of them to go to a hotel, but Ava wouldn't go. When she refused, so did Iliana. Pepper and Dan are staying here and Pence has stationed a patrol car out front. I think we're okay."

"Want me to come over?"

"Nope, no more room at the inn. And unless you're a praying woman, there's nothing to do. Just wanted to keep you in the loop. Next time I ask you for a favor, Dot, do me a favor in return and tell me to pound sand."

44

That night, Frank wants to go out for dinner, just the two of us; because I've been so distracted, he feels we're disconnected. There's nothing worse than being married and feeling lonely. I felt like that when I was married to Mark, who was married to his work until he met the wasp-waisted Melinda.

We head downtown to one of our favorite Mexican restaurants. There's no better guacamole on the planet. Frank has a beer. I have a margarita, on the rocks, no salt. We both order the evening special, chicken pozole. The owners are happy to see us, so is the waitstaff. Everyone is cheerful. Frank has saved up a bunch of things to tell me, little things about the house and the garden, funny anecdotes about his clients and his subs. For a moment, I can almost believe things are back to normal.

The sirens start as we are ordering flan for dessert. A don't-you-dare look flashes across Frank's face and just as quickly disappears.

"Go ahead," he says. "Look at your phone. I know you want to."

There's a text from the comm center. *Trouble at Fran's house. The chief wants you there, Code 3, lights and sirens.*

* * *

Frank comes with me rather than taking an Uber home or sitting in the restaurant until I get back, because knowing me, who knows when that would be. We pull up in front of Fran's. All the lights are on. Pence's car is parked in the driveway. There are two other patrol cars on the street, but no fire truck, no ambulance. No ambulance means no injuries, unless the ambulance has already come and gone.

Fran opens the front door, dressed in her bathrobe, her frame silhouetted against the inside lights. Pence comes out next. I adjust my eyes. The front of the house is covered in graffiti. The words BITCH and LIAR tagged over and over in black and red. Pence motions for us to stay in the car, looks up and down the street, then waves us inside. He closes the door, turns the lock. Fran's fireplace poker is leaning against the hallway wall, not by the fireplace where it belongs. Ava is curled up on a living room chair. Iliana is kneeling next to her. I can't hear what they're saying.

"Cody." Fran takes my arm, walks me into the living room. "He came here about thirty minutes ago. He was drunk. Yelling at the top of his lungs for Ava. Pepper chased him off. Now she's out looking for him. Eddie went with her. I called 911."

Judging from what he's wearing, Pence has been called away from a dinner far more elegant than the one Frank and I were sharing. He asks Fran if she wants to file charges. Vandalism? Trespassing? Drunk in public? He tells her he has room in the jail. Cody could bunk with his father, two Wilsons for the price of one. We groan. He grimaces at his own lame joke.

Ava gets up, crosses the room until she's close enough to Pence to step on his feet. "No jail. Please no jail. He needs help. He's a victim. Just like me."

Pence looks at Fran. "Same here," she says. "I don't want to file charges. Just get him help."

Pence notices Frank for the first time. "Nice to see you, Frank. Lucky you, tagging along with your spouse. I sent mine home in a cab. She wasn't happy." He looks at me. "What do you think, Dot? You know the players here. When we find him, should we arrest him or put him on an involuntary mental health hold?"

"I can't answer that." Pence looks confused. "You're asking me to diagnose a young man I barely know and to do it without a proper psychological assessment."

"Dr. Meyerhoff, these are exigent circumstances. Considering we don't even know where Cody is, you do not have the time to do your mumbo jumbo thing with inkblots and tiny animals in a sandbox." He looks at his watch. "Just give me the freaking crib notes, if you would. In plain English. I promise not to sue you for breach of ethics."

I'd like to tell him that the Psychology Licensing Board has no such compunctions about censuring psychologists who violate their code of ethics. But this is not the time to explain the finer points of professional psychology.

"From what I have observed as a friend of the family, Cody is experiencing a period of emotional dysregulation."

"English, please."

"He's agitated. Freaked out. His entire life has been turned inside out and upside down. He feels like a victim. He believes he and his mother have been betrayed both by Ava and by his father."

Pence holds up his hand to stop me. "TMI. All I need to know is, is he a suicide risk?"

"Yes."

"Is he a risk to others, including my officers?"

The front door opens. Pepper comes in. Followed by Eddie. They both look exhausted.

"In the wind," she says. "Nobody's seen Cody or heard from him."

"Perhaps you could answer the question I just posed to Dr. Meyerhoff, as she seems reluctant to do so. Is he a candidate for a victim-precipitated homicide?"

Pepper sits at the dining room table. Eddie flops on the couch. "That's what you're calling suicide by cop these days?" There's a bluish bruise blooming on his head.

"Suicide by cop?" Ava gasps. "What does that mean? Oh my God. Please don't let him hurt himself."

Pepper leans forward, her elbows on her knees. "He's just a kid. They run into trouble and think it's the end of the world. I'll bet he doesn't really want to die. Still, we got some hot dog rookies out there looking for him. No telling how our guys will react if Cody waves a gun or a knife in their direction."

Pence coughs. "So, Officer Hunt, you're saying you think he needs psychiatric hospitalization?"

"You're asking me? Ask the doc."

Pence rotates to look at me. "I can't answer that question, either," I say. "That's up to the admitting doctor at the hospital."

"I don't have an admitting doctor here, Dr. Meyerhoff. All I have is you. Let me rephrase my question. Dumb it down to its basic elements. If we catch him, do we take him to a hospital or to the jail?"

"Hospital," I say. "Definitely hospital."

"Thank you." He swipes his hand across his forehead as if getting an answer out of me is hard work. He turns to Ava. Points his finger. "Don't go to school, don't go to work, stay home, stay away from the windows until we find him. And let me know if he tries to contact you. Do not, under any circumstances, try to protect him. Do you understand?"

Ava grabs his arm. "Please don't hurt him, this is all my fault. Cody didn't do anything bad, I promise. He's never hurt me. Ever. He doesn't mean what he says. I know him better than anyone. He doesn't want to kill himself. Just find him. I'll talk to him. He'll listen to me."

Pence smooths her hand off his sleeve as if he were carefully removing something sticky. "Not to worry, young lady. My guys are trained. They know what to do in these kind of situations with these kinds of people."

Ava pulls back. The look on her face speaks volumes. Young lady? These kinds of people? Who is this condescending idiot? She's right. Pence is an idiot. Classroom training is not comparable to real-time action. Real-time action in a stressful high-risk situation, with amped-up cops facing an unstable teenager who is waving a gun in their faces, begging them to shoot him before he shoots them.

45

Before heading to the jail, I drop Eddie off at his apartment and leave Frank at home. He isn't happy. He wants me to wait until tomorrow to see Lonny. We have a brief tug-of-war. I tell him I'm afraid to wait. Cody is decompensating. He's drunk and he has a gun. The risk of him killing himself grows greater every minute he's left alone to gnaw on his resentments. If Cody kills himself because I didn't do everything I knew to do to prevent it, I couldn't live with myself. I'm only now learning to live with Ben Gomez's death. I don't think I could recover from two suicides.

Lonny will talk to me. I'm certain of it. He's a card-carrying narcissist masquerading as an ordinary citizen, a harmless nice guy with a boatyard. Narcissists love to play cat and mouse with their supposed inferiors. The first day I met him at his house, he was too cool, too slick. His hospitality just a bit condescending. Then he barged in on me at my office twice without calling first or making an appointment. If that doesn't reek of desperation, I don't know what does. He's cornered and he knows it.

I kiss Frank goodbye. He tells me to be careful. I tell him Lonny will be locked up and I'll be talking to him through bars. He tells me to call if I need anything and to come back soon because he needs his sleep and he won't be able to sleep until I'm home.

By the time I get to the jail, it's almost 9:00 p.m. Visiting hours are over and the officer staffing the front desk appears to be having trouble staying awake. He's one of those about-to-retire guys who's just watching the clock until his pension kicks in. He's not happy to see me. I doubt he's happy to see anyone. I tell him I want to talk to Lonny Wilson. He raises his eyebrows.

"The guy with the missing kid? He doesn't even know his kid's MIA. He's been sleeping it off most of the day. Didn't touch his dinner."

I tell him it's not safe for me to be alone with Lonny. He tells me he hasn't got any staff because they're all out looking for the Wilson kid. The best he can do is shackle Lonny to a table that's bolted to the floor. Or I can come back tomorrow. I take the first option.

There's a short, dark hall leading from the front desk to the visiting room. I can see Lonny through the barred window. His hands are shackled to a short chain attached to a metal table. He's unshaven and wearing an orange jailhouse suit two sizes too big. His head is bowed, his hair hanging in lank strands. There's dirt under his fingernails. He picks his head up as I open the door, squints at me with gummy eyes. He doesn't seem to know who I am for a minute. When he recognizes me, he groans.

"Fuck me, what are you doing here?"

"Cody's missing. He needs your help."

Lonny strains at his shackles. "How am I going to do that? I can't even scratch my own ass."

I take a seat on the other side of the table. Out of his reach but not his smell. "You need to talk him into giving himself up and voluntarily committing himself to a psychiatric facility."

"Tell him to check himself in to a nuthouse? Why the hell would I do that?"

"Because you put him there. You're the one who did this to him."

He jerks back as if I'd smacked him. Curses under his breath and swings forward, hitting his head on the table. It takes him a minute to sit up again. Blood is trickling down one cheek like a tear. He swipes his face on his sleeve, leaving a red smear.

"You need to protect him from himself. He's suicidal."

"You made him like that, you and Ava. Not me. What are you after? How much do you want?" He shakes his head, his hair whipping around his face, trying to wake his alcohol-soaked brain. "That girl is lying. If it was me who got her pregnant, she woulda come to me for money. And I would have helped her. Given her money for an abortion, whatever she wanted."

"Come to you? Are you kidding? She was scared to death of you. You raped her. Forced yourself on her. Traumatized her so badly she's been hiding from you for years."

"I told you before. I did some bad shit in my drinking days. But I'm a different man now. I don't drink anymore."

"You're drunk right now. Stop wasting my time. Where's Cody?"

"I'm not saying I never made a mistake. I'm being honest here. I drank a lot in those days. Sometimes I had blackouts."

"Tell me where Cody's gone."

"How do I know? He doesn't tell me where he goes."

"He's drunk, Lonny. He's driving. He has a gun."

Lonny looks at the ceiling, his head cocked to one side, calculating his next move.

"I do remember this one little babysitter. I drove her home after we had a party. I shouldn't have because I was hammered, but Cody was crying or sick or something, so Marlene stayed home and I drove the babysitter."

"Does he have a favorite hiding place? A place he likes to go to when he's angry or in a bad mood?"

"I was feeling friendly, so I kissed her. She was a nice kid. She didn't resist. I thought she liked it. I did it again. When she didn't push me away, I figured she was okay with it. Probably angling for a bigger tip like they all do. I don't call that rape, I call it getting lucky."

"Bastard." I lift out of my chair. I want to slap the smirk off his face, break every bone in his body, throttle him with my bare hands. He's trying to break me, get under my skin. He's a narcissist and narcissists love torturing their prey before they go for the kill. Lonny looks pleased, like he's just landed a punch and has me against the ropes. I didn't come here to fight, I came here to help Cody. If I back down, Lonny wins. And if Lonny wins, Cody could die. I force myself to calm down and back my chair a few inches away from the table. All we ever have in life is what's in front of us; the past is the past and the future isn't here yet. The man in front of me, for all his bluster and outsized ego, is chained to a table wearing a filthy jumpsuit and facing criminal proceedings. He's the one against the ropes, not me.

"You weren't lucky, she was too terrified to resist. She was only thirteen."

He frowns like this is news. "Really? She must have looked older. I don't go for little girls."

"Cody's not at Marisa's. Where else would he go?"

Lonny shrugs. "Beats me. He doesn't have a lot of friends."

"Cody knew you were drinking. He hid it from Marlene."

"Marlene's the one you should talk to. Back in the day, she was tired all the time taking care of Cody. We hadn't had sex in months. I was horny as hell. I'd watch her nurse him and get aroused. Bet you think that's sick. I'm a man. I have needs, so I got it when I could. But I never raped anybody. Never had to. My friends called me Lucky Lonny. Women liked me."

There it is, a vulnerability, a chink in his armor.

"Every woman except for Marlene?"

His eyes narrow and his mouth forms into a humorless rictus. "It's like I was invisible. It was just her and Cody. That's all that mattered. I was a cop. A good one. Now I'm ass-kissing fat fucks who pay me to fillet the fish they catch because they don't want to get their hands dirty." He raises his hands to his face. "I stink. I can't get the smell of fish off my hands." He leans in. "Marlene thinks she deserves better. I'm an embarrassment. She doesn't give a crap about anyone but her and Cody. She doesn't care about me, she doesn't care about Ava, she doesn't care about that babysitter. I worked my ass off for years and she and Cody turn on me."

"Tell me where Cody might be hiding. He's been protecting you. He knew you were drinking and didn't tell anyone. He hid your guns to keep you from killing yourself. Now it's your turn to protect him."

"Whatever he did, he did on his own. I never asked him. The kid's a little off. Always has been. Tell him for me, as soon as I get out of this place, we'll take a fishing trip. Montana maybe. Someplace in the mountains."

"Now, Lonny. Cody needs you now. Not tomorrow."

"Then get me out of here. I'm chained to a freaking table. Bail me out, I'll do whatever you want. Look for Cody, take him to a head shrinker. You're the psychologist, tell me what to do."

"Why were you crying?"

He startles. "What are you talking about?"

"Somebody reported to the police that they saw you and Cody fighting. Both of you were crying."

Lonny rocks in his seat for a minute. "That fucking kid. He followed me. I was drunk. He thought I was going to off myself. Kept screaming at me not to do it because he needed me. I kept telling him to leave me alone. Find someone else to need."

"He loves you."

"He hates me."

"He doesn't hate you. If he hated you, why would he try to stop you from killing yourself?"

"Because he's a fuck nugget who doesn't know his ass from a hole in the ground."

"I can guess why Cody was crying when you were fighting, but why were you crying?" He doesn't answer. "If you don't care about what happens to him, why did you hit your head on the table when I told you Cody needed psychiatric care because of you?"

"I don't know. I fell asleep. I'm drunk, you know." He closes his eyes. Tilts his face toward the ceiling. Tears are rolling down his temples and into his hair. "He's like a goddamn dog. All he wants is a pat on the head. I'm so screwed up, I can't even do that. Tell him to leave me the fuck alone, forget I ever existed."

"He can't forget about you. Any more than you can forget about him."

"What do you want from me?" Lonny's eyes are red, he's swaying back and forth in his seat.

I lean in as close as I dare. "Take responsibility for your actions. Stop blaming everyone else for what you did. Marlene isn't responsible because she didn't want to have sex. Iliana isn't responsible because she didn't fight back. And Ava isn't responsible because she exposed you. Want to help Cody? Admit that you raped Iliana. Stop whining. Take your punishment. Show some courage. Give Cody a shred of something positive about you that he can hang on to."

46

It's been twenty-four hours, thirty-four minutes, and fifty-eight seconds since Cody went missing. Ava's out of her mind, blaming herself, over and over. She's convinced that if anything happens to him, it will be her fault. Still under virtual house arrest per Pence's orders, she spent most of today pacing and complaining that keeping her inside is a total waste of time. She made Cody run away, she should be the one to bring him back.

Fran found a friend to keep the café open. Eddie insists she's wasting money. He's perfectly capable of running the place. According to Fran, who went to his apartment to check on him, he's still nursing his head wound and is wobbly on his feet. She'd rather close the café than risk having him fall headfirst into the deep fat fryer.

Dan has gone home. Sharon was afraid to be alone. But, at my insistence, they are coming to dinner tonight. It feels like eons ago that I made Ava pledge to introduce Sharon and Iliana. Iliana is leaving tomorrow, so it seems like an opportunity to cash in on that pledge, get our minds off Cody, and take a small step toward making a connection between Ava's adopted family and her birth mother. Iliana thinks it's a good idea. She's eager to meet the woman who raised Ava. She wants to thank her and, out of some residual guilt that clings like a cobweb, explain her decision to place Ava for adoption.

I don't expect Sharon and Iliana to become friends, but I do think it would help Ava if she didn't have to choose between mothers or, more likely, defend her choices every time she opted to spend time with Iliana and not Sharon. She's spent enough of her life filling the chasm in Sharon and Dan's relationship, distracting them from their own difficulties. Sharon's insecurities could cause trouble and trouble is the last thing Ava needs. Better to have Sharon meet the real Iliana than be tormented by the Iliana she imagines is stealing Ava's affection.

Frank insists on coming with me so he can help in the kitchen. Fran thinks the occasion calls for a feast, roast beef, scalloped potatoes, green beans, and ice cream. I think everyone, including me, will be too nervous to eat.

Fran greets us at the door, grumbling about cooking Ava a veggie burger made in a laboratory that produces fake meat. She doesn't understand why anyone who won't eat meat will pay big bucks to eat Frankensteinian vegetables that are made by a chemist to look and taste like beef. Why not eat meat in the first place?

Ava gives her a hug. "I told you not to cook something special for me. I can eat everything but the roast beef."

"At my table, everyone has a full plate. End of discussion." Fran points Frank to the kitchen and marches off.

"I'm trying to persuade Iliana to stay longer." Ava takes a seat next to Iliana on the couch. Iliana looks tarnished. Some of the brightness in her face after the interview with Bergen and the DA has worn off.

"I need to get back to Marisol. I promised her I'd only be gone for the weekend." Iliana smiles at Ava, touches her face. "I'll be back. There will be depositions and a trial." Her backpack is sitting on the landing like a watchful eye.

The doorbell rings. Ava opens the door. Dan and Sharon are standing on the doorstep, holding hands, waiting to be invited in. Dan is wearing an out-of-fashion suit. There are shiny spots at the elbows and the back flap refuses to lie flat. Sharon, on the other hand, looks quite fashionable. She's wearing a simple pair of black slacks and a loose-fitting collarless shirt. Her hair is shorter, sporty, not the teased and sprayed blowback she had when we first met.

Iliana stands, her legs shaking. Sharon gives her a quick once-over, head to toe, comparing her large frame to Iliana's compact body. Iliana extends her hand. Sharon bats it away and asks for a hug instead.

Dan steps forward. "Give her a little space, Sharon. We only just got here." He takes her hand and leads her across the room to two side-by-side chairs.

"So, Iliana—I hope I'm pronouncing your name right—are you enjoying Fran's hospitality?" Dan rests his hand on Sharon's leg. She pushes it off. "This must be quite something for you, after so many years, seeing Ava all grown-up. She was such a cute baby. I have pictures if you'd like to see them."

Neither the smile on Sharon's face nor the lilt in her voice cover her real intention. To thrust a knife into Iliana's heart and twist it. I watch for Iliana to parry. She doesn't move, doesn't say a word, just sits on the edge of the couch, still as stone.

Dan clenches his teeth. Ava glares at me, like it's my fault for pressuring her into this meeting, which isn't going well and should never have happened.

"I understand you live in San Francisco. Will you be taking Ava back with you?" Sharon tosses off the question as if she's asking about the weather when losing Ava is what she fears most.

"We just got here, Sharon," Dan says. "Give it a rest. How about we hold our questions until after dinner when we know each other a little better?"

Sharon disagrees. Insists that it is better for the digestion if everyone gets to know one another before they eat. Dan gives up without a fight. The tyranny of weakness is powerful and Sharon's an expert at weaponizing her emotional fragility.

Ava's adoption is the elephant in the room. Now that Sharon has opened the door, out of meanness, anxiety, or a combination of the two, there's no way around it. We could plunge in or we could spend the next hour making superficial small talk.

"Thank you, Dan," Iliana says. "I'm fine with it, really. Compared to yesterday's interview, this is easy." She turns to face Sharon. "I presume you know that I was assaulted when I was thirteen. Ava was conceived as a result of this assault. The reason for my visit is to ask the district attorney to file charges against my assailant. I understand the man who has been identified as my rapist is your close family friend. This must be shocking. I'm so sorry." She folds her hands on her lap, looks directly at Ava and me. "Until yesterday, I don't think I could have said those words out loud."

"We didn't know about the assault when we adopted Ava, did we, Dan?"

"You couldn't have known, Sharon," Iliana says. "I doubt the man who raped me ever knew I was pregnant. You have no reason to blame yourselves for anything. I'm happy you adopted Ava. I didn't want her to go to an institution, I wanted her to have a family."

"Could we talk about something else? Please." Ava's voice is strained.

Sharon keeps talking, all the while fidgeting with the hem of her shirt, twisting the material around her fingers. "This man and his wife are, were, our closest friends. I can hardly believe it. Never in a million years would Dan or I have let Ava be alone with him had we known he could do such a thing. You must think I'm a terrible mother."

"This is not about you, Mother." Ava's eyes are narrowed, the muscles around her jaw so tight she can barely talk. "It's about holding Lonny accountable. It's about Iliana and me getting justice for what's been done to us." I can't imagine what it has taken out of her to keep propping Sharon up, year after year, filling her insatiable needs for reassurance.

"You're wrong, mija." Iliana puts her hand on Ava's leg. "This is about all of us. I used to think that what happened to me was my problem only. But it was you who helped me see that the man who hurt me hurt us all. And that he needs to be punished for what he's done." She turns to Sharon. "Please understand that I am not in competition with you for Ava's love. A child deserves all the love she can get. She can never have too much. We may have gotten to this moment in different ways, on different paths. However, we got here. I am very grateful we had this chance to meet because we share something precious—we love Ava." She looks at Dan and Sharon, Fran, and me. "All of us."

The rest of the evening goes by in a flurry of food. The conversation stays light. Sharon and Iliana do their best to be cordial and express interest in the minute details of each other's lives, the way women do. It's a bit forced, but sometime after the Caesar salad and before the roast beef, they find a connection between Sharon's brief stint as an LVN and Iliana's medical transcription service. Dan is silent, monitoring Sharon's every word. Fran distracts herself from the main event by playing hostess, Frank by being her sous-chef. Ava is unusually quiet, sneaking looks at her watch like the evening is crawling by at glacial speed. An unexpected shower pummels against the windows, taking us all by surprise. This leads to a brief diversion into a discussion of climate change. Ava excuses herself from the table as Frank is clearing the dishes to make way for dessert. She steps out onto the front porch. The rain is sheeting down at an angle. I go out and stand next to her.

"Looking for Cody?"

"I can't stand it. We're here stuffing our faces and pretending to be nice to one another. Because of me, he's out there, all alone, wet and hungry and scared."

"Dessert's on, lemon meringue pie." Fran sticks her head out the door.

"Not hungry," Ava says. "I ate too much already, Aunt Fran. It was delish."

"Get your skinny butt in here anyway. Turning down lemon meringue pie won't bring Cody back. Only Cody will bring Cody back. Cody and the cops. Sounds like a singing group, doesn't it?" She disappears into the house.

Ava scans the street again. "Cody's out there," she says. "He's watching us. I can feel him."

47

It's 10:00 a.m. Sunday morning. I'm still in my bathrobe, Frank's in the kitchen mixing up a batch of Bloody Marys. Iliana's on the train to San Francisco, Ava's probably in her room crying, Fran's asleep, and Cody's still missing.

There's a knock on our front door. It's Pepper, in uniform, her patrol car idling in the driveway. My stomach flips.

"Is it Cody?" She nods. "Is he dead?"

"Not yet. He's down at the jail, in a tree, armed to the teeth and drunk as a skunk."

The streets surrounding the jail are blocked. Deputies aren't letting anyone through, including the press who caw like crows the minute I get out of Pepper's patrol car.

"Who's the boy in the tree? What's his name?"

A fire truck and an ambulance are parked on the street, engines running. I half walk, half run to the lawn in front of the jail entrance.

"You can't stay up there forever, son." Pence is aiming a megaphone at the top of a huge California oak, its stout trunk covered in bark rough enough to tear a person's skin. I look for Cody. At first, all I see are leafy green branches. Then I spot him, crouched in the crook of two thick limbs, clutching a handgun to his chest. A rifle lays across his lap.

I run toward Pence. He's wearing a short-sleeved shirt with crossed golf clubs embroidered on the pocket, suggesting he had other plans for the day.

"Effing kid. He's been in that damn tree for forty-five minutes yelling for his father. He's armed and he's drunk. He won't come down and he won't drop his weapons. Only wants to talk to his father, who refuses to come out of his cell. Says he's not going to be part of putting his kid in jail."

"Cody knows me. Let me try."

There's a commotion behind the police barriers. Sharon and Marlene are arguing with a deputy. Marlene breaks through the barrier tape and runs at us. Her shirt is untucked on one side and she has a black eye.

"What the hell is going on here?" Pence wheels around to face his troops. "This is an active shooter scene; keep the family and every other damn person behind the crime tape."

"He's my son. Let me talk to him."

Marlene reaches for the bullhorn. Pepper grabs her, spins her away, apologizing as she does, her voice low but firm. "The chief has the situation under control, Ms. Wilson. Best to leave things to the professionals."

Pence turns toward Cody's tree. "Your mother's here, son. You don't want her to see you like this, do you?"

Cody leans forward, pushes some branches aside. His hair is matted under the ball cap he wears everywhere. The one with Wilson's Boatyard embroidered on the front. His skin is sallow and his cheekbones grown so sharp they cast shadows on his face.

"I want to talk to my father." His words slur.

Three firefighters are squatting under the oak tree, spreading a giant yellow tarp over the ground. I don't want to think about what the tarp is for.

"You're killing your mother. You know that, kid." Pence is drumming his fingers against the bullhorn. "She's right here, crying her eyes out." No response. "You don't want to hurt your mother, do you?" Still no response. He turns off the bullhorn. "Where are my hostage negotiators?"

Pepper walks toward us, brushing dirt off her uniform. Sharon is standing at the edge of the crime scene tape, her arm around Marlene's shoulder, keeping her upright. Marlene looks like a ghost.

"Mutual aid. Working a hostage situation in Gilroy."

Pence turns back to the tree, flips the switch on the megaphone. "Okay, kid, let's make a deal. Come on down, then you can talk to your dad."

"Him first. Then I'll come down. Maybe. If I want."

"You can't stay up there much longer. You must be hungry. How 'bout a pizza. I'm buying."

Cody reaches for a paper bag. Pulls out a can of beer and a sack of chips. He waves at us, chugs the beer, and throws the can to the ground. We watch as it sails through the air like a falling leaf. He jams a fistful of chips in his mouth and starts on another beer.

"You must have been a Boy Scout," Pence says. "Came here prepared." He shifts from one foot to the other. "I want to help you. I really do. But you have to show me something first, son. Throw down your weapons. Then we can talk about getting your father out here."

"I'm not your fucking son. Tell my mother to go home. I want to talk to my father or I shoot myself in the head."

Cody disappears in a flurry of leafy movement. Thick branches closing in behind him. We stare at the tree. The crowd holds its collective breath. Pigeons swoop over our heads, watching the unfolding drama from the best seats in the house. Cody reappears holding something in his hands. A rifle shot cracks the air. Marlene screams. The deputies pull their weapons. A pigeon falls to the ground dead.

"Stand down." Pence aims the megaphone at his officers. "Holster your weapons. Do it now." He turns back to the tree. "I get it, son. You proved your point. You know how to shoot." Pence's voice is shaking. He sounds like he's underwater.

Cody pulls back. I can't see his face anymore.

"This is not a contest, son. I got nervous officers here. They know how to shoot as good as you. They're just waiting for me to give them a go sign. I'm begging you, don't make me do something I can't undo."

There's no response. The upper branches move, then stop. I hold my breath.

"Last chance, kid. Promise me, if I can get your dad out here, you will throw down your guns and come out of that tree."

Two chattering gray squirrels bounce from branch to branch, chasing each other in circles down the trunk of the tree.

"Do I have your promise?"

"I'm not promising anything until I see my father."

"You," Pence turns to a burly cop with a hard face, his eyes hidden behind sunglasses. "Get that idiot father out here if you have to drag him by his ears."

"Where's Dan?" I ask. "He can talk Lonny into coming out."

Pence looks at me as if he'd forgotten I was standing next to him. "I already talked to him. He refuses to do anything for Lonny except kill him with his bare hands."

"Then let me talk to Lonny," I say. "I talked to him the night he got arrested. He hates me so much, he'll talk to Cody just to prove me wrong. I know what makes him tick, where he's vulnerable." Pence backs away from me as if he needs physical distance to think. I follow him. "I'm your best option. Your hostage negotiators aren't available. Dan isn't available. Marlene is an absolute wreck. Physical force should be your last resort. There are reporters all over the place. I can see the headlines now. 'Kenilworth Police Chief Authorizes Brute Force to Get a Jail Inmate to Follow Orders.'"

Pence turns around slowly until we're face-to-face, shooting daggers at me with his eyes. If looks could kill, I would be lying dead here on the grassy knoll in front of the jail, next to a dead pigeon. He gestures for a correctional officer to escort me to Lonny's cell. "Dr. Meyerhoff," he says, "whatever you do, don't make me regret this."

I walk toward the jail, losing confidence with every step. I know how to get to Lonny. I understand his soft spots. It's Cody I'm worried about. He thinks what he wants most in this world is the truth. But what if I persuade Lonny to tell the truth, that he raped Iliana and Ava is Cody's half sister? Might the truth Cody craves push him over the edge? Cause him to shoot himself? And would I be the one who helped it happen?

48

Lonny is standing on his bed, looking out a small, barred window.

The officer bangs his baton against the bars of his cell. "Get off the bed, Wilson. You got a visitor."

Lonny turns. The minute he sees me, he jumps down and throws himself against the bars. I step back a foot.

"What are they doing out there? I heard a shot. Don't let them kill my kid." He's shouting, his voice disturbing the unhappy occupants of the cells on either side.

"He wants to talk to you. He won't cooperate until you come outside and talk to him."

"I'm not helping any freaking cop kill my kid. And I'm not helping you put him in a nuthouse." He turns back to the window, steps up on the bed again.

"This won't end well for Cody without your help."

"Not doing it. Not helping you kill my kid."

"Nobody wants to kill Cody, except Cody." Lonny doesn't turn around. "If you won't agree to talk to him and he kills himself, you'll carry that guilt for the rest of your life."

"He won't listen to me. He hates me. I wrecked his life."

"He's out there in a tree begging to talk to you."

"He just wants to tell me how much he hates my freaking guts before he shoots me and offs himself."

"Are you afraid of your own son?"

Lonny whirls around, jumps down, takes three long steps toward the cell doors and me. "I'm not afraid of anyone."

"You're afraid of the truth. You're afraid to admit what you've done. Cody is confused. He doesn't know how to live with what you did."

"How's it going to help him to know what I did?"

"Because you're messing with his sense of reality. He doesn't know what's true and what isn't anymore."

"Tell him to forget I ever existed."

"You'll always be his father, even if he never sees you again. Don't make him pay for what you did."

"He hates me."

"He doesn't hate you, Lonny. He loves you. He's aching for you to reach out to him. He wants to know that you understand how much you hurt him. How what you did has changed his life. You can salvage your relationship. People do it all the time. Murderers do it. You can do it."

He backs away from the cell door and starts to pace. He's talking to himself. He stops walking and faces the wall, hands flat like he's ready to do push-ups. I wait. He turns around, closes his eyes, crosses his arms over his chest. His breath is coming in long intervals. I watch the rise and fall of his jumpsuit, the way his Adam's apple moves, the rhythmic pulse of a small tic under his jaw.

"If I go out there, you have to promise to call off the cops. No guns, no jail time, no nuthouse."

"He's suicidal, Lonny. He needs professional help."

Lonny uncrosses his arms. "Then no deal."

"Just until he stabilizes. Probably no more than a week. He's confused. He's suffering. Is that what you want for him?"

"You deaf? No jail, no psych, or no deal."

"Your son is destroyed because of what you did."

"Then he needs to man up. Pull himself together."

"Like you've pulled yourself together? Wearing so much armor nothing gets in or out. You told me all Cody wants is a pat on the head and you can't even do that for him."

"I was drunk when I said that."

"In vino veritas."

"What the fuck does that mean?"

"People under the influence tell the truth." He squints. "Cody wants you to see him, not save him."

Lonny startles. He takes a deep breath. Begins to pace around his cell. I can hear shouting from the outside. A roar goes up. He listens. It stops. He keeps pacing. His eyes are averted, but I know he's watching me watch him. He likes making me wait.

"One minute," I say. "Make up your mind in one minute or I'm out of here to tell Cody you don't care if he shoots himself in the head."

"I never said that."

"Might as well have, because if you don't go out there, that's what's going to happen."

He mutters something to himself, goes to the sink, turns on the water, scoops a fistful in his hands, wets his hair, and slicks it back with his fingers.

"Could his mother visit?" He checks his reflection in the dented metal plate that serves as a mirror.

"Of course."

"And they won't do anything to his brain? No voodoo shit? Not going to dope him up on meds?"

"Maybe something temporary to calm him down. Then talk therapy, group support."

He tugs at his jumpsuit, flattens the collar, and straightens his

shoulders. "I am not a coward. And I'm not afraid of my son."
He calls for the guard to open his cell.

"How do I look?" The guard shrugs, looks at me for the answer.

"You look fine," I say. "Like somebody's father." I say this, not because I believe it, but because that's what he needs to hear.

49

Lonny Wilson, standing in the sun in his orange jailhouse suit with the words *KPD Inmate* stamped on the front and back in large black letters, doesn't look like anybody's father. He looks like a convict. His hands are manacled, his feet shackled together with a short, thick chain, and he is surrounded by armed officers. He squints in the noonday sun, unable to shade his eyes. There's a rustle in the topmost branches of the oak tree.

"Where are you, son? Lemme see your face."

Pence commands an officer to relinquish his hat. He puts it on Lonny's head, tucking in runaway strands of hair, then bends to Lonny's ear. "Get him out of that tree before he does something to himself." He holds the megaphone in front of Lonny's face.

"Talk to me, son."

"Tree." Pence nudges him. "Get him out of the frigging tree."

"Come down, please, Cody."

Cody peers out from his leafy alcove. "I hate you. You ruined my life."

His voice shoots out of the tree like an arrow aimed at Lonny's heart.

"I get it. I do. I hate myself. I'm sorry." There's no response.

"Come down now, okay? I used to be a cop, remember? I know how these guys think. They don't have all day to wait for you to make up your mind. I don't want you to get hurt."

Pence takes the megaphone away from Lonny. "Take your time, Cody, no one's in a rush. We want this to end peacefully."

He moves the bullhorn back to Lonny. Lonny doesn't look happy to be upstaged.

"Listen to me, son. I know how this goes. Come down out of that goddamn tree before they kill you."

"You don't give a shit about me. Tell me the truth. Is Ava my sister?"

Lonny drops his head, muffling his voice. "Half sister."

Pence elbows him in the side. "Louder."

"Half sister."

"I said louder."

"Half sister, Cody, she's your effing half sister." His voice streaks through the air, scattering in all directions. "That makes me her freaking father. Happy now?" Sweat is dripping off his chin, staining his jumpsuit. Cody pulls back and disappears behind a wall of green leaves. "Say something. Goddam it. Talk to me."

Cody sticks his face out again. "They're just making you say that to get me to come down."

"Nobody's making me say anything. Man up, kid. Face the music. Don't embarrass yourself or me." Lonny shuffles his feet in the grass. "Here's the honest-to-God truth. It was a long time ago. I messed around with a babysitter. I thought she wanted it. You're a guy. You know how guys are. They're calling it rape. They can call it whatever the hell they want. I didn't know how old she was and I didn't know she got pregnant. Happens to millions of guys."

Lonny's not trying to help Cody, he's trying to make a case for his defense in front of the press.

"I wish you were dead." Cody's voice is hoarse.

"Then do it. Shoot me," Lonny yells back. "What are you waiting for?" He shuffles toward the tree. An officer tackles him. Two more pile on top. The scuffle is over before it starts.

"That's enough," Pence says. "Get him the hell out of here." He takes the bullhorn up and walks forward. "Okay, Cody. I kept my end of the bargain. Now it's on you, buddy. Come down out of that tree, please. Don't make me come after you because I will." He tells one of his officers to get the nonlethal beanbags ready.

"Fuck no. I'm not coming down 'til I'm ready, maybe never."

I see Ava out of the corner of my eye. She's with Dan, begging a police officer to let her past the crime tape.

I tap Pence on the shoulder. "Ava's here. Cody will listen to her."

"Let the teenage girlfriend of a suicidal suspect talk to him? Brilliant frigging idea, Doctor. She's part of the reason he wants to kill himself. The longer he stays in that tree, the more dangerous the situation. Look at the crowd, he could shoot any of them. I don't want a mass murder on my hands."

"He wants to kill himself because of what his father did. He doesn't want to kill anybody else."

"Whatever. I'm a cop, not a shrink. My job is to keep people safe, him included."

"If you won't let Ava talk to him, let me. I got Lonny out of his cell, didn't I? Don't forget about the reporters. You don't want anyone reporting that you were so eager to get back to your golf game, you used force on an emotionally disturbed teenager who was hiding in the top of an eighty-foot-tall tree."

I grab the bullhorn before he can stop me.

"Cody? It's me, Dr. Meyerhoff."

"I don't want to talk to you."

I squint at the top of the tree; not even the leaves are moving. "Ava's here. You're scaring her. She doesn't want you to hurt yourself."

"Put her on. I want to talk to her."

"It's up to the police chief, not me. I'll ask him." Pence makes a slashing gesture across his throat. "He says okay, but first you have to throw down all your weapons."

I poke Pence. Point at Ava. He waves at the officer obstructing her path. She dashes across the lawn so fast she nearly knocks me over.

"Ava's standing next to me, Cody. Can you see her? She wants to talk to you, but the chief won't let her until you throw your weapons down."

There's a pause. A rifle flies out of the tree and bounces on the ground. Pence pantomimes that Cody has more than one weapon.

"All of them, please, Cody. All of them."

He throws down his handgun. Another minute passes and a spearfishing gun comes sailing out of the tree. Now he moves forward, balancing on a long branch.

"Is that all?" I say.

"Yeah!"

He could be lying, no way to know. I hand Ava the bullhorn. Her hands are shaking. She raises the megaphone to her mouth.

"Can you hear me, Cody?" Her voice is thready. She repeats herself, louder this time. "You're scaring me. Please don't hurt yourself."

"I don't want to talk to you."

"You just asked for me."

"I hate you. I don't want to ever see you again."

"I wish none of this had happened, Cody. If I had known how this was going to turn out, I would never have started looking for my birth parents. I mean it."

"Liar. I hope you go to hell." He's starting to lose his voice.

Pence bends down. "Two minutes." He holds up two fingers for emphasis. "If he isn't down in two minutes, I'm going to have the fire department knock him out of the tree with a fire hose. If that doesn't work, then I'm going for the beanbags."

"He's been in that tree for over an hour," I say. "He's shot his gun once. All he killed was a bird and he did that on purpose to show us he could shoot. He doesn't want to kill anyone but himself. Give us more time." I take the bullhorn from Ava.

"Cody, this is Dr. Meyerhoff again. Think about this. If you kill yourself, Ava will feel guilty for the rest of her life. So will your mother. Killing yourself is like killing her too. She's already hurting from what your father did. You're only adding to her pain."

Ava asks for the bullhorn back. Pence tells me not to give it to her. He's at the end of his rope. So is Cody. I ignore Pence and hand the megaphone to Ava. She walks toward the tree.

"I get it, Cody. I know what you're thinking because I've thought it too. You're thinking that you're half him and that makes you no better than he is. I have half of his genes, same as you. I also have half of Iliana's genes. Like you have half of Marlene's. You are who you are. Neither one of us is who Lonny is." She doesn't wait for him to respond. "You're not responsible for what Lonny did. You don't have to find the answer to why he did it. Neither do I. We're only responsible for what we do, no one else." She bends over for a brief moment; the megaphone is heavy for her slender arms. "It's hella confusing to love someone who did bad things. You can love Lonny without accepting his bad parts. It's okay. I'm learning to do that with Dan and

Sharon." Cody is still perched on his branch. Barely moving. It's hard to see the expression on his face. "Are you listening to me? Killing yourself isn't going to change anything. You've been my best friend for forever. Now you're my brother. I'm going to help you. You're going to help me. Please come down. We can help each other. I don't want you to die." She sinks to the ground crying.

Two crows settle on top of the oak tree, screeching at Cody to find somewhere else to sit. He pulls back, out of sight. A minute passes. First one, then another branch starts to move, each one lower than the one before. Now I can see him making his way downward. He's moving slowly, carefully, like someone who wants to live. A minute passes before we see his legs dangling off the lowest branch. He sits, his upper body hidden from view. Two minutes pass, then three, then four. Suddenly, there's a flurry in the tree and he jumps to the ground, his hands in the air. Three KPD cops rush him, knock him over, tie his hands behind his back with plastic straps, and march him to the open doors of the waiting ambulance. He walks slowly, his head down. All the fight gone out of him.

Per my instructions, Cody's being transported to the psych unit at Kenilworth Community Hospital for an evaluation. They'll keep him there until he's no longer suicidal.

Ava watches the ambulance pull away. Tears slide down her cheeks. She looks at me.

"Couldn't he have just gone home?"

"He's suicidal, Ava. I couldn't take the chance. You wouldn't have wanted me to take the chance."

"He's going to blame me, if he ever talks to me again."

"I did this, not you. If he's going to blame anyone besides his father, tell him to blame me."

Dan and Sharon rush toward us, reaching for Ava. I watch them walk away, their arms around one another, a creature with six legs. Pence is giving a statement to the press. He's using the oak tree for background. Camera lights and TV cameras wink in the shade of its leafy canopy. Cody needs protection. And therapy. I did my job as a psychologist. If anyone is to blame or to thank, it's the ghost of Ben Gomez.

50

It's October. The Japanese maple in our yard is turning a deep red. People who think California has no seasons should come to Kenilworth, where the pistachio and liquid amber trees line the streets like torches, their goodbye-to-summer leaves showing crimson and chartreuse. I'm in the living room, watching Frank through a window as he fertilizes plants for the last time until spring. I have clients scheduled for most of the day and a coffee date with Pepper for yet another conversation about her return to street patrol. I intend to recommend to Pence that she get her old job back after the first of the year, but I'm waiting to tell her until we get closer to Christmas.

After meeting with Pepper, I am heading to Moss Point with Frank, Ava, and Fran. Sharon and Dan have invited us to dinner. They want to thank me for helping Ava and for contributing my time pro bono. They'd like to pay me, but they know how much time I spent and they don't have the money to cover my fees. I tell them the best way to compensate me is with a home-cooked meal.

Ava's still living with Fran, working part-time in the café with Eddie and going to college. She enrolled too late to get all the classes she wanted, but at least it's a start, long overdue in my opinion, to thinking about her future. I laughed when she told me she plans to major in psychology.

Lonny Wilson has pled guilty to child rape, sparing Iliana the pain of having to testify in open court. Hard to imagine her fending off whatever questions Lonny's bulldog attorney would have flung at her as he tried to invalidate her story and reduce the length of his client's sentence. The last nail in Lonny's coffin came after the results of the court-ordered DNA test agreed, with a ninety-nine percent probability, that he was Ava's father. His sentencing comes up in six weeks. We all plan to be there, Fran, Eddie, Ava, Dan, and Sharon. We want to support Iliana when she gives her victim's statement to the judge. Ava wanted to make her own statement, but the law still doesn't consider children of rape to be victims.

Cody refuses to see Ava. Marlene told Sharon that his therapist says he needs more counseling before he can face her. He goes to a support group for kids whose parents are incarcerated. He really likes the group. It's the one place he feels as if he belongs. He doesn't have to worry that somebody is going to make fun of him because his father is in jail. Pence has asked the DA to drop all criminal charges against Cody with the exception of drunk in public. He's using it as leverage to pressure Cody to stay in therapy.

Sharon and Dan have been going to marital counseling once a week and family counseling with Ava every other week. According to Fran, they're getting along better. Less blame, more listening. The therapist is helping them accept that it's perfectly normal for an adopted child to want to get to know her birth mother. She's also helping them get used to Ava's efforts to learn about her cultural heritage. Ava's taking Spanish lessons and she and Sharon are going to a Mexican cooking class at the local community center.

Dan goes to AA and has his own therapist. He is questioning his judgment about Lonny and feeling guilty for letting Sharon think it was her fault they couldn't conceive. He was resistant to the idea that paying money to talk to a stranger instead of a friend would be helpful and equally surprised that he feels better.

Sharon goes to Al-Anon and Co-Dependents Anonymous. She's making new friends. Learning how to set boundaries. She and Marlene are still friendly, but it isn't like it was before. Marlene has lost so much, how could it be the same?

Ava has her own therapist and goes to Alateen, a support group for teens whose parents are addicted to alcohol or drugs. She hopes that one day Cody will join her. Fran thinks Alateen has been helpful. She just wishes Ava would stop spouting AA slogans every other minute and go back to talking like a normal human being.

I asked Fran how Dan and Sharon feel about Ava continuing to live with her. She said their therapist thought it was a good thing. It would give them more time to work on their relationship, as well as their individual problems. Living away from home might help Ava figure out who she is and what she wants out of life because both are essential developmental tasks for someone her age. Essential developmental tasks sounded to Fran like psychobabble, a highfalutin way to describe running away from home. Which is how she thinks Sharon and Dan still see it, despite what they say to the contrary.

I do stay in touch with Iliana by text. She and Marisol have never been happier. They love having Ava in their lives. Iliana's continuing to see her therapist, going twice a week instead of once. Everything that's happened has stirred up feelings from the past and she still has a lot to work on. She says her therapist told her that traumatic memories have no expiration date. Then she quoted a psychologist who studies Buddhist teachings, who said that our minds have Velcro for the bad stuff and Teflon for the good. When she said that, I wrote it down. I'm thinking of having it made into a poster for my office at headquarters.

Pepper is waiting for me in our usual back booth. Eddie is carrying a tray of dirty dishes to the kitchen, Ava is making a fresh pot of coffee, and Fran is nowhere to be seen. There are hardly any customers this late in the afternoon.

Pepper leans over the table, whispering because she doesn't want Ava to hear her.

"Imagine ten Codys, drama queens, every one of them, boy or girl. The slightest thing, a breakup, a bad grade, the cafeteria runs out of french fries, and they want to jump in front of a train. Give me a bad guy crook any day of the week. They don't cry when you yell at them, don't get their feelings hurt when you cuff them and throw them on the ground. It's an even playing field. I need a freaking PhD to deal with these kids."

"By the way, how's school going? Still working on your master's?"

She ignores my question. I wonder if she's changed her mind about becoming a therapist. If cuffing bad guys and throwing them down is what makes her happy, she isn't going to like the therapist life, which involves days of sitting quietly and listening.

"Most of these kids are the way they are because Mom and Dad, if there is a dad, are crap parents. Cops are expected to be all things to all people. I'm not a priest, I'm not a doctor, I'm not a psychiatrist, and I'm not a freaking babysitter. I'm a cop. I put bad guys in jail. End of story."

"Hey. Fresh coffee." Ava shows up at our booth. "Mind if I join you?" She sits without waiting for an invitation. Pours coffee for

Pepper and me and sets the pot on the table. Eddie's training her in his style; don't ask to join, wait to be asked to leave.

"I saw Marlene at my mom's house the other day. I asked again when I could see Cody. She said he wasn't ready. She isn't sure he'll ever be ready to see me. He blames me for everything, including his parents' divorce. I've texted him about a hundred times. He never texts back."

"That's his choice," Pepper says. "You don't have anything to apologize for."

"That's what my therapist said. I feel bad. He's so miserable. Not only won't he talk to me, he won't talk to Marisa or Astra or anybody he used to know."

"You didn't make him miserable," I say. "Short of torture, one person can't make another person miserable."

Pepper leans over the table. "I know you didn't ask me, but I was telling the doc, I deal with teenagers all day long. They can't see into the future. They think everything is shit and will stay that way forever. If Cody was here, I'd tell him the same thing I tell the kids at school. Ask yourself, will whatever this is matter next week?" Pepper looks at Ava, then me. "Am I wrong?"

"Hella wrong." Ava stands up, coffeepot in hand. "Cody's my brother. My only brother. What happens to him will matter to me for the rest of my life."

51

The sun is starting to set as we drive over the hills toward the coast. Ava wants Frank to pull over so we can watch for the green flash. She has never seen one and neither have I. It's something that happens when the sun goes below the horizon of the ocean and light rays bend through the atmosphere. Frank thinks the whole thing is a myth and reminds us that if we stop, we'll be late for dinner. Fran doesn't think stopping is a good idea, either, unless we like overcooked food.

The yard in front of Dan and Sharon's has been newly planted with echium, asters, ice plant, and agapanthus, all blooming in the moist ocean air. A colorful contrast to the fields of wild grass surrounding the house.

Sharon continues to look well. Dan is wearing a collared shirt instead of his usual t-shirt and jeans. There are cut flowers in vases around their small living room and in the bathroom. Dan offers us wine. Sharon places a tray of canapés on the coffee table. I imagine they don't entertain very often, or if they do, it's more potluck and barbecue style. Dan raises his glass for a toast. He and Ava are drinking iced tea.

"We want to thank you all for helping . . ." he stumbles over his words ". . . our daughter and us. Bottom line, it's been a tough couple of months, but it's getting better. We're getting better. It would have been tougher without your help." He gulps his drink.

Sharon stands. Smooths her hair, getting ready for the spotlight. "I'm not going to lie. I have my moments. And I feel terrible for Marlene and Cody. But the important thing is that Ava . . ." She stops. Takes a deep breath. "I mean the important thing is that Carmela is happy and we're all getting better in therapy. Or trying to." She looks around the room. "That's it. I'm going to check on the food. I cooked butter chicken for us and tofu for you, sweetie. I want to make sure it's done enough."

Ava stands up. "Mom," she says, "tofu is done before it's cooked. I'm sure it will be fine."

"Got it," Sharon says. She looks embarrassed. "I'll be right back."

"Wait a minute, please. It's my turn and I have something I want to say." Ava raises her glass of iced tea. "I want to thank everyone here, including my parents. And I want to apologize. I said a lot of stuff I'm sorry I said."

Sharon starts to reassure her everything is okay. Dan stops her. Tells her to let Ava finish.

"Like you said, Mom, some things are better. But to be honest, because of me, some stuff is broken and will stay that way."

Sharon tries again to say something. Dan puts his hand on hers and she quiets down.

"Dr. Meyerhoff says changing things takes a long time. We didn't get here in a hurry, it took eighteen years. I just hope it doesn't take another eighteen to fix it all." Ava laughs. She's joking and not joking at the same time. "There is one thing we could fix now. We could fix my name. I know our family therapist said you should call me whatever makes me comfortable. I've been Ava for eighteen years. Now I'm Carmela. But I'm still

Ava to myself. I don't know how to be two people. I don't want to give up my past. Growing up here, in Moss Point with you, that's me. Having another family, being part of another culture, that's me too. It's going to take time to figure this out. So, please, all of you, continue to call me Ava, like you always have. When I'm with Iliana and Marisol, when I make friends at college, they can call me Carmela."

"She's grown up a lot." Frank rolls over in bed and looks at me.

It's eleven o'clock at night. I'm trying to get comfortable, despite my super-full stomach. In addition to butter chicken, we had rice, salad, rolls and butter, ice cream, and cake, followed by presents all around. It was like Christmas. Dinner was Dan and Sharon's present. The wrapped boxes were from Ava. An Instant Pot for Fran, a case of pinot noir for Frank and me, an apron to give to Eddie. Ava wanted to get something for Pepper but she didn't know what, so she bought her a diary with blank pages because she thinks Pepper won't be a cop forever. She probably won't be a therapist, either, because in Ava's opinion, Pepper talks too much and likes to order people around.

Frank raises up on one elbow. He looks serious. "I know I bitched at you for getting involved. My bad. If it wasn't for you, things would have turned out way different."

"I think Ava and Iliana deserve the credit. They were both very brave."

"So were you from behind the scenes, pulling strings, greasing the skids."

"Fran really bore the burden . . ."

"Stop." He raises his hand. "Modesty is not allowed. You did a helluva of a job. Say thank you."

"Thank you, Frank."

"You're welcome, Dot. Now can we go to sleep?"

ACKNOWLEDGMENTS

For many reasons, this was not an easy book to write. I am grateful to my wise and brave beta readers, Ann Gelder, Doris Ober, Edna Marie Cole, Mysti Berry, Lloyd Russell, and Kathryn Frank for their thoughtful spot-on feedback. Ann Gelder's amazing critique literally saved the entire project. Jason Hemsted and Lori Kelly of the Des Moines Police Department helped with research. Dr. Joel Fay helped with the grittier aspects of cop culture. Paula Kamena, Esq. and Dr. Mark Kamena generously shared their knowledge about child sexual abuse, law, and alcohol addiction. Lorraine Dusky's online site, First Mother Forum (firstmotherforum.com), is an invaluable and poignant resource for anyone involved in the adoption process.

My agent, Cynthia Zigmund, has been a steadfast partner for almost a decade. I look forward to more of the same as we partner with Open Road Media, who have graciously contracted to relaunch my back list and release this new addition to the series. As always, my husband, Steve Johnson, has been a rock. He's done way more than his half share of keeping our lives together and never complained as I plagiarized his entire life for the character of Frank.

ABOUT THE AUTHOR

Ellen Kirschman, PhD, is a police and public safety psychologist, a volunteer clinician at the First Responder Support Network, and a sought-after speaker and workshop facilitator. Kirschman has been awarded by the California Psychological Association for Distinguished Contribution to Psychology and the American Psychological Association for Outstanding Contribution to Police and Public Safety Psychology. She co-authored *Counseling Cops: What Clinicians Need to Know*; authored two self-help guides *I Love a Cop* and *I Love a Fire Fighter*; and writes a mystery series featuring police psychologist Dr. Dot Meyerhoff.

THE DOT MEYERHOFF MYSTERIES

FROM OPEN ROAD MEDIA

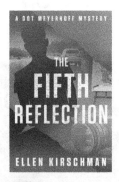

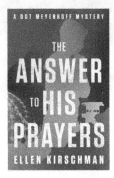

INTEGRATED MEDIA

Find a full list of our authors and
titles at www.openroadmedia.com

FOLLOW US
@OpenRoadMedia